THE
UNBORN

David Shobin

THE LINDEN PRESS/SIMON & SCHUSTER
NEW YORK
1981

Published by The Linden Press/Simon & Schuster
A Simon & Schuster Division of Gulf & Western Corporation
Simon & Schuster Building
Rockefeller Center
1230 Avenue of the Americas
New York, New York 10020
THE LINDEN PRESS/SIMON & SCHUSTER and colophon
are trademarks of Simon & Schuster
Manufactured in the United States of America

10 9 8 7 6 5 4 3 2 1

Library of Congress Cataloging in Publication Data

Shobin, David.
   The unborn.

   I.   Title.
PZ4.S5585Un   [PS3569.H567]   813'.54   80-18333
ISBN 0-671-25626-2

The brain of the human fetus exhibits recordable electrical activity as early as the eighth week.

—Allan C. Barnes
Intra-Uterine Development

The Unborn

1

Omega.

The red light signifying termination flashed on the programmer's console: end of printout. Pattner, the programmer, had just queried the computer about the significance of previous data. The computer's response should have been simple enough, for a recent technological advance enabled its hardware to assess all parameters of a printout. If the printout was incomplete and not inclined toward logical interpretation, the computer generally indicated "insufficient data." But now it signaled omega. It simply wasn't answering.

"Omega again," said Pattner.

"What the hell's that supposed to mean?"

"Don't know."

"Punch it out once more."

"I already ran it through twice."

"You suppose the old boy could be thinking again?"

"Could be."

"Okay. Wrap it up and put what you've got into memory."

Pattner activated the memory circuit and tried to put things into perspective. For the past few months, the computer had been showing signs of near human irrationality. The technology that enabled the computer to analyze its own responses had also, it seemed, endowed it with the ability to freely associate within its own memory banks.

Through the process of scanning its memory for data retrieval, the computer had begun to unify apparently unrelated events to the point where they appeared plausible. In a sense, it hypothesized. But too often the hypotheses had been expressed in almost human terms. And, recently, the computer's responses appeared truly peevish, irrational, or sarcastic.

The hospital computer was the country's second largest, surpassed only by the facilities at NASA. But its scope was far more complex. The designers had constructed its memory banks to store every known facet of medicine. When called upon, it could regurgitate the most trivial medical fact and integrate related requests into a unified, precise printout. Officially referred to as the Medical Integrative Computer, it was nicknamed MEDIC.

One of MEDIC's most valuable facets was its tabulation and evaluation of data from the hundreds of ongoing research studies within the hospital and surrounding university. Every day the data collected from each research project was programmed and submitted to MEDIC; every evening MEDIC reviewed and evaluated the information for the scientists to make the necessary adjustments in their projects.

MEDIC's initial spectacular performance made its recent erratic behavior all the more bothersome. The programmers called MEDIC's hypothesizing "thinking," although they seriously doubted that it actually thought in human terms. Still, it freely associated events in a sequence so much more logical than what was called for that no one doubted that some form of minor mechanical evolution was occurring. What was most perplexing was why MEDIC had begun to think when it did.

After weeks of mathematical tinkering, the team of pro-

grammers developed a program whose title provoked incessant bad jokes and wry puns. It was named Freely Relating
Event Union Detection. They called it Freud.

Freud proved to be no joke, however, living up to its
name. The program was everything they expected. It tabulated all the freely related events and had them cross-
indexed. One by one, variables were eliminated.

The answer lay in the computer's input. All the data
programmed into MEDIC had one basic similarity: it was
dead, isolated medical fact from either the recent or remote past. But there was one exception. In a far corner of
the hospital lay the only laboratory that fed live data into
the computer. The data came from volunteers participat-
ing in sleep research. As they slept, their brain waves were
transmitted to MEDIC for analysis. Freud finally revealed
that MEDIC's strange, humanistic activity coincided with
the sleep patterns of these subjects.

"A fuckin' dreaming computer," said Pattner.

The supervisor corrected him.

"MEDIC doesn't dream. It free associates while the
subjects dream."

"Same difference," said Pattner. "First we've got a computer thinking, and then it starts to dream. There's no
telling what could be next."

As if on cue the emergency light flashed bright orange
on the console. The computer was malfunctioning. Pattner
quickly snuffed out his cigarette and pressed the Interrupt
button to terminate all circuits. A slow, sibilant drone
whirred softly as the series of cogs stopped operating. On
Pattner's right, the supervisor was checking the individual
circuits. A quick survey revealed that they should all be
functioning normally. Yet they weren't. The supervisor
looked at Pattner.

"First time that's happened," said the supervisor. "Press Override," he snapped.

Pattner punched the button and a single computer unit began to operate, its tapes winding slowly. Simultaneously, the console's typewriter began its staccato lettering in front of them. It typed one word.

Floating.

The supervisor looked to Pattner.

"Jesus Christ. What the hell is that?"

Pattner pressed a sequence of buttons and several more units began their mechanical hum. The tapes turned together for a moment and then jolted to a stop. Another printout appeared.

Commence Dialogue.

Pattner and the supervisor stared at the typewritten letters. And then all the computer units jerked into operation at once. Their tapes turned faster and faster, the noise level in the room increasing in intensity. Soon the sound was deafening, a cacophonous screeching of locomotive wheels.

"Did you hit Re-set?" shouted the supervisor.

"I didn't touch a damn thing," Pattner yelled back.

"For Chrissake, the thing can't start by itself!"

The two scientists stood alone, amazed at the display before them. Deep within its mechanical interior, MED-IC's brain pulsed to life.

2

Narrow rays of morning sunlight filtered softly through slats in the blinds, warming the velour of the bedspread. Flecks of dust, wafting lazily upward on rising thermals of air, were set into a blizzard-like spiral by a sudden rustling of sheets. She got off the bed and began to put on her clothes.

"Where are you going?"

"Out."

"Out where?"

"Just out."

He sat up and swung his legs over the side of the bed, his calves prickling with gooseflesh.

"It's cold in here."

No answer.

"Come back in the bed. I want to talk."

Again, no reply. She put on her bra backwards, hooking it in front before swinging it around and inserting her arms under the straps. Her linen slacks were slung over a chair. When she reached for them he came off the bed toward her.

"Do you mind if I put on my pants?"

"Go ahead. I'm not stopping you."

"Good."

She reached for her slacks again, but this time he held her wrist.

"Samantha—"

"I asked you a million times not to call me that."

"All right, whatever you say. Sam. What're you, just going to walk out?"

"Why not? I thought we had agreed to that."

"We had. But there's still a lot we have to talk about."

"Let go of my wrist."

He released her. A warm breeze blew through the room, ruffling her tawny hair. She stared at his nakedness.

"I'll get your pants."

"What's wrong? My nudity bother you?"

No, she thought. It didn't bother her at all. She had always found his lean body and good looks very appealing. The only trouble was that he knew it, too; the resultant egotism lent him a cool, wary aloofness that she had no use for now. There was nothing more to discuss. She wanted to leave.

"Would you mind if I left without rehashing this over and over?"

"I don't mind at all."

"Good. I don't feel very well anyway."

"Come off it! Not all women have morning sickness. Christ, you don't have to be so serious. It's not like you."

She frowned.

"I don't know," she said. "I was less serious before I was a pregnant lady."

"And I'm supposed to feel sorry about that?"

She shrugged. "Why should you be sorry? I said it wasn't your fault."

"No, but you implied it. You make me—us—sound like some kind of moron, like, Gee, Jerry, I forgot to put in my diaphragm. Or, Golly, I took my last pill three days ago. Or—"

"Stop it."

"Stop, now?" he said, sitting up. "Isn't it a little late

for that? No, sir. We ain't no morons. Especially you, with your phi bete and magna cum. A couple of sophisticates, we were. No dumb screw-ups for us. Hell, if I can remember your exact words correctly, they were, 'Oh, Jerry, it feels so good, please don't stop, oh God Jerry, fuck me harder, I want you to come in me!' You're amazing!"

Samantha slowly shook her head at his risible display of emotion. The gap between them widened further, their divergent viewpoints irreconcilable. Her flexibility jarred harshly with his preconceived notions. It was time to go.

"That's me," she quipped. "The Eighth Wonder of the World." She finished dressing and gathered up her belongings.

"This is a hell of a time to tell me, after we finish making love," he said. "Very manipulative."

"We didn't make love. Like you said, we fucked."

"Call it whatever you want. Same difference. Did you honestly think I'd feel any different afterward than before?"

"I didn't know what you'd think. Maybe I was just horny. That happens to all us pregnant girls. First we have morning sickness, then we screw our brains out."

"Not funny. You waited until we finished for a reason."

Losing patience, she was a mime. "Gosh, the suspense is unbearable. Okay: what reason?"

"The usual. You want me to marry you."

She nearly laughed at the humor of his remark. But then she caught herself, and a sad smile of chagrin curled her lips. How little he understood.

"You have no idea how pathetic you sound. In many ways you're a pitiful, conceited child. The last thing I want is to marry you. Nobody could insinuate himself between you and your righteous self-image."

"So why did you even bother to tell me you're knocked up?"

"Why? Well, maybe I thought that, as the prospective father of this child, you might want to know it exists."

Anger suffused his cheeks.

"What the hell makes you think I'm ready for fatherhood? Your kid's, or anybody else's? I've got years before I'm ready to be a father. Maybe never."

She mellowed a bit. "Look. It's nobody's fault. It just happened. A simple equation: one sperm plus one egg equals one baby."

"And you're trying to tell me you're actually going to keep the thing?"

"It's not a thing. It's a baby. My baby. Yours too. But I think I'm going to go this one alone. No one will ever have to know whose baby it is."

"I'm not interested in secrets; I'm interested in careers. Our careers. You know damn well I have a year left in med school. And you have at least two years before you get your doctorate. Are you ready to give all that up?"

"I'm not giving anything up. Mothers can teach and study at the same time."

"That's a lot of crap. You think you can do it now, but wait till you have a few sleepless nights under your belt. Up to your knees in empty bottles and dirty diapers."

"I never said it would be easy."

"More likely impossible. What's gotten into you, anyway? You're not the kind of person who'd want to bring up a fatherless child. You're so vocal about women's rights, I never thought you were against abortion."

"I'm not. Abortion should be for women who want it. I don't."

In frustration, he became self-conscious and crossed his

legs to hide his sex. She picked up her sweater and started for the door.

"You're making a mistake, Sam."

"Let me worry about that."

"How're you going to feed the kid? Food stamps?"

"If I have to."

"Did you tell your parents?"

"Nobody knows but me, you, and the doctor. And it's going to stay that way."

"There goes money from home."

"Look, I haven't had an allowance since I was thirteen. After that there was babysitting, the supermarket, or any other job I could find. Now I have an instructor's fellowship. But if I need food stamps to get by, so be it."

She opened the door, paused, and addressed him again. "You make me sorry I told you, Jerry. I knew you'd want me to have an abortion."

"So why did you?"

"Maybe I thought every man has the right to know when he's going to be a father. Or maybe this was one of those times when I just wanted to be with you."

"You might have something there. If you're interested in extra money, I could always spread the word around."

Tears filled her eyes.

"Go shit in a hat," she said, and slammed the door.

3

Route 50 snakes slowly westward on its lazy journey through the swampy lowlands surrounding the Chesapeake Bay. The highway is born at Ocean City, whose Atlantic waters, early in May, still retained the chill of the recent winter, but were becoming tepid due to an unseasonable week-long heat wave. At first the road heads away from the sea, inland toward Salisbury and from there over the brown and gray marshland to Cambridge. But then the two-lane strip of tar turns abruptly north, weaving its way between the shallow inlets and scum-covered bogs until, after several miles, it widens into a four-lane highway, no longer elastic tar but rigid concrete. Then west again, over the gleaming Chesapeake Bay to Annapolis and, farther on, to Washington, before finally settling into the gently rolling hills of Virginia. Route 50 is not a particularly scenic road; the surrounding landscape is generally flat, or at best only slightly hilly, and is interspersed with patches of sapless pine. Its most characteristic feature is its spectacular mediocrity.

Deeper into Virginia the tilled brown acres are transformed by the first verdant flush of green. Seedlings in even furrows push through the sandy loam to inch their fragile stalks skyward, tight leaf-buds bursting through their protective sheaths. This is tobacco country, and the weather-beaten shanties and prefabricated villages of migrant workers mark the corners of the land. Farms give way to estates, and estates to plantations—the genteel touch of aristocracy. Far off the road, green oases shield stables housing thoroughbreds and their spindly-legged foals. Undulating hills replace the flatness of the bay, and the fresh hint of the lush warm summer to come lingers in the breeze.

Jonathan Bryson drove over the final stretch of one such hill, retracing the last leg of the route he had followed from New York two years previously. He breathed deeply, invigorated by the fleeting traces of will-o'-the-wisp that moistened the morning air. The hill crested and gave way to a spectacular expanse of valley. The view never failed to inspire Bryson. Looming in the distance was a massive complex of glass and steel, a glistening phoenix arising from nowhere but toward which all roads headed. The central hub of buildings sent a spoke-like maze of tunnels beckoning to the periphery of the valley. The world converged on Jubilee General.

Jubilee General Hospital was the model of medical regionalization with which all other medical centers were compared. Construction had begun in 1977, and the entire complex was federally funded. Located between Washington and Richmond, the hospital was the climax of years of intensive investigation and planning.

Regionalization of medicine was high on the list of government priorities. During the decade of the 1970s the Department of Health, Education and Welfare concluded that one way to curb spiraling medical expenditures was to eliminate costly duplication of services and facilities. The existence of scores of identical small community hospitals was pointless, the H.E.W. reasoned, if even better medical care could be provided by one large, centrally located medical center. The center would encompass all the hospital beds, facilities, and patient services formerly afforded by the small "caretaker" hospitals. Instead of ten maternity units in a fifty-mile radius, there would be one unit with ten times as many beds. The center would have one CAT scanner instead of the community's six. Rather than five smaller open-heart surgical facilities, there would be one larger one. This was the core of the concept of regionalized medicine.

By elimination of local community hospitals, costly inter-hospital rivalry for identical services could be prevented. Since all patients would be referred to one large institution, under-utilization of existing facilities was impossible. Instead of the eighty-five or ninety percent occupancy rates of community hospitals—rates which invariably meant financial loss for management and increased costs for patients—Jubilee General was consistently one hundred percent occupied.

The input of federal funds proved to be too massive: the community hospitals waged a brief, losing skirmish. One by one the small hospitals yielded to the enormity of Jubilee General. This was not unexpected. For not only was Jubilee General the penultimate medical center, it was also an academic mecca, a universe of medical research, education, and development. It housed its own medical and professional schools and even advanced undergraduate schools. The foremost medical laboratories and testing facilities were located within its walls, providing every known diagnostic service and many experimental ones. In addition to providing care for every patient in the northern Virginia community, it was a major referral center for patients from across the country. In intent and actuality, it was regionalization made complete. Jubilee General was not just a hospital. It was its own city.

The sheer enormity of the megastructure made obscure

each individual ward, lab, or research area. In addition to MEDIC—the most sophisticated medical computer in existence, the Jubilee General complex contained schools of medicine, dentistry, pharmacy, and nursing; the hospital housed 3600 beds, 200 research labs, scores of clinical labs, and floor after floor of architecturally precise modules for ancillary patient services.

At thirty-seven, Bryson was the head of the Sleep Research Laboratory. He had held that position for two years since being lured from his struggling private practice of neurology in Manhattan.

From his first day as project director, he had had an adequate budget and sufficient staff to help him get his projects under way. He was allotted an initial $20,000 budget, a full-time secretary, a research associate, and complete access to auxiliary hospital and university facilities. He was also allowed ample free time to supervise the residents in neurology clinic twice a week, attend ward rounds, grand rounds, and selected conferences. All that remained was to put his time and the department's money to good use.

The department had no set goals for him. He was expected, however, to use the initial funds as a springboard toward obtaining other project grants. Such grants traditionally came from government agencies, the private sector, or nonprofit-charity funds. Private interests, such as drug companies and manufacturers, offered the greatest monetary potential.

Of competitive necessity, pharmaceutical companies were anxious to market new products. But the road from invention to final consumer marketing took many years, sometimes decades. Only after extensive animal trials would the Food and Drug Administration consent to human experimentation, and then under rigidly controlled conditions, usually in a university setting. New medications intended for sleep—either sedatives or hypnotics—were always under development. The goal was to invent the ideal sleeping pill: one which would induce sleep within minutes, maintain normal somnolence for six to eight hours without awakening, cause no hangover, and have no potential for habituation, abuse, or addiction. Of the dozens of sleeping pills available to the patient, none fully met these criteria; all had flaws in one area or another. It was evident that the first manufacturer to invent the ideal sleeping pill would reap windfall profits amounting to hundreds of millions of dollars.

Initial aspects of new drug investigation—formulation, dosage levels, toxicology, and most animal studies—were done by the pharmaceutical company. After obtaining FDA approval, the final stage before marketing—the human trials—had to be conducted by unbiased and reputable researchers such as Dr. Bryson, whose conclusions were more apt to be accepted than those of the parent company. The administrators and department heads of Jubilee General lost no time in establishing their own department of sleep research.

By late spring Bryson had two projects nailed down and others that seemed promising in the works. The first was an animal study, funded by H.E.W. and channeled through the National Institutes of Health. The cancer epidemiology division of N.I.H. had been disturbed by numerous case reports of mouse uterine cancer in long-term users of Somnapar, a tertiary carbinol hypnotic. The project was given to the sleep research laboratory, but Bryson shared the grant with a Ph.D. in the department of pharmacology. Pharmacology controlled the animal lab, and most of the work would be done by them.

The second project was a straightforward sleep study on a new benzodiazepine derivative. The drugs in the benzodiazepine family, such as Valium, were either tranquilizers or hypnotics, depending on their chemical formula. The incredible financial success of Valium led other drug companies on a scramble to cash in on the benzodiazepine boom. By alterations in the chemical formula, they hoped to retain the basic properties of the benzodiazepines while adding a safe but alluring new quality for the drug-consuming public.

Sleep studies were just that: careful observations of the sleep behavior of volunteers. Most volunteers were students from within the university, paid by the hour for their time. It was a much sought-after job. Some students paid for their entire graduate educations by sleeping in the lab three days a week. There was only one inconvenience: all sleeping was done during the day in a fully lit, soundproofed room, and the volunteers were wired to an electroencephalograph, or EEG. The EEG recorded their brain waves for later analysis.

Sleeping EEGs were fairly constant. Brain waves were divided into four groups labeled alpha through delta. Each group had a characteristic waveform appearance determined by the frequency and amplitude of oscillations on a graph. While alpha waves were associated with wakefulness, delta waves were found in deepest sleep. A fifth group was associated with REM activity, the "rapid eye movements" of dreaming.

A decade earlier, sleep researchers had discovered that a night's sleep was divided approximately into ninety-minute intervals. Each interval, or sleep cycle, began with near wakefulness and progressed steadily to deep sleep before returning to wakefulness. A certain period of time was devoted to each stage of the cycle. If the subject was tired, a proportionately larger amount of time was initially spent in deep sleep before reverting to other stages. The intervals between sleep cycles were devoted to dreaming and REM sleep.

REM sleep was essential to the quality of a night's sleep. No matter how much time was spent in other sleep stages, if REM activity were suppressed, the subject invariably felt fatigued or irritable after awakening. The EEG served to delineate the length of all stages of slumber and REM sleep. This was of utmost importance in investigation of a new hypnotic: its effectiveness would be diminished if it either abolished REM activity or decreased the amount of time spent in deep sleep.

Students were accepted as volunteers in the study only if they fulfilled certain criteria. There could be no history of neurologic disorder or psychiatric treatment. Females could not be pregnant. Prior insomnia was cause for exclusion. They could not participate if they had previously used other hypnotics regularly, or if they admitted to frequent drug or alcohol use, including hallucinogens. And their physical health had to be good. After acceptance their first week in the program was devoted to obtaining baseline sleeping EEG recordings, without drugs. After their sleep pattern was established and recorded, the experimental hypnotic was administered.

Bryson conducted the study according to the "double blind" technique. Under this format, neither the subject nor the person conducting the study knew whether a sleeping pill or a placebo had been administered. The pills looked identical, and were distributed according to a code. Not until the study was completed would the code be revealed and the results analyzed.

Like all researchers at the hospital, Bryson's data was computer analyzed. But early in the course of the sleep study, he added a new technique. Instead of sending the EEG results to the computer, Bryson decided to channel the brain waves directly into MEDIC. Relying on past skills, he designed a computer program whose language reflected each EEG spike. The computer-coded brain waves were then continuously transcribed to MEDIC during an entire sleep cycle. The following morning, the computer submitted its analysis of the subject's dreaming pattern, noting such parameters as the amount of time spent in REM and deep sleep, total sleep time, and the effect, if any, of the placebo or hypnotic on sleep quality. Thus far, the morning analysis had proved both time-saving and beneficial. Bryson had no reason to suspect that his ingenuity was causing a problem until several months later, on that morning in late May, when he received a call from Pattner in the computer center.

"Dr. Bryson, we're not sure what's happening in your lab, but your data's got the computer dreaming."

"Dreaming?"

"Well, not exactly. Daydreaming would be a better choice of words. We suspect that whenever you run a sleep study, MEDIC's brain gets a little fuzzy. It wanders."

"What is it you've been drinking, Mr. Pattner?"

"Wish I was, Doc."

"It so happens that I know something about computers. And I'm sure its brain can't wander. Who suggested that?"

"Freud did."

"Smoking those funny little cigarettes, maybe?"

Pattner grew exasperated, realizing how foolish his hypothesis must sound. "Doc, this is very complicated, believe me. It would take a long time to explain. The reason

I'm calling is to let you know that your computer program is making MEDIC nuts."

"What am I supposed to do? Change my study?"

"Nothing like that. It's not interfering with anything important. But you should realize that when MEDIC acts crazy, you might get some crazy results on your data analysis. You might want to interpret the data with a grain of salt."

"All the analyses seem fairly coherent so far."

"Okay. I just wanted to let you know."

"Thanks, I appreciate that. And Pattner—"

"What's that, Doc?"

"Give my best to Freud."

Bryson replaced the receiver with the faintest hint of uneasiness.

4

Samantha crumpled her note paper and tossed it in the trash. However she tried to rearrange her budget and expenses, she still came up short. Assets: her father's half of the tuition; her biology fellowship; a small allowance from her mother; and a five-year-old Pinto. Debits: her half of the tuition; apartment rental; food and clothing; and upcoming obstetric and pediatric fees. She tried to figure all the angles, but finally concluded that even if she sold her car, moved to less expensive quarters, and collected food stamps, she was still $1,000 in the red. She had to find another job.

Her visit with her department head had been a disappointment. Odd jobs in research biology were nonexistent. The department budget was a meager slice of the university's pie. The plums had already been scooped up by the top professors, leaving only a withered crust for administration. Other than her fellowship, there was simply no money available for research of any kind.

She encountered the same dilemma in other departments. Basic science departments received little of the revenue funneled into the university. The bulk of the money was siphoned off by the hospital and its many subdivisions. A logical individual, Samantha made her way to the hospital.

The medical staff coffee-shop was crowded at midday. Samantha fought through a sea of white coats until she found a place at the counter. She ordered coffee and pondered her next move. The employment office seemed a likely place to start, but it probably offered only full-time positions of the white- and blue-collar variety. Perhaps if she could meet the chief of service of one of the clinical departments, he might apprise her of any money-making ventures under his jurisdiction. In her mind she contemplated the various clinical departments. She knew of surgery, internal medicine, and of course obstetrics. Her own doctor, in fact, was on staff at the hospital. She turned to the unshaven intern next to her.

"Excuse me, do you know where I can find the department of obstetrics?"

He glanced at her, dabbing ketchup from his lips. The woman beside him was clearly the most attractive female he had seen in weeks.

"You're much too quiet to be in labor."

"It's natural childbirth."

He looked at her waist.

"More like immaculate childbirth. You're not even sporting a belly."

"Thanks. But I don't mean obstetrics like I'm-going-to-deliver obstetrics. I mean the department office."

"Why didn't you say so?"

"Why didn't I say so. Why do I get the feeling it's hard to get a straight answer from you?"

"Probably because you're right."

"Okay. Let's start again. Do you know where I can find the department of obstetrics?"

"Which part?"

Patiently. "The office of the chief of service."

"Chief of service, or department chairman?"

"I give up. You win." She finished her coffee in a gulp and picked up her check. "Thanks for nothing."

"Hold it, I'm serious." He smiled. "The OB department is spread out over four floors. Where you go depends on what you're looking for. What are you looking for, anyway?"

Samantha put down her check. "Actually I'm looking for a job."

"In the OB department? Are you a nurse?"

"No. I'm a graduate research assistant in biology. I'm looking for a part-time job, and the hospital seems like the only place on campus with money."

"That it is. But why did you pick obstetrics?"

"It seems as good a place as any to start."

"Did you check the bulletin board?"

"What bulletin board?"

"The one outside the coffee shop. Lady, you are in a fog. It's about twenty feet long. You can't miss it; it's covered with notices. Rooms for rent, ski trips, odd jobs. There's a big call for sperm donors."

"Thanks a heap."

"No, I suppose you don't fit the job description. But check it out. Maybe you'll find what you're looking for."

Samantha thanked him, paid her check, and stepped out into the corridor. Hundreds of posters and announcements cluttered the bulletin board. Indeed, sperm seemed to be in demand for several research projects. Samantha spent twenty minutes perusing the notices. There were several positions that might suit her. Animal labs had to be tended, psychological profiles needed investigation, and someone was needed to lend her body to teach medical students how to perform gynecologic exams. She quickly discarded that one and was about to give up when another posting caught her interest.

A research lab needed volunteers to do nothing but

sleep. Someone was willing to pay selected participants five dollars per hour of simple somnolence, eight hours per shift. Samantha briefly computed that by "working" three days a week at such a job, she could gross over $1,000 in a little more than two months. Not bad. She could sleep as well as the next person. She jotted down the telephone extension of the lab.

Before she could change her mind, Samantha found a hospital telephone and called the sleep research lab. She expected to speak to a lower-echelon bureaucrat, but the woman who answered the phone had an encouraging politeness. She was anxious to meet Samantha and gave her easy, concise directions to the lab. Eight floors up and across three corridors, in the research building nearest the hospital, Samantha arrived at her destination. A plump woman in her fifties waved her inside the office.

"Samantha Kirstin? I'm Mrs. Rutledge." Her handshake was warm, firm. "Dr. Bryson just left for the clinic. He asked me to show you the lab and have you fill out an application."

"Dr. Bryson is the boss, I presume?"

"He's head of the lab. Actually he's a neurologist; he's in the neurology clinic now. Are you familiar with our sleep projects?"

"No, but I'm a quick study."

The older woman smiled. "It's very simple, really. And it can be quite pleasant. Are you a medical student here?"

"I'm a grad student in biology."

"Good . . . good. Most of our volunteers are med students. Some of them think they know it all, and they consider my explanation of the project a waste of time. Have you heard of the EEG, the electroencephalogram?"

"The machine that records brain waves?"

"Exactly. In sleep research the essential tool is the EEG. In the project Dr. Bryson is conducting now, we're measuring the effect of a new sleeping pill on the EEGs of sleeping volunteers. Apparently the pill's effect on the brain waves has a lot to do with its success as a drug. At this time of year, final exams are coming up, and two of our participants have dropped out. Would you be available to take part?"

"What do I have to do?"

"You have to be able to relax, and, if possible, to sleep, with electrodes pasted to your scalp. The only other tool in our trade is a bed with clean sheets in a soundproof, lighted room."

"Sounds like a porno movie."

Mrs. Rutledge laughed. "My dear, based on some of the dreams our male volunteers say they have, I sometimes think that myself. Come, we're in the middle of a session now. Would you like to observe?"

"Sure."

Mrs. Rutledge led Samantha into a large back room. The pens of a three-channel electroencephalograph were tracing waves onto moving strips of graph paper. The machine itself was connected to a computer console, and Mrs. Rutledge explained how the readings were transmitted directly into MEDIC. But most interesting was a four-by-eight-foot glass window, which Samantha knew had to be mirrored on the other side. Through the window she watched a young man turn in his sleep.

He floated through his reveries like an embryo turning gently in the womb. He came to rest on his back, the sheets rumpled in a white pile at his feet. He wore only a pair of blue briefs. The electrode wires attached to his scalp were plugged into a jack on the headboard.

Mrs. Rutledge pointed to the EEG pens. They had completed a waveform and began a rapid series of squiggles.

"He's dreaming," said Mrs. Rutledge. "Watch his eyes."

The young man's cheeks made small spasmodic jerks. His lips pursed, then relaxed again. The whole face lost its tenseness, the jaw dropping open slightly. At the same time, Samantha was aware that his respiration had increased. Then slowly, perceptibly, the eyes began to roll under closed lids. Like moles burrowing under sod, the eyes wandered aimlessly, first to the side, then up and down. Occasionally the sleeping man would squint, and the lids would quiver. The rolling eyes searched through darkness, following the path of fantasy. It reminded Samantha of the gentle twitching of a sleeping puppy.

The sleeper lay still on his back, legs spread apart. A bulge began to push his briefs upward. Samantha felt her cheeks redden as the erection grew. She glanced at Mrs. Rutledge and saw that she noticed it too.

"An interesting dream, no doubt."

"I feel like I'm intruding," said Samantha, embarrassed.

"Nonsense. You should know from your biology that this is normal when men dream. Still . . ." she winked at Samantha, "too bad we're not advanced enough to know how to videotape his dreams."

Samantha laughed, caught off guard by Mrs. Rutledge's eroticism. The older woman didn't look the type to entertain such notions. Yet she probably saw it every day, and coped with it through humor.

"Do I have to dress like that?"

"Any way you want," said Mrs. Rutledge. "Naked, pajamas, bra and panties, whatever suits you. You can wear a raincoat if you want."

"Maybe he should have," said Samantha, gesturing through the glass.

Mrs. Rutledge smiled. "Shall we give him some privacy?"

"I don't know," said Samantha. "This is starting to get interesting."

But then she nodded, and they went back to the outer office. Mrs. Rutledge sat at her desk and motioned for Samantha to do likewise.

"What do you think, Miss Kirstin? Would you like to participate? The work is easy, the pay is good, and you leave the job refreshed. I put the notice on the bulletin board just this morning. I don't mean to pressure you, but this type of work is popular, for obvious reasons. I don't know if the position will still be vacant by tomorrow."

"You've sold me, Mrs. Rutledge. I think this job should be a yawn."

"Very good, then," Mrs. Rutledge said, smiling at the pun. "Are your graduate studies flexible enough that you could arrange them around project hours?"

"I think so. I teach two mornings a week, but the rest of the time is pretty much my own."

"Then that leaves only the formality of the application. Are you in good health?"

"Yes."

"Do you use drugs on a regular basis?"

"No."

"Have you ever had a sleeping problem?"

"I sleep like a log."

"Okay. Fill out the rest of this questionnaire and sign it at the bottom."

Samantha scanned the page and filled in the blanks and

biographical information where required. Question fourteen made her hesitate. It stipulated that female applicants could not be pregnant, to protect the fetus against
any untoward effects of the new drug under investigation.
The question called for the date of her last period. After
a moment's thought, she filled in the date as one week
before. Then she completed the remaining questions,
signed the application and the required consent form, and
returned it to the secretary.

Mrs. Rutledge glanced at the paper and placed it in a
folder. "When can you start?"

"I have a class tomorrow, so I suppose the day after
that."

"Perfect. I'll see you in two days then, nine o'clock
sharp. Dr. Bryson should be here too. He'll want to meet
you before you begin. One final thing: try not to get too
much sleep tomorrow night. Some people have trouble
sleeping in the daytime. If you're tired, the first day will
be less anxiety-provoking, and you'll relax easier."

"Should I bring anything with me?"

"Just whatever you'll be sleeping in."

Samantha said goodbye and left the building feeling relieved. She was not quite two months pregnant and knew
that with her slender figure her pregnancy wouldn't become
evident for another three. By that time, if she were paid
regularly, she would break even financially for the year.
And once she was a participant, perhaps they would allow
her to continue if she signed a waiver.

As she walked outside and across campus, something
was bothering her, a nagging annoyance she couldn't quite
pinpoint. She sifted through her thoughts as she walked
until she finally came to grips with a lingering fear. She
was worried about the drug, knowing that some medica-

tions in pregnancy were unwise. But sleeping pills? Thousands of pregnant women must take them. Certainly she had friends who had used all sorts of drugs in pregnancy, and their babies were fine. Why should hers be any different?

She didn't know the answer, and knew that she would never know. Once she took the medication, she wouldn't rest easy until the baby was born. But there was no sense fretting about it now. She was doing what had to be done. It was a simple matter of survival.

5

Even in early summer her apartment trapped heat like a
furnace. The air was thick and motionless when she returned from the lab, stifling her. Samantha drew the sash
to the curtains and pried open the window. A breezy gust
swirled into the room, pumped by unseen outdoor bel-
lows. The wave of cool air upended a picture on her book-
case. Samantha righted it, gazing at the photo, musing at
the memory it evoked.

The picture had been taken two years previously. She
and a girlfriend had spent a week in Provincetown. It was
the first vacation Samantha allowed herself after three years
in college. A straight-A student, Samantha realized that
she no longer had to study with such punctilious compulsion. Good grades came to her naturally, iron filings
drawn to a magnet.

It was time to unwind and take stock of her life. It was
also a time of awakening sexuality. For three years she
had channeled her libido into scholarship, with little opportunity for romance. Though there was no dearth of requests or potential suitors, she dated rarely. When she
wasn't studying, she was working at various collegiate jobs
for tuition and pocket change. But now, Samantha closed
her books, packed a suitcase, and drove with her friend
to the beach.

It had been a sybaritic week. Samantha luxuriated in the
sun and water, her pale skin metamorphosized to a deep
tan. She swam for miles in the surf, her tall body gaily

outdistancing the throng of male onlookers. She borrowed her friend's Adidas and learned to jog. At the end of her brief morning run, she was surrounded by men who fell over one another trying to capture the attention of this laughing golden child-woman.

She instantly liked one of them. She had first noticed him playing touch football with a group of men on the beach. He was clearly the best-looking man among them and she took him up on his offer of a stroll down the beach.

She learned that Craig was a graduate student at Yale; that he was one of the most outrageously conceited men she had ever met; and that his conceit was matched only by his childishness. Nevertheless, a determined Samantha helped him roll up his towel as she slung his camera over her shoulder, leading him by the hand back to her own blanket. There, her girlfriend took a picture of them. Then Samantha escorted Craig to lunch.

Now, two years later, alone in her apartment, Samantha smiled at the photo. It was framed, a glossy color-enlargement that bore the inscription: "To S.S.: May there be many more nights like that one. Craig." S.S., she recalled. That's what he had called her: Sunny Sam. Even now she laughed at the enigmatic inscription. She concluded that it signified a kind of crepuscular rationalization on Craig's part, for their final evening together had been a dismal failure.

Bold though it was, Samantha's intent in pursuing Craig had been to prove something to herself. She wasn't interested in physical conquest; in fact, the thought made her a little uneasy. She hoped that the few days she spent with Craig in Provincetown might develop into an intense, exciting relationship, and bring out the hidden side of her. But

Craig proved, their first evening together, that sex was all he had in mind. He pursued her relentlessly, and it was all she could do to fend him off. When she finally decided to give in, on the last night of her vacation, it wasn't because he overpowered her. Rather, Samantha had grown truly fond of him. When they began to make love, she wanted desperately to relax. Instead she felt her tension rise. Craig seemed to be in an incredible hurry. He made love like a football player, she thought, racing toward the end zone while she awaited the kickoff. Her anxiety, like too much champagne, made her want to burst forth in giggly bubbles. But when he climaxed before entering her, her tension was released, and she found herself laughing uncontrollably from the innate awkwardness of the moment. Before she could explain or apologize, Craig beat a hasty retreat.

His inscription, she concluded, had to be a symbol of his ego's refusal to admit defeat. She had kept the photo because she liked the way she looked in it. It was the onset of her adulthood, of her ability to flirt and be flirted with. In her bikini she looked very adult indeed. Her straight, reddish-blond hair fell just beyond her shoulders; and her eyes, more green than hazel, had the unrestrained twinkle of awareness, of the freedom that accompanies maturity.

More experience that summer led her to believe that she had little in common with men her own age. She was still friendly with them, and had formed many cheerful, easygoing bonds. But her independence seemed to challenge them, to put them ill at ease. Sometimes she felt like an older sister in their midst. She began to seek out the company of older men. During the next two years, she rarely dated anyone less than ten years her senior. And then came the exception.

At twenty-six, Jerry was three years older than Samantha. From the outset, she knew that their bond was purely physical. For the first time in her life, someone evoked a lust in her that made her ashamed. Samantha understood that their liaison was a chimera, animal magnetism, pure and simple. When they made love, it was as if each was unaware of the other's presence. They copulated with self-indulgent intensity, oblivious to their surroundings. When they made love, they might just as well have been masturbating alone, one's body a tool of the other's gratification. Samantha knew that their relationship was predestined to fail. But she felt powerless to stop. Being with Jerry was an exercise in lip biting. She half cursed, half laughed at her compulsion. Damn, she thought, red-faced, she clung to him as though he were made of plastic, a six-foot vibrator. Only when Samantha discovered that she was pregnant could she extricate herself from their mutually insatiable appetites.

Alone. The sensation was not new to her. She could easily turn to the older men she had dated in the preceding months, but the complication of pregnancy was not something she could impose on them. She would persevere in solitude, as she had done before. And she would succeed. The past bore witness to that. And if she didn't, well, she'd call in the troops—the Red Cross, or Interpol. Life couldn't be all that hard. If worse came to worst, she could always leave town.

Four years before, the summer after her freshman year, Samantha had become estranged from her parents. The minor disagreement between them had grown to an altercation of major proportions. Samantha's desire for complete independence from her pampering family had caused

the rift. But she couldn't help it. They were suffocating
her with their attentiveness. At a time when they wanted
to mold her future into an elaborate protective soufflé, all
she wanted was to cut her own piece of cheese, thank you.

The falling out could easily have been remedied with
a modicum of communication and compromise on both
sides. But Samantha found herself unwilling to negotiate.
Her headstrong stubbornness made the break complete. She
and her parents still spoke to one another; in many ways,
theirs was a normal family relationship. But she condoned
no financial support, and made fewer trips home. It was a
struggle in the beginning, but she soon earned a comfortable scholarship. Samantha was pleased with her circumstances.

When she entered graduate school, her attitude toward
parental support mellowed. Secure in her success, she was
touched by her father's graduation present of half her tuition expenses. She still insisted on working part time, more
as a gesture of self-reliance than from absolute need.

Samantha felt comfortable in her decision to keep the
child. When she discovered she was pregnant, she was surprised that she wasn't upset; but even more astonished
that she actually liked the idea. Sure, she thought, her
desire for motherhood might displease her more radical
feminist friends. But in this matter personal politics played
no role. Anyway, she bought her bras at Bendel's: they
were too expensive to burn.

Samantha was amazed at her own ease with the idea of
being a single parent, of raising a child her own way. And
she was confident of her ability to succeed by herself. Telling her parents about her pregnancy would only complicate
things. She would tell them later. For now, she would go
it alone.

Financially, there was not only the problem of the doctor bills. She already had grand, elaborate plans for her child. The initial $1,000 she would earn in the sleep lab would provide for her most pressing needs. But after the baby came in December, she would spare no expense to provide the best for her child. That might mean teaching additional classes the following semester to pay the bills, but the sacrifice would be worth it. The baby would need clothing and furniture, toys, and as it grew older, every conceivable educational device to develop its mind. It would need a mature, devoted mother's helper for those times Samantha was absent. When she was home, she planned to spend every waking moment with her child.

Though it was now barely more than an embryo, Samantha dreamed of holding and touching her child, of nurturing it, of watching it grow. She yearned for mothering. She tried to picture her baby, but the image was diffuse. And she had already begun considering names. She hated cute names and had to stifle a laugh when her married girlfriends chose what she called "ethnic and religious chic" names like Ryan or Megan, Joseph or Mary. She wanted a name with character: strong, simple, and basic. Perhaps Tom, or Jim. A Susan, a Joan.

Her mind whirled, a gallimaufry of diverse thoughts, of plans, worries, and imperatives. She had to unravel the medley. Samantha put on her jogging shoes and a loose-fitting running outfit, locked the door to her apartment, and went across the street to the park. Exercise would calm her.

Her doctor okayed jogging until midway through pregnancy, provided it was done in moderation. She padded onto the asphalt walkway, the beginning of her two-mile circuit, keeping to the shade of the trees. It was an interesting sensation: her breasts, slightly fuller, bounced freely, without restraint, and she self-consciously slowed her pace when someone approached. She felt like the engineer in a locomotive, aware of the freight aboard, terrified that a false step or stumble might jar loose the train's tiniest passenger. But that minor worry would not stop her from running. Samantha knew it kept her mind keen and her body healthy. Now, the thought uppermost in her mind was her own health. Exercise and proper diet would keep her fit and trim. She would avoid pollutants, steer clear of chemical additives . . . but oh, God, the drug! Please, she thought. Let me get the placebo!

Worry quickened her pace. Perhaps if she were super healthy, super strong, the benefit of physical conditioning could offset any adverse effect from the sleeping pill. Samantha returned to her apartment in record time.

6

He was more rugged than handsome, but very attractive nonetheless. Somehow Samantha had expected someone much older, professorial, with white hair and a long lab coat. Dr. Bryson looked young enough to be someone she might meet socially. His light brown hair matched the tan of his Levi's, and his blue eyes reflected the denim of his work shirt. His casual attire lent him an air of easy informality, and Samantha felt herself both comforted and stimulated by him.

Dr. Bryson reviewed the project in much more detail than Mrs. Rutledge had done. Samantha lost the train of his words. She kept staring into his eyes, wondering if she might do something embarrassing in her sleep. Dr. Bryson felt her gaze and interrupted himself.

"Is there something wrong?"

"What? Oh, no. I'm still with you."

"All right. So that's the whole thing in a nutshell: the effect of the medication on the quality of your sleep. We'll do baseline tracings the first three times you're here. You won't get the pill or the placebo until the fourth session. All we need now is three eight-hour EEG recordings. Are you ready to start?"

"Lead the way."

A clothes closet and bathroom were adjacent to the sleeping area. Samantha changed into her nightwear, long flannel pajamas covering her underwear. As a pre-bedtime ritual she emptied her bladder and washed her hands and face. She stared at her image in the mirror, sighed, and opened the door to the sleep room.

Dr. Bryson was sitting on a chair by the headboard, adjusting the electrode wires. Samantha entered the room self-consciously. It was embarrassing to enter a bedroom in children's pajamas and lie down next to an attractive stranger. Keep telling yourself it's for the money, she thought.

He motioned for her to lie on the bed. He attached the electrodes to her scalp and plugged the other ends into jacks on the headboard.

"All set," he said. "Ready for action."

"It's your bedroom. What have you got in mind?"

He smiled at her. "You're tinkering with my professionalism, Miss Kirstin. Right now all I have in mind is sleep. Your sleep. So close your eyes and relax. If you sleep, fine. If not, just relax and think pleasant thoughts. You can toss and turn all you want; don't worry about the wires. You can't strangle yourself."

"Wanna bet?"

"Well, let's just say it would be a first. If you need any kind of help, even if it's to go to the bathroom, press this button on the headboard. Otherwise Mrs. Rutledge will let you know when the eight hours are up. Do you have any questions?"

Unexpectedly Samantha thought of the baby, and felt a fleeting note of panic. "Are you sure I'll be all right?"

"Of course you will. Why?"

"Oh, I don't know. New surroundings, I guess."

"Fine. Remember, we're just outside if you need anything."

He closed the door and she leaned back on the mattress. Deep breaths, she thought, slowly in and out. Get your body to relax. Start at the toes and work up.

Samantha tried to concentrate on yoga meditation, but it was difficult. Her line of concentration was being distracted. Thoughts twinkled in her subconscious, fireflies on a summer night. Bryson's eyes seemed to stare at her, and in her mind's eye she stared back. Too blue, his eyes. He awakened thoughts in her that she was unprepared to deal with. She sensed her vulnerability—a feeling quite new to her, an emotion she never experienced before. Now was not the time, she thought. She rolled on her side and forced her mind to become blank. It was an effort; the struggle into lethargy was keeping her more awake than asleep. But she kept at it. Eventually she felt less need to keep turning and was content to lie still. Slowly her limbs became heavy. Her distraction was yielding to confusion, and confusion to slumber. Thoughts receded inward. Before she fell asleep, Samantha felt a warm sensation in her lower abdomen. It was the barest trembling, the slightest fluttering of butterflies, a quivering radiation of serenity. Comforted, she slept.

Outside Bryson gazed at her through the mirror, puzzled. She was certainly different from the other participants. Most of the medical students had a voluble sarcasm he found offensive. Her humor was more an incisive wit than a semblance of raillery. Outwardly she was an attractive, pleasant young woman. But the attitude of nonchalance he found so refreshing had a filigree of apprehension. Was there something she was holding back?

He reviewed her application. Samantha Kirstin was twenty-three and unmarried. She was a graduate student at the university working toward a Ph.D. in biology. Her biography was very straightforward, very uninformative. What he really wanted to know was, What is she doing here now?

He watched her sleep. The EEG revealed that she had rapidly passed through REM sleep and was on the verge of deep sleep. She had unconsciously tossed off the covers. She lay on her back, chest rising and falling with each breath. The flannel pajamas amused Bryson—a child's self-consciousness in an adult's body.

The EEG traced the waveform of delta sleep. Bryson noted its characteristic rhythm as he downed the last of his coffee. He was about to refill his cup when he noticed a subtle change on the oscilloscope. At the end of each delta wave, a little blip appeared. At least, he thought he noticed it; he wasn't sure. His eyes narrowed and he gazed intently. It was gone. He suspected it was an artifact; an electrical quirk? He adjusted the fine tuner to focus on the delta waves. They were perfectly normal.

Bryson looked at Samantha. She was motionless, eyes perfectly still, with no sign of REM activity. He looked from Samantha back to the oscilloscope. Had he imagined it? He rubbed his eyes with the back of his hands.

Bryson poured himself more coffee and returned to the electroencephalograph. There were no blips. Slowly, his sleep subject came out of delta sleep and slipped into theta and beta waveforms. The small bursts of REM activity he thought he had seen did not reappear as the pattern changed. Soon the sleep cycle was complete, and a new one began.

A REM spike appeared, not a blip but characteristically tall. Bryson knew that Samantha had to be dreaming. As he studied the screen, her limbs twitched, and she rolled on her side. She pursed her lips and propped up the pillow under her head, sleeping all the while.

He was perplexed. Could it possibly have been some sort of interference, static in the tracing? It was as if he were recording two different subjects on the same channel. And that was impossible.

The telephone rang. It was the computer center.

"Doc, what's going on over there?"

"Nothing special. Why?"

"Something strange is happening here. All the computers have gone haywire. As close as I can determine there may be some connection to the circuitry in your area."

"What do you mean, 'circuitry?' "

"I'm not exactly sure. But it looks like the problem is related to some sort of interference between MEDIC and your link-up. There's no pattern to it. It's pretty much at random. Are you performing one of your sleep studies?"

"As a matter of fact I am."

"Do you suppose you could hold off for a while?"

"What good would that do?"

"It's like I explained to you before: when your people are dreaming, MEDIC goes nuts. There's no rhyme or reason for it. It just happens. Our programs get fouled up, the tapes stop turning, and all our circuits seem to home in on your lab. And then MEDIC really gets screwy. The best I can describe it, I would say it's talking to itself."

"So why don't you turn it off?"

"That's just it, we can't. We don't seem to have complete control."

"Listen, I'm really sorry. Is there anything particular you'd like me to do?"

"Well, do you suppose you could work out a different time for your project? As far as I'm concerned, it wouldn't be so bad if MEDIC was dreaming at night. But during the day, it screws up our whole schedule. I know your study is important, but we've got other responsibilities too."

"I could try. Sure, why not."

"By the way. Let me ask you. There's a couple of things that MEDIC said. Here, let me get the printout," said Pattner. "Do the words 'Floating' and 'Commence Dialogue' mean anything to you?"

"Not really. What do they mean?"

"I don't know. They came up on MEDIC's printout just before I called you. Maybe five minutes ago."

Five minutes . . . There it was, nagging him, the slightest hint of wariness. He glanced at Samantha. She was sleeping soundly. He checked the oscilloscope: the waveform traced a normal sleep pattern. Yet, exactly five minutes earlier, the bizarre blips that intrigued him might have been on the screen.

"Mr. Pattner," he said, "my console goes directly into MEDIC, correct?"

"Yes. Your lab is the only one in the hospital or university that transmits live data."

He felt a sort of free-floating anxiety as his mind struggled to put things into perspective. "Mr. Pattner, let me think about this for a while. I'll try to work out something with my studies. If I come up with anything, I'll let you know."

Pattner rang off and Bryson hung up. He looked through the mirrored glass into the sleep room, feeling confused. The blips, the call from the computer center, Samantha's bizarre EEG pattern . . . were they somehow related? Maybe the blips were purely imaginary. Coincidence. Maybe not. But Bryson decided that sometime in the next day or two, he would have a long talk with Samantha Kirstin.

7

"Cream and sugar?" he asked, reaching for the stainless steel containers on the counter top.

"Black is fine, thanks," said Samantha, lightly touching the back of his hand.

Bryson glanced at the fingertips resting on his wrist. Usually he shied away from such physical contact. He wasn't a toucher. But now he felt . . . different.

Samantha finished her first cup of coffee and ordered another.

"You drink that stuff like a Brazilian."

"My only vice," said Samantha. "I adore coffee. I'm hooked on the caffeine. You don't think that can hurt, do you?"

"Hurt what?"

She hedged, looking away.

"Hurt my body. Physically. Have you ever read anything about that?"

"Sure. Coffee's great stuff, the perfect laxative. Makes you regular as clockwork."

"But you don't think all that caffeine could, say, derange my chromosomes?"

"Not that I'm aware of. Why do you ask?"

"Just curious."

There she goes again, he thought. She puzzled him. It was this enigmatic quality, plus the events in the sleep lab the preceding day, which led him to invite Samantha to coffee this morning. He was surprised by the way he blurted out the invitation, a proposition which drew a raised eyebrow and whimsical smile from Mrs. Rutledge. As a general rule, Bryson never had dealings with the sleep study volunteers outside the lab. He remained professional, aloof. But Samantha impressed him as unique. She was more mature, more clever. And she gazed at him now with a stare he found disquieting. He fumbled for small talk.

"This is your second graduate year in biology?"

"Mostly zoology," she corrected.

"What does it consist of?"

"A lot of seminars. And I'm an instructor in undergraduate biology. Did you take Bio One?"

"I had to, in pre-med."

She nodded. "I would say half of my students are pre-med."

"How long before you get your degree?"

"I should finish the requirements for my Masters by the end of the fall semester. After that, another eighteen months or so for my doctorate."

Bryson listened to the details of her academic life. Samantha's pleasant conversational tones captured his attention. She spoke of recently changing concepts in traditional zoology, and of how such changes would influence the direction of her career. Interesting though it was, Bryson hoped Samantha would talk more about herself. What he really wanted to know was whether or not she lived alone.

I don't get it, he thought. He knew he was becoming uncharacteristically interested in the girl. Since his annulment, he had not allowed himself to become entangled in the private lives of any of the women he met. The memory of his hurt was still clear, the pain still fresh. He found that devotion to medicine did more for his peace of mind than any analyst's couch. Now research was his only mistress, filling his day, sleeping with him at night.

He was no monk, however. Jonathan Bryson dated occasionally, but rarely with the same woman more than two or three times. It was safer that way. Women satisfied his physical needs, and to that end he was gentle and considerate. But he steered free from commitments. He had little reason to fear offending anyone. There were thousands of single women in the Jubilee General complex. If one of his bedmates grew possessive, he bade his farewells and moved on to the next. Now, though . . .

Her stare was unwavering. She raised an inquisitive eyebrow.

"Are you still there, Dr. Bryson?"

"I'm sorry. What?"

"I said, how long will it be before I'm given the medication or the placebo?"

"As soon as we have enough baseline tracings. As I said, it takes three sessions. Sometimes four."

Samantha brushed a stray lock of hair from her forehead. "By the middle of next week, then, you think?"

There was definitely a frown on her forehead. It was the same expression of vague concern he had seen the day before in the lab, when she asked him if everything would be all right. Was something bothering her?

"Yes, I think so. Middle of next week. Are you in a hurry?"

"No. I was just thinking out loud," she said, as she touched his hand again. "You'll be there in the lab, won't you?"

"Not for the next few days. I'm going to a conference out of town this weekend. But don't worry. Mrs. Rutledge can answer all of your questions."

He glanced at his watch. "Looks like I've kept you too long, Miss Kirstin. Mrs. Rutledge is probably wondering where you are. Thanks for joining me this morning."

"Call me Sam, Dr. Bryson, okay?" she asked, finishing the last of her coffee. She smiled at him and pushed herself away from the table. "Have a nice weekend. Hope you enjoy your conference."

"Thank you."

He watched her walk away, puzzled by the melange of personal interest and professional concern he felt for her. He suppressed the thoughts, content to simply watch her walk. Shoulders straight, head held high, Samantha disappeared around a corner. Something in the way she moved . . .

Bryson returned to the university the following Tuesday, going directly to the lab rather than home. He wanted to be there when Samantha Kirstin awakened. It was strange how his thoughts strayed to her during the conference. He was showing the kind of interest in a woman that he hadn't allowed himself to feel in years.

His timing was perfect. As Mrs. Rutledge welcomed him back, Samantha tossed in her sleep, nearing the end of her session.

"How's it going, Rosie?"

"Very good, very good indeed. I confess I'm growing fond of our new sleeper. She's a very pleasant young woman."

"No problems, then?"

She looked at him quizzically.

"Were you expecting problems?"

"No. Not really."

"It's curious that you should ask that," said Mrs. Rutledge. "Everything is proceeding quite well. Samantha and I have had delightful chats together. She's very poised, with her own special charm. Yet I have the sensation that she's troubled."

"Troubled?"

"Yes, that something's on her mind."

"Something specific?"

"No, she's mentioned nothing. And I wouldn't want to pry."

They looked through the mirrored glass together for several minutes. Samantha was in the final stage of REM sleep. Bryson inspected the markings on the oscilloscope. At first everything appeared perfectly normal. But then, as the waveform changed, blips began to appear.

The blips. He hadn't seen them since Samantha's initial sleep session, if he really had seen anything at all. Yet now here they were again, appearing taller, stronger than he recalled them. He watched intently, calling to Mrs. Rutledge.

"Rosie," he said, pointing toward the screen, "have you noticed those markings on the 'scope while I was gone?"

"Which markings?"

"These, over here."

But as he drew her attention to the blips, they began to fade, before she could perceive the change.

"Damn."

"What was it you saw?" she asked.

"I'm not sure."

An EEG pattern of wakefulness filled the oscilloscope. In the sleep room, Samantha opened her eyes. Mrs. Rutledge went to assist her.

As Samantha dressed in the bathroom, Mrs. Rutledge tidied up the sleep area. Bryson sat on the desk top and mulled over his thoughts.

The damn blips, he thought. What did they mean? The researcher in him struggled for an answer, but at this moment there was none.

Bryson was also perplexed by the intensity of his concern for the girl. It shouldn't happen, at least not to him. He had to remain objective, to maintain perspective. Yet all weekend his thoughts had been intruded upon by Samantha. And no sooner did he return from his conference than he went to the lab. But most significant and troublesome was Mrs. Rutledge's evaluation that something bothered Samantha. Rosie had picked up on the same hints that he had.

All right already, he thought. It was time to admit he was interested in her. When they had coffee together, he had broken his cardinal rule about not fraternizing with the students. It was time to go for all the marbles.

Samantha, yawning, combed her hair and greeted him sleepily.

"Welcome back, Dr. Bryson. How was the conference?"

"Fine, Sam. And now that we're on a first-name basis, I'd like you to call me Jon."

"Welcome back, Jon," she said. Samantha pressed her hips against the desk ledge, leaning beside him. They exchanged polite smiles, and an air of tension enveloped them, neither speaking. Samantha sighed, looked away, and rummaged through the papers on the table top.

"What are you looking for?"

"I could have sworn Mrs. Rutledge left a chocolate bar here this morning."

He laughed. "Rosie's got a sweet tooth, Sam. It's probably in her stomach by now. Tell you what: can you cope with your hunger for another hour or two?"

"I doubt it," she laughed.

"Even if I promise you a great meal?"

"Is that an invitation out to dinner, Dr. Bryson?"

"Jon, remember? No, it's the promise of a culinary delight, at my place."

"Great! I'd love it."

"Seven?"

"I'll be ready," she said. With a wink, she was gone.

8

A small pile of minced green herbs was heaped on the corner of the chopping block. Beside it, a handful of peeled shallots awaited the chef's knife. Empty eggshells were clustered around a half-filled bottle of vermouth.

"Where did you learn to do that?" she asked.

"Make béarnaise sauce?"

"No. Crack eggs with one hand."

"My form of survival training," said Bryson, as he began mixing the egg yolks with a wire whisk. "Being a bachelor in Manhattan is not everything it's supposed to be. New York restaurant cuisine is a delight to the palate and a terror to the pocketbook. So, as a lover of good food, I had to learn the basics."

"A filet with béarnaise sauce isn't my idea of the basics."

"It is, believe me. The complicated dishes take hours."

"You're a regular Julia Child."

"Except for our dress size."

He had Samantha prepare a simple salad while he finished the sauce. Soon the steaks were ready and he uncorked a bottle of St. Emilion. She brought the dishes out to a small glass table on the apartment's terrace while he went to the oven for one last item. Bryson returned with a breadbasket lined with a red linen napkin. Warm bread steamed in the cool breeze of a late spring dusk.

"Is that fresh bread?" she asked, as he poured the wine.

"The real thing, cross my heart."

"I can't believe it. Okay, go on and complete the sentence."

"Which one?"

"A loaf of bread, a jug of wine . . ."

He laughed. "You're jumping the gun, aren't you?"

"Not really. When a man invites a woman to his apartment for dinner, that's one thing. When she accepts it's another."

"And which is it with you, Miss Kirstin?"

"Blimey, a touch of the formal, eh wot?"

"Force of habit. I feel a little uncomfortable when I ask a woman to come to my home, even when I have the most honorable intentions."

She sampled the wine, looking directly at him. "And what are the good doctor's intentions tonight?"

"Strictly professional, I assure you."

"Shit."

"Better try your steak before it gets cold."

"Spoilsport."

She knew that her boldness was defensive, her way of reacting to the tenseness of the situation. The humor of her bravado defused anxiety, made all the more mellow by the wine. Still, she was embarrassed by the braggart in her; aggressive sexuality was not her true character.

Steak, salad, bread, and wine: the meal was as superb as it had been simple. She asked him about himself and was aware that he skipped over any reference to his personal life, past or present.

Bryson was annoyed at his garrulousness and chided himself for not coming to the point. His intention had been to get to know Samantha Kirstin better, more as a subject in his project than as an individual in her own right. To that end he hoped that the social circumstances of his invitation would make her relax and allow him to understand the workings of her personality. But she proved to be the perfect conversationalist, in that she was an astute listener. At any pause in the conversation she adroitly turned their discussion back toward Bryson, and he found himself rambling on, encouraged by Samantha's pertinent questions. She was clever, witty; and in spite of his uncontrollable effusiveness, he wanted to keep talking and talking. She had an uncanny understanding of his foibles which made him want to say yes, yes, that's it. . . .

"Aren't you curious why I invited you here tonight?"

"Yes. But I'd rather not ask and take all the mystery out of it."

"It's not all that mysterious. Very simply, I think you have an unusual EEG."

Her eyes widened in mock concern. "Oh God. Will I live?"

He smiled. "Until you're a hundred. But as far as your EEG goes, you have a kind of tracing I've never seen before. It looks perfectly benign, yet I can't quite explain it. Here, let me draw it for you."

On the back of a paper napkin, Bryson illustrated the various types of normal EEG patterns. Beside it, for comparison, he reconstructed Samantha's EEG as he remembered it from the afternoon.

"This is what your EEG looked like on the oscilloscope," said Bryson, pointing out the various features. "These lines are normal waveforms—here, here, and here. Now, look at these small oscillations a little farther on. That's your normal REM pattern, both in timing and in duration. Compare that to this portion of the tracing," he said, indicating the blips he thought he noticed earlier in the day. "Do you see any difference?"

She cradled her chin in her palm, elbows on the table. "It's a good thing you didn't become a gynecologist. Women would be too embarrassed to get undressed in front of you."

"Come on, I'm trying to be serious."

"I'm sorry," she said, comparing the waveforms. "Let's see. They look the same to me. Except maybe these little ones are shorter and squigglier than the others."

"Very good. That's precisely it."

"Huh? What's precisely it?"

"What you call squiggles have one more difference from your normal REM pattern. Your normal REM waves occur where they should, at the end of one sleep cycle and the beginning of the next. But these little ones occur when you're in delta sleep. You couldn't possibly be dreaming then. At least I don't think you could."

"So what does it mean?"

He shrugged. "Wish I knew. We occasionally see abnormal EEGs in patients with neurological problems, like head trauma or epilepsy. But on your application you mentioned none of that."

"I've always been as healthy as a horse," she said, devouring two slices of bread as if to prove it.

"And you don't use any drugs or medications?"

"Oh, I mainline smack, but nothing serious."

He laughed and sat back. "You know what's so astonishing about you?"

"Yes, but say it anyway."

"I could tell someone else they had an abnormal EEG and they'd have a stroke worrying about it. I mention it to you, and you act like you couldn't care less."

"Oh, I care all right. But since you're the brains behind the sleep research lab, I figure you know what you're doing. I also think that if there were something seriously wrong, you would let me know."

"I would," he nodded. "This is more puzzling than serious." He thought of telling her of his conversation with the computer center but demurred. "I have some good brandy inside. Could you give me a hand with these plates?"

He washed the dishes while she dried. Night had fallen, and the evening air carried a chill. Bryson closed the sliding door to the terrace and led Samantha into the living room. His townhouse condominium had a stone hearth fireplace, and he tonged the pieces of firewood into their iron cradle.

"The last three logs in the cord," he said.

"Never too late for a fire, hmm?"

"Hell, it won't be June for another week yet."

"I love a fire. Back home we have fireplaces in practically every room. I always watched the late show by a fire, even in August."

"Where's home?"

"Long Island. A little place you never heard of called Laurel Hollow."

He filled her snifter with Courvoisier. "I know Laurel Hollow. I used to pass it when I was going sailing. A friend of mine docks his boat in Cold Spring Harbor."

"No kidding?"

"Honest. I probably drove by your house a couple of times."

She smiled. "I would have waved, but I didn't recognize your car."

"More likely you can't see a car from your window. I

didn't think any house in Laurel Hollow had less than thirty rooms on a fifty-acre estate, all perfectly concealed from prying eyes."

"Would you settle for eighteen rooms on ten acres?"

"You're serious, aren't you?"

She nodded. "Part of a proper upbringing. And something I was very happy to leave behind."

"Problems at home?"

"More like annoyances than problems," she said, folding her legs under her on the sofa. "I guess they come with the turf."

"The unhappy rich girl?"

"Sort of. My father's never at home. He's always flying around the world on some kind of real estate deal. Mother is sweet, but very prim, very polite. Like a well-trained lap dog. She belongs to the right clubs, and is perpetually smiling. All she can say is, 'But of course, darling.' "

He laughed aloud. "I bet she tries hard, in spite of what you say."

"Don't get me wrong. She means well, and in some ways I feel sorry for her. I'll give you a for-instance: I have an eighteen-year-old brother, just us two kids, you know? My father gave him a yellow racing Porsche for his birthday. The brat is really spoiled rotten. He didn't have the car more than a week when he totaled it, drunk driving. A minor miracle he wasn't hurt. But the last time I called home, they had bought him another Porsche—blue this time. Talk about pathetic."

"So you left home."

"Not right away. Mother went to Vassar, so naturally I did too. But they had me come home once a month and on every holiday. It was as if I had never left Long Island. Between my parents' supervision and the cloistered atmosphere at school, I felt like I was in a nunnery. The only thing that kept me going was freshman biology. I really loved it. I must have spent every afternoon in the lab."

"When did you cut the cord?"

"That same year. After the first semester, I couldn't take it anymore. I wanted to major in biology, so when my parents and my advisor weren't looking over my shoulder I sent off applications to half a dozen schools that had good bio programs. After my freshman year I transferred to George Washington."

"Your parents must have loved that."

"They did everything to get me back. That summer my father bought me a catamaran I had wanted since I was in high school."

"You sail cats?"

"I'm crazy about them. I'll say this for my dad: even though he was an absent father most of the time, he taught me to be independent. When I was thirteen, I fell in love with my first small catamaran. I wanted it for my birthday. Mother's afraid of water. Can you believe that? Living on the North Shore, just off Long Island Sound? Anyway, she convinced my father not to buy it for me. He told me that if I wanted it I'd have to buy it myself. That was a switch: up until then I'd had anything I asked for, and the next week I was baby sitting. My mother was mortified. Father was furious that I actually got a job, but he was too stubborn to give in. From then on I've always worked."

"Did you get your catamaran?"

"Two of them. The one I was saving for I bought when I was fifteen. And the one my father bribed me with, I sailed all summer until he realized I was serious about transferring to G.W. The next day, he sold it."

They talked about sailing for the better part of an hour. Bryson again found himself monopolizing the conversation, aware that Samantha was charting the course of their dialogue as skillfully as if she were planning the tack of a sailboat. He grew more impressed with her. As she studied him talking, he studied her back, the camaraderie born of sailing developing into something greater, an encompassing feeling of mutuality and closeness, of touching and being near.

Still sipping brandy, Bryson was aware that Samantha had him begin the long tale of his arrival at Jubilee General. His private practice of neurology in Manhattan had been a struggle. In fact, up to then his whole life had been a series of struggles. After working his way through college, Bryson married his childhood sweetheart who, it turned out, did not have the same commitment to monogamy that Bryson did. After several of her sordid affairs, he bailed out. The annulment was swift but humiliating. Escape from mental haziness that followed seemed to lie in choosing the right career. Bryson set his sights on computer science, returned to college and took a master's degree in that field. But though he excelled in this area, he soon realized that even the finest jobs in the computer industry offered little intellectual stimulation. He longed for human contact. A career in medicine seemed ideal, but he knew his chances for admission to medical school were remote. Bryson scored well enough on the pre-med entrance exam, however, to earn himself a place on the waiting list of a medical school in Boston. For once, luck turned his way. He was accepted.

Medical school proved brutal. Clinically and diagnostically, he excelled. But the sheer weight of memory work wore him down, worsened by the nights and weekends he worked to earn money for tuition. Toward the end of his second year he was ready to quit. Apparently, so were a dozen others in his class. With the reduced class size, Bryson was awarded a small scholarship, enough to provide sufficient financial aid to enable him to only have to work weekends. This proved to be the impetus that sustained him. From then on, Bryson devoted himself to his studies. By the time he graduated, he was elected to Alpha Omega Alpha, the national medical honor society.

In med school, neuroanatomy had fascinated him, perhaps because of his computer background. In a sense the intricate workings of the brain and nervous system were those of a computer, though infinitely more complex. But like a computer, a short circuit or power failure would be reflected in a defective human printout: a limp, a speech defect, paralysis. The key to diagnosis lay in determining the exact site of the power failure.

Although Bryson did his internship in Boston, he was attracted by the glamour of New York. One of the more prestigious residency programs in Manhattan took him on for three years of training in neurology. Here his life took an upward turn. His skill, confidence, and exuberance earned him a reputation as the young lion of the department, and he was made Chief Resident in his final year. Bryson began to envision an enviable private practice on Park Avenue. Thus emboldened, and assured of success by his superiors, he took out a $30,000 loan from the Chase Manhattan Bank. On July first of that year, after completing his residency, he rented a five-room office on 72nd Street and Park Avenue. There soon followed the hiring of a receptionist, two nurses, and an answering service; purchasing a costly malpractice insurance policy; and outfitting his quarters in the latest art deco. The only thing that did not come was referrals.

The first six months of practice were disastrous. Bryson saw barely three dozen patients, most of them Medicaid recipients. A smattering of token hospital consultations was tossed his way. He was forced to take on menial medical jobs here and there to supplement his income, but it was barely enough. By the end of his first year in practice, Bryson's total debt was $40,000.

The second year proved better, as did the third. Persistence, word of mouth, and constant availability rewarded him with a slowly growing private practice. Bryson was finally able to live with a modicum of comfort. His reputation grew and soon patients had to wait four weeks, then six, for an office visit. If success was not yet his, it was clearly just around the corner. But along with success came a growing list of non-medical responsibilities: reams of paperwork, administrative dilemmas, and never-ending hospital committee meetings. They impaired his ability to be a complete physician, a consummate healer. Late one night, after resolving one of his interminable personnel disputes, Bryson concluded that private practice was not for him. He longed for medicine for its own sake, for pure science and research.

Jonathan Bryson began to daydream. He recalled his early student days in the laboratory and the glee that came with unfettered discovery. As he tapped a patient's knee with a reflex hammer, his mind wandered to thoughts of test tubes and distillation flasks. He would gaze endlessly into the pupils of a patient and become lost in the reflected retinal sheen, letting his thoughts stray to vaccines and guinea pigs. He was conscious of his progressive mental lapses even if his patients were not. He realized that the time had come to rechannel his energies and give his career new direction. If his fantasy lay in research, that was where he would turn.

Two and a half years after completing his residency, he began leafing through scientific periodicals, searching for vacancies in medical research. Months passed; little worthwhile was available. Bryson grew edgy. He found himself anticipating each Sunday's *New York Times* with its listing of openings in the health professions. Nothing suitable came up. He likewise scanned the medical journals, and twice placed notices under "Situations Wanted" that went unanswered. Then, nearing the end of his third year in practice, he came across an item in the *Journal of the American Medical Association* about a position in sleep research at Jubilee General. He sent off his resume the next morning.

It was late now and they were both a bit drunk, part from liquor and part from the euphoria of shared reminiscence. He still hadn't learned enough about her.

"Why did you apply for the job in the lab?"

She seemed to collect her thoughts.

"It's something I'm interested in. In physiology, they taught us the mechanics of sleep. I heard about the job from some friends who are med students."

Her eyes darted away, a hint of deceit. He knew she was lying.

"Is it the money?" he asked. "I know we pay well."

"Anyone can use extra money."

"You're not anyone. You come from a wealthy family and you have a good instructorship. Why should you need the money?"

"I have some expenses."

"Another catamaran?" he asked, smiling.

She didn't return his smile. When she replied, it was a whisper. "If only it were." She pushed herself up from the couch. "It's getting late. Thank you for dinner. It was delicious."

He came over to her. "Hey, I didn't mean to pry. I apologize if I'm getting too personal. It's just that . . ."

"That what?"

He shook his head. "I don't know. It's a feeling I get from you. If you're in some kind of trouble . . ."

His eyes beckoned, and she looked deeply into them.

Samantha touched his cheek. She ached to tell him. "Thank you. Maybe someday." She turned to leave.

"Who's Jerry?"

She started. "How do you know about Jerry?"

"You talk in your sleep."

"What did I say?"

"Just something about Jerry. Who is he? A boyfriend?"

She averted his eyes. "Someone I used to know."

He moved closer, and they were nearly touching. He saw the sadness grow in her. Her eyes misted, and she turned her face away. With his fingertips, he turned her chin back to him.

"Let me help you," he said.

It was the shattering of ageless china, like a hundred lines etching her face and then being suddenly pulled apart, the void within her filling with a sadness that surprisingly poured forth in long, racking sobs. He put his arms around her, and she cried on his chest, clinging tight.

He smoothed her hair, touching her neck. She looked up at him and wiped the tears from her eyes. He kissed her gently on the forehead. Their sudden closeness comforted her. It was warm, tender and unexpected. Her eyes fastened on his, and their faces were drawn slowly together,

nearer still until eyes closed and lips touched, unmoving,
the barest, silky caress of mouth on mouth. They clung
together softly for minutes, and when she finally moved
away her opening eyes saw his open too, and the sadness
in her yielded to yearning, a slowly growing ache that
burned within her, and this time their kiss was hungry, insistent, tongue seeking tongue, and she pressed herself
against him with a fierceness, frightened by her intensity
but not wanting to stop.

They sank onto the rug before the fire. He held her by
the waist, and they lay on their sides, embracing. Her fingers traced the back of his head through his hair. He
touched her lips, her nose, her cheeks, gently sculpting the
contours of her face. For a long while they searched each
other's eyes in the firelight, and then she again pressed
against him eagerly, and he rolled onto his back. They
were both impatient. He lifted the blouse from her slacks
while she undid the buttons on his shirt. Soon they were
naked, and legs entwined as they rolled from side to side,
mouths locked together. In his hunger he held her breast
firmly, almost harshly, and when she drew away, he knew
he had hurt her; but she said no, her breasts were tender,
please touch me here, and she guided his hand to the
dampness and warmth between her thighs. In a minute
she sighed, and her fingers caressed the muscle of his belly,
then reached lower to hold him firmly, eagerly. Then they
were both ready, hurriedly but unpreparedly, and he rolled
away from her, whispering of protection. But she held him
fast, arching herself toward him. It was safe, she said, she
was due any day; and he rolled back toward her, cupping
her buttocks. She guided him into her, their joining a
smooth, undulating carousel, a slippery softness of merging and coming apart, of slowness and then rapid quick-

ening, until she crushed her hips against his, whimpering softly, holding him close until he too was spent, breathless, the urgency easing.

He held her for many minutes. The sadness was gone from her, and contentment took its place. They parted slowly.

When Samantha sat up, she was shockingly pale.

"Are you okay?" he asked.

"Too much wine," she said, and arose unsteadily, walking toward the bathroom. She closed the door behind her, but the sound of retching was unmistakable.

She stayed in the bathroom a long while. Bryson thought of going to her, but granted her privacy. He stoked the embers in the fire. As he stared at the coals he frowned, wrestling with his thoughts. It was back again, that feeling of uncertainty, of things hidden, unsaid. There was something happening here, if only he could piece it together. Samantha's words . . . what had she said?

And suddenly he saw it, and the light of recognition blazed brighter than the fire before him. In his mind's eye, he pictured her application form; he could see every line. He recalled the entry where she listed her last menstrual period. She had written the date of 2 weeks before. How, then, could she be due any day? Could she possibly be mistaken? Maybe she was on the pill, or had an I.U.D. No, those women usually remembered their periods. And Samantha was much too intelligent to use nothing at the wrong time of the month, to risk getting pregnant, unless . . .

The realization struck him with such intensity that he nearly burned himself on the hearth. The ruse about her periods, the tender breasts, the vomiting . . . idiot! A freshman medical student could make the diagnosis. Annoyance gave way to reflection, and he pictured her before him. The sadness he had seen was legitimate. She was indeed in trouble. No wonder she needed a job.

He went to his bedroom, put on a robe, and returned with a long-sleeved shirt for Samantha. He lay on his stomach before the fire. Samantha finally came out of the bathroom and sat next to him, wrapped in a bath towel. He handed her the shirt. She discarded the towel and put it on. Her color had returned.

"Mmmm," she murmured, snuggling next to him. Her breath smelled of his mouthwash. She relaxed and closed her eyes.

Samantha was dozing. Bryson knew that he had to talk to her, to let her know he knew. He felt drawn to her, wanting to comfort her and help her. He brushed her cheek with his lips.

"You're pregnant, aren't you, Sam?"

Startled, she opened her eyes, realizing that he knew, the statement irrefutable.

"How could you tell?"

"I'm a doctor, remember?"

"I knew you were a closet gynecologist."

"You couldn't be very far along."

"A little more than two months."

"You still have time, then."

"For what?" she said, looking directly at him. It was a statement, not a question, its meaning clear.

Bryson pursed his lips. "Well. That's a big step."

"I know."

"Are you Catholic?"

"No. It has nothing to do with religion or being anti-abortion. I'm not. I just want to have the baby."

"That must have been a tough decision. I guess you thought it through."

"I did. But it wasn't as tough as you think."

"This Jerry, is he the father?"

"He's a nobody."

"A nobody who got you pregnant, you mean."

"He's not to blame. If one has to assign fault, it was as much mine as his. There was never a question of marriage, of doing something that's wrong for both of us. So right now, he's just a memory."

"And you need a job."

She inhaled deeply, thoughtfully. "Having a baby's not inexpensive. I do need the money. I know it was wrong to lie to you when I applied for the job. But I looked everywhere else on campus, and I couldn't find a thing. I was just hoping that . . . I don't know. I'm sort of glad you found out. I was scared out of my wits about what the drug might do to the baby. Now the whole thing is academic."

"You're not interested in the project?"

"How could I be? I was kidding myself to think I wouldn't worry. And the form said that female applicants couldn't be pregnant. Now that you know, I feel relieved."

"There still might be a way."

"Thanks, but I wouldn't want to take the chance."

"You don't understand. If I were a totally committed scientist, which I'd like to think I am, I should exclude you from the study. But there may be a very legitimate, scientific reason for keeping you in the sleep project: simply to study a pregnant woman's EEG. And since your EEGs are already interesting, there may be a lot to be gained from it. Your "squiggles" may even have something to do with being pregnant. So, Sam, if you want to stay in the study, I could arrange for you to get the placebo every time."

"No sleeping pills?"

"Not unless candy makes you sleepy."

"And nobody would know?"

"Not for a couple of months, when it would make itself obvious."

"Are you sure it won't harm the baby?"

"I'm sure," he smiled.

Samantha relaxed against him, comforted, and closed her eyes.

"Doctor, you're an all right person."

She nestled next to his shoulder and was soon sleeping soundly. Bryson lay awake looking at the embers, not wanting to move and disturb her. He would not allow himself to feel sympathy for her; she had made her decision with full consideration of the alternatives and the consequences. Still, her dilemma touched him, and he knew he would help her if he could.

He kissed her cheek tenderly and smiled to himself. Just his luck. The first woman who had interested him in years turned out to be pregnant.

9

"Can you make anything out of that, Mac?"

Joachim MacFerson studied the EEG tracing. As head of the section of neurophysiology, he had more experience with the workings of the nervous system than anyone within the university confines. His subspecialty was developmental neuroanatomy, a field which charted the growth and function of the maturing nervous system. MacFerson's reputation was nationwide, but the piece of graph paper before him baffled him.

"Beats me. I never saw anything like it. You think these little oscillations might come from the fetus?"

"That's what I was hoping you could tell me," said Bryson.

MacFerson shook his head. "I don't know. It's possible. There has been some work in the EEGs of newborn infants, but not this early in fetal development."

"At what stage were they studied?"

"Usually during labor. Most of the studies dealt with predicting faulty neurological development at a later age, say at one year old, based on the EEG pattern during labor. They would compare the fetal EEG, or FEEG, with the year-old infant's EEG, and see whether there was any relation between the stresses in labor and abnormal neurologic function. Some of these guys say they can predict brain damage from the FEEG."

"So researchers conducting FEEGs are interested in long-term neurobehavioral follow-up."

"Basically, yes."

"How do you do an EEG on a baby still in the uterus?"

"Around '69 or '70 a new electrode was developed. It was inserted vaginally, into the uterus and onto the baby's scalp. After that, they were able to get pretty reliable continuous FEEGs."

"What sorts of things did they look for on the tracing?"

MacFerson scratched his head in recollection. "If I remember correctly, they were interested in FEEG changes associated with too much medication, lack of oxygen, fetal heart rate decelerations, or forceps deliveries. Stuff like that."

"So with the electrode," continued Bryson, "they would perform an FEEG, and see if transient changes in the waveform were associated with neurologic abnormalities when the kid was older?"

"Right."

"Do they read a fetal EEG the same as an adult's?"

"No. They're read according to standardized terminology for newborn EEGs. Newborn EEGs have characteristic pattern classification. A set of random variables is used to define the amplitude, frequency, and bandwidth of the signal."

"In my tracing, can you eliminate this blip as a fetal signal because I haven't used an intrauterine electrode?"

"Hell no. I can't say that at all. We know that the fetal nervous system is developing as early as eight weeks of pregnancy. It could be that your pregnant patient has high neuro-conductivity, and early impulses originating in the fetus are reflected on the mother's tracing."

"Then it's possible?"

"Sure. We know that babies dream. But no one has studied how early in fetal development that occurs."

"Babies are one thing, but how about an unborn fetus?"

"Definitely. A fetus has an EEG and dreams, too."

"You sound pretty certain of that. How can you tell?"

"There was a study a couple of years ago by a group of Scandinavian investigators," replied MacFerson. "They took incubating baby chicks and delaminated their shells, putting a glass cover on top of the egg. Through it, they could see that the unhatched chicks had occasional rapid eye movements. So they concluded, probably correctly, that unborn babies dream. At least, baby chicks do."

"Interesting. So if these are fetal signals on my tracing, all I have to do is monitor my subject for a week or two, and see if any pattern develops."

"Why waste your time? Let MEDIC do it."

"How could I do that?"

"In some of the fetal EEG studies, computers were used. You see, when you do research like this, there's a massive volume of data generated. In a couple of weeks you could accumulate thousands of pages of graph paper, and it would be tough to be precise about the meaning of relative patterns by your own visual analysis. I don't see how you could consistently evaluate that much data."

"The computer analyzed the tracings for them?"

"Yes. For FEEG analysis, they used a minicomputer in a disc operating system configuration. Data were transcribed to digital magnetic tape and analyzed with an offline version of an FEEG program. A typical program classified the EEG patterns into categories like low voltage, high voltage, voltage depression, etcetera. Saved a lot of time."

"Sounds like it should. If I were to divide my subject's EEG into one-hour intervals, MEDIC could analyze each epoch in about two seconds."

"That's what computers are for. Still, when you talk

about EEGs at two months of fetal development, you're sailing on uncharted waters. You might be able to get an interesting paper out of it."

"More than that, Mac, more than that. Right now we're talking hunches. But if this turns out to be what I think it is, I might be onto something big. Of course, I need a lot more data before I could draw a reasonably scientific conclusion. And do me one last favor, Mac: keep this under your hat. I don't want anyone to hear about this prematurely, before I can show them something solid."

MacFerson promised and Bryson spent the rest of the morning in the university library reviewing obscure articles on fetal electroencephalography. After several hours of perusing the journals, he knew MacFerson was right. There was very little written on fetal EEGs, and most of it dealt with tracings taken during labor. There was nothing about electroencephalography early in fetal development.

The field was wide open.

Bryson felt his excitement grow. If Samantha's baby, barely more than an embryo, did indeed emit brain activity recordable on an EEG, it was an incredible finding. If he could chart the pattern of electrical activity of the developing fetal brain, he could enter a whole new area of drug comparison. The promise of a new source of research funds would be unlimited. Once he developed an EEG terminology for the normally maturing fetus, he could propose a standard to which other fetuses could be compared. This alone would be a remarkable achievement in science. It was also something the drug companies were bound to seize upon, affording him greater opportunity for study.

Bryson grew heady with anticipation. Was this the elusive discovery he had been seeking since coming to Jubilee General? Ever since he abandoned private practice and set his sights on research, Bryson hoped that one day he would make—perhaps stumble onto—a fascinating, seemingly unimaginable discovery, one that held great hope for mankind. Like Pasteur, Koch, and Lister, he would use that discovery as the cornerstone for decades of intensive, satisfying investigation. It was a staggering concept, to be the man behind it all. It was a scientist's promise, and a scientist's dream.

He felt unable to contain himself. As the person who had shared his aspirations over the past two years, Mrs. Rutledge might best understand his mounting exhilaration. He phoned her and recounted his conversation with MacFerson. If Mrs. Rutledge was surprised when he mentioned that he'd learned Samantha was pregnant, she didn't show it. Her concerns, if any, dealt more with Samantha's responsibilities as a single parent. Although it was too early to go into details, Bryson related what he thought he might find, and how he would arrange for Samantha to receive the placebo. Mrs. Rutledge was thrilled for him. Bryson promised to be more definitive about his plans when he next saw her. As a parting shot before she hung up, Mrs. Rutledge wondered aloud if Bryson's scientific curiosity didn't carry an element of personal concern. She knew a crush when she saw one, she laughed. Bryson replaced the receiver, shaking his head. Was his interest in Samantha all that obvious?

That afternoon he phoned the computer center. Once again he spoke with Pattner. The following afternoon, he said, he would conduct another sleep study on the same subject whose EEG provoked Pattner's previous call. He would do it toward the end of normal working hours so as not to hinder computer functioning if another disturbance occurred. Pattner was agreeable. Then Bryson phoned Samantha. He told her not to come to the lab in the morning, but rather at four in the afternoon. He would explain why when he saw her.

The next afternoon, Samantha arrived at the lab early. With Mrs. Rutledge in the other room, she kissed Bryson on the cheek.

"Mixing business with pleasure?" he asked.

She sat down primly. "All right. I can be as professional as you. You owe me thirty-five dollars."

"For what?"

"For the seven hours I should have worked since nine this morning."

"Tell you what: I'll pay you twenty dollars an hour for two hours of work, if you call it that, if you can come every day, four to six."

"Why so generous?"

"Because you're pregnant."

"It's a little early for a baby shower."

He smiled. "Yesterday I did some research in the library. It's becoming more and more plausible that your unique EEG comes from electrical impulses arising in the baby. If I can prove that's true, you're worth your weight in grant money."

"Then maybe I should command a higher fee."

"Are you asking for bids?"

"Not if I have to open my premises for inspection."

"Then I win on two counts: most recent inspector, and highest bidder. What I'd like to do, Sam, is a simple two-hour tracing. We'll do it the same as a regular sleep study, except that I'm going to attach one of the scalp electrodes to your belly, just above the pubic bone."

"You're serious about the brain waves coming from the baby, then?"

"Very. This could be a medical breakthrough."

"Now I'm confused. You explained the other day that when I have REM activity, I'm dreaming. I'll buy that; I saw it myself on one of your other volunteers. But suppose you can prove that the impulses do come from the baby. Does that mean that the baby has REM sleep?"

"Probably."

"Then if REM sleep is associated with dreaming, what on earth could a two-month-old, one-inch-long, unborn baby be dreaming about?"

Bryson knitted his brow, breathing in and out deeply.

"Good question. I haven't the faintest idea."

"But you're sure that they dream?"

"That's what I'm going to find out. If they don't actually dream, I wouldn't be surprised if the developing nervous system had some sort of electrical activity. It's a phenomenon of all brain cells, regardless of developmental stage."

He went on to describe the experiment MacFerson explained with the unhatched chicks.

"The fetus certainly has enough sensory input to give it the stuff dreams are made of," he continued. "Other researchers have put miniature telescopes into a uterus containing a four-month-old fetus. They haven't looked specifically for rapid eye movements, but we know from their observations that these babies move their arms and legs, breathe in and out even though their lungs are filled with fluid, and respond to stimuli. If the central nervous system can integrate that information, who knows what might be happening in their brains?"

"Okay, counselor, I'm convinced. If it's the Nobel Prize you're after, I won't stand in your way. When do we start?"

"As soon as Mrs. Rutledge finishes preparing the sleep room."

"And you're sure, Jon—really sure—this can't hurt the baby?"

"I'm sure. Promise."

Soon Samantha was in the sleep room, wired loosely to the console. She had pulled her jeans down to just above the top of her pubic hair, where the electrode was secured.

"How soon will you know the results?" she asked.

"It shouldn't take long. The computer will analyze the EEG pattern by tomorrow morning. I'm going to ask the programmers to pay special attention to any unusual REM patterns. After a week of pattern analysis, we'll find out if anything significant has developed. Sweet dreams."

He turned off the light and asked her to try to remain on her back to keep the electrode from being detached. Outside, Mrs. Rutledge joined him. They observed through the glass as Samantha wiggled into a comfortable position. Once again, it didn't take her long to fall asleep.

When he first came to the lab, before he had begun relying exclusively on his oscilloscope and MEDIC's computer analyses, Bryson had employed a standard six-channel electroencephalograph, rather than the miniature three-channel unit he still used. But the standard model soon lost its value. MEDIC's evaluations rendered its ink pens and graph paper obsolete. But now Bryson took it out of storage, dusted it off, and hooked it up to the console. It produced precisely that tangible, graphic tracing that he now wanted. Should he get results, no one would rely on his word alone.

Bryson watched the printout. A green light on the panel above it indicated that the waveforms were being transmitted to MEDIC. Within minutes the pen on the graph traced a characteristic REM pattern. He glanced again at Samantha, the twitching of her eyelids indicating a dream. The pattern changed, and she moved rapidly into deeper sleep stages.

Then the blips appeared.

It was still early in the tracing. Bryson nudged Mrs. Rutledge, who now acknowledged what he had previously alluded to and what she had not previously seen. Samantha had barely entered a non-REM pattern when the strange markings inked themselves onto the paper. Mrs. Rutledge watched in awe. But the markings had changed since Bryson had first seen them. Now they were darker and more strongly etched, the pen oscillating vigorously. The markings were powerful, and stood out clearly from Samantha's background theta waves. The blips appeared at random. Whereas on the oscilloscope they had seemed to trail a delta wave, now they enigmatically popped up anywhere, as if at will.

Bryson wasn't surprised at the telephone's ringing.

"When did you start?" asked Pattner.

"About twenty minutes ago. Any problems?"

"No, it's too late in the day for any serious trouble. We had a short wind-down, must have been right after you began. Now everything's working okay. If the interference from your lab is no worse than this, we might be able to live with it."

Bryson was mildly amused. As he listened to Pattner's explanation, he wondered if the programmers would ever come to grips with what he considered to be seemingly minor annoyances.

Bryson hung up the phone and stood before the mirrored glass. Samantha appeared to be perfectly comfortable, lying quietly. He watched her for a long while. Then slowly, unexpectedly, she rolled onto her side and curled into a fetal position.

Bryson looked at Mrs. Rutledge, and she at him. Perhaps it wouldn't have seemed so strange if Samantha's hands hadn't pressed against her abdomen, holding the electrode firmly to her skin.

Something was happening right in front of him, something he could not comprehend. His hands felt clammy. In the back of his mind, he recalled what Pattner had asked him during an earlier conversation: a reference to the words "Floating" and "Commence Dialogue."

The sudden scratching of the EEG pen startled him. The tracing resumed, and a lazy REM pattern appeared on the graph. In the sleep room Samantha's hands relaxed, and she rolled onto her back, stretching. In a few moments her eyes opened. He went into her room and sat on the bed.

"Are you all right, Sam?"

Her stare was vacant, glassy-eyed. He shook her shoulders lightly.

"Sam?"

Slowly her pupils narrowed, and she looked at him in recognition.

"What's wrong?" she asked.

"I don't know. I was about to ask you the same thing."

"I'm fine, but your hands are freezing."

She twisted away from him, lay back on the mattress, and yawned.

"How long was I asleep?"

"Not long."

"Funny. It seemed like I was sleeping forever. I have the feeling that I want to tell you something. But I can't remember what. Hell, I wish you guys would let me sleep."

Bryson smiled at her, somewhat relieved.

10

"Nature accepted that giant step in the zoological hierarchy," Samantha explained to the class. "The evolutionary implications were inevitable."

Her lecture, in the final week of spring semester, dealt with the transition of certain vertebrates from aquatic to terrestrial life. Recent discoveries in zoology shed more light on the manner in which the ancestors of man arose from the depths of the sea to lead a land-based existence. It was a vibrant, ever-changing area of new ideas and discarded notions. Protean though it was, Samantha felt at home lecturing about this facet of zoology; for the ascent and development of man had a steady, relentless immutability that could not be fundamentally altered by newer theories about the past. She had planned to make this the subject of her thesis.

A talented speaker, Samantha had a keen grasp of her subject, commanding the attention of her class. The students listened with rapt attention. She was a peripatetic teacher, walking about the lectern as she spoke, emphasizing important points with the jab of a finger. Although her presentation was a lesson in celerity, she was never so quick as to leave her listeners confused. She spoke with the fluid ease of one who has total familiarity with the subject.

"The original terrestrial phyllum became subdivided into three groups, the result of climate and geography. Of these, the . . ." Abruptly, she paused.

Her mind had become suddenly blank in the middle of the sentence.

Samantha knitted her brow and turned away from the class, toward the blackboard. Had she forgotten the material? Impossible. She knew the subject inside out. In fact, she knew precisely what she wanted to say; she was just having some . . . difficulty . . . constructing the phrase. Within her brain, vague, irrelevant thoughts popped like flashbulbs, interrupting her concentration. And then, she once more had it all together, for just as suddenly, her mind was clear. She turned back to her students.

"I'm sorry, class," she smiled. "My train of thought is like a railroad: it has its temporary derailments. Now, as I was saying before: the most important species to evolve from the . . . from the three original subdivisions of . . . of . . ."

Again, Samantha was speechless. Inwardly, she was furious with herself. Behind the lectern, unseen, her toe tapped in rapid agitation against the wooden floor. Once more, her mind was totally vacant, except for the strangest pinging, tiny cerebral jolts of thought and word which made no sense to her. What was happening to her? She looked out over the class, a sea of inquisitive eyes staring at her with curiosity and confusion, bewildered by their teacher's antics. Samantha felt herself flush. This had never happened to her before. She felt awkward, embarrassed, as she had at her first dance class years before. Then, from the back of the classroom, a snicker. Soon the room rustled with the susurrant tones of hushed conversation.

"I'm sorry," she said, without further explanation. "Class dismissed."

As far as she could determine, there was no explanation for what had happened to her. She was totally perplexed. As the students shuffled from the room, Samantha avoided their glances by self-consciously leafing through her notes, aware, all the while, of distant, whispered speculation about Miss Kirstin.

Damn! At twenty-three, she thought, I'm a bit young for senility. She had been noticing these momentary lapses for several days. But none of her vacant spells was so long and annoying as the one she had just experienced. She had heard of pregnancy depression, of postpartum blues, but this was ridiculous.

Samantha gathered up her belongings and hurried across campus to the medical school library. She found two texts on obstetrics and a weighty tome of psychiatry in the stacks. In a quiet alcove, Samantha spent the next hour reading about psychological changes peculiar to pregnant women. As she expected, pregnancy induced a number of mental and emotional alterations, ranging from minor quirks to serious psychiatric disorders. Changes in mood, outlook, and attitude were typical. There were several reports of aberrations in the functional capacity of the brain, such as thought processes, which the authors attributed to subtle degrees of cerebral edema or chemical imbalance. Bizarre dreams were common.

The findings comforted Samantha. Maybe she wasn't losing her marbles after all. Perhaps lapses in concentration occurred in many pregnant women. Still, it was something she would eventually mention to Jon. But she was anxious to get his impression of her dream.

She telephoned Bryson, and they agreed to meet for lunch. Leaving the library, Samantha's pace was more leisurely. She maneuvered through the midday crowds and was soon at the hospital entrance. In the coffee shop, Bryson waved her toward his booth.

They ordered their food. Samantha didn't want to mention the episode in class yet, content in her discovery that it was probably a normal behavioral phenomenon of pregnancy. Bryson carried the conversation, expounding further on electroencephalography, and on Samantha's EEG in particular.

"I still don't know if I buy what you were saying yesterday," said Samantha, picking at her food with a fork. She fenced with her lunch, spearing a piece of chopped steak here, a bit of asparagus there. "It's hard to believe that a shapeless blob of cells has cerebral activity."

"It's not shapeless at all," said Bryson. "When you're entering your third month, all of its features are recognizable, though not fully formed. In fact, the brain at this stage is probably more developed than other parts of its anatomy. And I didn't say it has cerebral activity. I said I think it does."

"Out with it, man. Do you think it dreams, or not?"

"I think it has definite neuroelectrical activity."

"You're a big help."

"I'm a scientist, not a prophet. The preliminary signs point to dream-like activity, but I won't commit myself for another week or two, when I have more data. This morning's computer analysis said the pattern was suggestive of REM activity, nothing more. Now it's your turn. What about this dream you had?"

"It was weird," she began. "When I awoke this morning, I thought I had dreamed it during the night. But the more I think about it, the more possible it seems that it happened during my last sleep session."

"What was it about?"

"I dreamed I was in a deep canyon looking upward toward a cliff. I was at the base of a waterfall, only there was no water. Then, from the top of the cliff, water tumbled around me in a cascade. Except it wasn't water. It was a stream of numbers and letters, millions of them. All pouring down onto my head, while I stood there looking up into this alphabet soup. And then I woke up."

"Definitely a sex dream."

"Why do you say that?"

"It's the old water-into-the-canyon dream. Very Freudian. This canyon didn't happen to be surrounded by hair-like trees, did it?"

"You're impossible," she said, feeling infinitely relieved.

"I never said I was a psychiatrist," said Bryson, looking at his watch. "Hey, you're going to be late for your substitute class."

Suddenly hungry, she snatched up the remainder of his hamburger. "Okay. See you later."

He watched her push open the coffee shop doors. She bounced when she walked, exuding spritely confidence. He dared not disturb that ebullience by telling her of his vague apprehensions. Anyway, he wasn't sure what he was worrying about. He was on the lookout for anything disturbing that might arise in Samantha's sleep studies, and if something did, there'd be a perfectly logical explanation for it and ample time to tell her.

He continued the daily afternoon experiments with Samantha during the next two hectic weeks. Her initial reluctance was gone, and she proved to be an eager participant. So eager, in fact, that he was perplexed. Samantha began to orchestrate the passive aspects of the sleep study. She arrived every weekday at precisely three forty-five. She had extra time, now that school had recessed for the summer. After chatting with Bryson or Mrs. Rutledge, she entered the sleep room at four o'clock, awakening at six on the dot. She was sometimes unsteady when she got off the bed, appearing dazed; but she soon snapped out of her funk, and left.

She and Bryson spent their evenings together several times a week. Their initial intimacy continued, and their relationship assumed warm and personal tones. He knew more than ever that he cared for her, and her effervescence in his company led him to believe that the feeling was reciprocal. Theirs was a complex relationship, lovers' simplicity obscured by overtones of employer and employee, professor and student, and complicated further by the fact of her pregnancy. They agreed to live in the present and not concern themselves with the future, with impending motherhood that would have an uncertain but undeniable effect on them both.

In the lab, the dark, frenetic markings on Samantha's EEG were no longer blips, but had become vibrant oscillations overshadowing Samantha's own background waveforms. They clearly dominated the tracing. Every day there was an instance, first of several minutes but later lasting up to half an hour or longer, when Samantha curled up and clutched her abdomen. Bryson noticed that the EEG pens stopped their charting each time she assumed that fetal position. He had no idea what to make of that, and it too concerned him; for when it happened, he had the most unusual sensation of some sort of reverse flow, a feeling so indescribable that he couldn't begin to relate it to Mrs. Rutledge.

The morning analysis from MEDIC was of little help beyond confirming that the fetus was probably dreaming.

The computer reported the markings as "REM pattern, atypical, unspecified." Bryson had hoped for more, but he knew that this was all MEDIC was programmed to reveal. Its assignment for the sleep research lab was to evaluate the electroencephalographic pattern of dreaming as it might be altered by a new hypnotic medication. Expecting more than that was beyond the scope of a machine. And yet there was something Pattner had said days before about MEDIC's augmented capabilities which made him wonder.

Toward the end of that week of recording, Bryson phoned the computer center and again spoke with Pattner. He wanted to know more about what Pattner had referred to as MEDIC's "thinking." The programmer did his best to explain the computer's apparent ability to freely associate unrelated events in a coherent fashion. He went on to describe development of the Freud Program, which linked MEDIC's deviant behavior to signals emanating from the sleep research lab. Up until recently, most of MEDIC's associations occurred during sleep studies; and while they were intriguing, they were generally innocuous. But then the shut-down had occurred, and ever since, there had been some sort of daily interference with MEDIC's functions.

"Did you get any more information on those isolated one-word printouts, like 'Floating'?" asked Bryson.

"Not one. But tell me something. Do you have any thoughts about what would make the computer act up like it has? Something new you're studying, perhaps?"

"No," he lied.

"I was hoping there was. This whole business with MEDIC acting up makes my supervisor very pissed. I'm afraid if we have any more screw-ups like the one a couple of weeks ago, he'll request the head of Data Processing to cut off your lab."

"What's your supervisor's name?"

"Roberts."

"I'll speak to him."

His conversation with the supervisor was hardly pleasant. Roberts let it be known that he wouldn't tolerate any more interference from the sleep research lab. They already had one serious but correctable malfunction, and certain of MEDIC's units were still performing erratically. When Bryson suggested Freud analyze Bryson's printouts Roberts refused to waste valuable time and effort on a preposterous psychoanalysis of a machine.

There had to be an explanation, Bryson thought, but he could expect little help from the computer center. He watched Rosemary Rutledge prepare her noontime pot of coffee. She was an excellent associate—efficient, polite, and not one to pry. Together, they had shared the mystery of the blips. But beyond that, she had never asked for an explanation. It was time to let her know precisely what he had learned so far.

Bryson asked her to take a seat. Over coffee, he related the events of the previous weeks to Mrs. Rutledge. She knew the chronology; he had only to fill in the details. He now told her of the applicability of what he learned from MacFerson and the library. Once again, he found himself growing excited over the potential in his discovery. As calmly as he could, Bryson went on to explain his thoughts on the unusual EEG pattern and his goal in studying the fetus. Then he related the puzzling computer malfunction, the computer's analysis, and the inexplicable fetal position Samantha assumed during her sleep periods when the EEG pens stopped charting—behavior that worried him.

"It sounds to me as though you've proved what you set

out to do," said Mrs. Rutledge. "You seem certain that the fetus is dreaming, whatever those dreams might be."

"Rosie, I'll probably never know what those dreams mean. And I suppose that over the next couple of months I could work out a standard EEG terminology for the developing fetus. What bothers me is this business of Samantha's curling up. I don't know what it is, or why it's occurring. But I think that unusual fetal position of hers—when the EEG pen stops—is affecting her. She looks so foggy when she wakes up. I wouldn't want her or the baby to get hurt."

"Do I detect a note beyond professional interest?"

He smiled. "She's a good kid, Rosie."

"Have you told her about the way she curls up during her sleep session?"

"Not yet. It would just make her worry."

"You underestimate her. She strikes me as a very independent young lady. I'm sure she could handle it."

"Handle what? All I know is that the fetus is sending strong EEG impulses to the computer, and that the computer is supposedly being interfered with. I can't figure out the significance of Samantha's fetal position, but it concerns me, not just because of the way she looks afterward, but because I think there's something else going on then. And I can't figure out what."

Mrs. Rutledge comforted him with a smile. "Tell her anyway. Maybe she can figure it out."

Samantha came to the lab for her afternoon session wearing a pair of running shorts and a loose fitting sweatshirt. She was drenched in perspiration, but showed no sign of fatigue. Her complexion was healthy and glowing.

"I didn't know you were a jogger," said Mrs. Rutledge.

"I've been running a long time, but I just picked up the pace recently. It makes you feel fantastic."

"How far do you run?"

"From the bio lab to here. About five miles."

"That's a lot of running."

"It's not as hard as you think. You can build up your speed and distance pretty easily."

Bryson entered the lab, having come from the clinic. He glanced at Samantha's attire and gave her a skeptical smile.

"Trying out for the Olympics?"

"Don't laugh. I bet I could outdistance you any time."

"Samantha's a jogger," interjected Mrs. Rutledge.

"Did your doctor say you could?"

"He said I could exercise in moderation." She stood up, yawned, and opened the door to the sleep room. "Nothing like a good nap after a long run."

"How can you be sure it won't hurt the baby?" asked Bryson. "All the pregnant women I know are supposed to take it easy."

"That's ridiculous. How many do you know, anyway? There is no documented study in the obstetric literature that indicates that appropriate exercise has a deleterious effect on the course of a normal pregnancy. In fact just the opposite may be true. By increasing the efficiency of the cardiovascular system, exercise may actually augment uterine blood flow and aid fetal development. See you at six," she said, closing the door.

Bryson and Mrs. Rutledge looked at each other in amazement and concern. Inside, Samantha undressed and attached the electrodes. She plopped onto the mattress and was soon asleep.

"When my sister had her three children," said Mrs. Rutledge, "the doctor wouldn't even let her go swimming. Things certainly have changed."

"Not that much."

"I wonder where she learned so much about exercise in pregnancy."

Bryson was wondering exactly the same thing.

11

She was alone in the bedroom when the cramps started. At first they were irregular, mild, menstrual-like sensations. She stared at the bland white wall. A red splotch appeared at its center and spread outward. Soon the cramps became intense, repetitive, causing her to double up. She rolled to the edge of the bed and put her feet unsteadily on the floor. Her legs were lead weight; the strength in her thighs was gone. And then the blood began. It trickled from her in red rivulets that streamed toward her knees. He was in the other room and she opened her mouth to call for help. The words wouldn't come. She shouted his name over and over, but there was no sound. She struggled to move. Her gait was clumsy, heavy and shuffling, near paralysis. A streak of blood trailed across the carpet. A sharp, crushing pain seared inside her, clutching her bowels. A gush of blood burst forth. It poured out, carrying with it large clots, jellied liver the size of plums. Something passed from within her, a ballooning pressure in her vagina that she couldn't restrain, suddenly spewing forth in the form of a purplish sac that thudded onto the rug. It was her baby. She cried soundlessly. The child struggled in its watery sphere, tearing at the gossamer walls holding it captive. The sac spilled open, its walls collapsing in a pool of fetid brown liquid. She tried to reach it, but was too weak. It started crawling toward her. She stared at it in growing horror. It was swollen, grotesque and deformed. It neared her toes. She tried pulling them away, but they wouldn't budge. It crawled onto her feet, a rancid gargoyle slithering toward her ankles. Its spider-like fingers dug deep into the bone. It started to bite her, gnawing at first, and then ferociously tearing her flesh into shreds. Excruciating pain fired breath into her lungs, and she was able to scream, shrieking a long, piercing wail. . . .

"Sam, Sam!" He shook her shoulders. She gazed at him sightlessly, unknowing. He slapped her lightly on the cheek. "Sam! Wake up, for Chrissake!"

Her eyes focused in recognition, and her arms leaped around his neck. She clung to him, trembling. At last she could cry, and she sobbed against his shoulder in relief.

"It's all right, it's okay." He rubbed her back soothingly. "It was just a dream, that's all."

In a few moments her tears ceased, and she eased away from him. A box of tissues was on the night table. She blew her nose and lay back, sighing.

"It was a horrible dream. I haven't had a nightmare like that since I was a kid."

"What were you dreaming about?"

She felt her abdomen, the soft, rounded curve just beginning to swell above the pubic bone.

"I dreamed I lost the baby . . . there was bleeding, a miscarriage. Only it wasn't a baby, it was . . . I don't know. I've got to get out of here." She threw off the covers and climbed out of bed.

"Now where are you going?" asked Bryson.

"I need air."

He looked at the clock. "It's almost two."

"I don't care. I have to clear my head."

"I'll go with you."

They dressed lightly. He locked the door of their rented

vacation bungalow, and they walked barefoot to the beach. A full summer moon illuminated the white sand. It was the middle of the season, but the resort town was nearly empty at mid-week. The beach was deserted.

Samantha walked to the water's edge. A wave rolled toward her, swirling around her ankles. Her feet sank into the wet sand.

"It was eating me alive."

"In the dream?"

She didn't answer but stared out across the ocean. He put his arm around her shoulders. The offshore pounding of the surf was a soporific, and she relaxed against him.

"What's straight out there?"

"I don't know," he said. "Spain. North Africa."

"I'm going for a swim."

"The water's cold."

"I don't care. Want to come?"

"Thanks, I'd rather fly. Remember *Jaws?*"

She smiled at him in response, stripped and waded into the water. When she was thigh deep she dove under the surface, and then broke through the waves in long, graceful strokes. Bryson put his hands in his pockets and watched her swim. Her freestyle was powerful, gliding through the breakers, her smooth shoulders shining in the moonlight. Fifteen minutes later she headed to shore.

When the water was waist high she stood up and waded inland toward him. He admired her lithe body. She was slender when he first met her, and now, nearly four months pregnant, her figure was still trim but more softly curved and proportioned, her pregnancy now undeniable. Water dripped from her shoulders and chin. Her recent penchant for athletics kept her lean, her muscles toned. Her breasts were firm and upright, more full and rounded with each passing week. In the cool moonlit air her nipples were erect.

She stopped just short of him, nearly touching, and searched his eyes. She lifted his hands from his pockets and pressed his palms to her breasts. She thrust herself against his fingers, writhing slowly. The sibilant whimper of a moan whistled in her throat.

"I want you."

He kissed her on the neck and ground her breasts against her ribs with the flat of his hands. She unzipped his trousers and pulled them below his hips. Then she sank to her knees and tongued him into readiness, gently kneading him and lathing the underside of his shaft. She pulled him down and had him roll onto his back. The sand was still warm against his shoulders. She climbed onto him, cool, salty droplets falling to his chest from her slick hair. Her body was unctuous, smooth and slippery, and she guided him into her. She leaned over him, waving her torso from side to side, nipples barely grazing his lips. He kissed one and then the other, then squeezed the base of her breasts firmly until the veins distended, and he widened his mouth around them, rolling his tongue over and over, sucking deeply.

My God, he thought, a breast feeder for sure, and he pressed his lips to her chest, cupping his cheeks with her breasts. It was tumult, and he buried his face in her flesh as she rode him furiously. Then her body quivered with a series of small spasms, and each time she said "Oh," the faintest whisper of release.

They lay quietly on their backs.

"When I was a little girl," she said, "if I had a nightmare, my mother would fix me Ovaltine."

He started to laugh, chuckling slowly at first, and then deeply, uproariously. His loss of control was contagious, and soon she was laughing too, tears running down their cheeks. They rolled together and hugged one another warmly. Soon the laughter subsided and they lay still.

"Hold me, Jon."

His grip tightened on her, and he nuzzled her forehead. She began to tremble.

"Are you cold?"

"No, I'm scared."

"The dream?"

"Let's go back."

They retraced their steps toward the cottage, holding hands, shuffling in the sand.

"Do you think I'm doing the right thing?" she asked.

"Working in the lab this summer?"

"No, I know that's right. I mean about having the baby."

"It's funny you never asked me that before."

"I never had second thoughts before."

"Nah," he said, reassuringly. "What are you worried about?"

"Nothing. Everything. It's so confusing, it's happening too fast. Sometimes I feel like there's something wrong here," she pointed to her temple, "inside my brain. I lose track of what I'm thinking about. And then I have a whole jumble of thoughts. Things pop into my head, out of the blue."

"Like what?"

"Like . . . wait a minute." She stopped walking and pressed her fingertips to her eyelids. "Like . . . did you know the average oxygen saturation of the placental inter-villous space is estimated to be sixty-five to seventy percent, but can be increased by maternal exercise and modifications in diet, body position, and altitude?"

"Sure. I learned that in the eleventh grade."

"C'mon!"

"Okay, you probably picked it up in one of your courses somewhere. The human brain has a tremendous capacity for recall."

Her chin quivered. "But the fetal brain," she said, raising her voice, "undergoes maximal neuronal and synaptic development by the eighteenth week, a process which can be accelerated in the animal model by substantial increases, according to Chinese researchers, of dietary RNA!"

He was no longer smiling. They reached the bungalow and he opened the door.

"And they make good lo mein, too. Look, Sam," he said, holding her by the shoulders, "I don't know where you learned that, and I don't know why those thoughts come into your mind. Maybe it's not recall. Maybe this happens to all pregnant women. But as for whether you're doing the right thing, that's not for me to say."

She pulled away and shook her head.

"It's not just the thoughts. I mean, they're there, but they don't really bother me. There are other things. I sometimes forget things. This crazy dream. And what the doctor said last week."

"You didn't tell me you had an appointment."

"I didn't tell you about the one last month, either. It wasn't any of your business then. But now I think you're entitled."

"What did he say?"

"He said my uterus is the size of a five-month pregnancy."

"What?"

"He said my uterus is the size of a five-month pregnancy."

"Is that possible?"

"Absolutely not," she said, shaking her head resolutely. "I'm certain of my dates. I'm regular as clockwork."

"In that case I don't understand."

"The doctor did a test in his office, an ultrasound, the one that shows a picture of the fetus?"

He nodded. "I'm familiar with it."

"At first he thought I was having twins. But the sonogram showed just one fetus. The baby's head is the size it should be in a five-month pregnancy."

"Okay, you're having a big baby. So what?"

"You don't understand! The rest of the baby's body is normal for a four-month pregnancy! It's just the head. The head is bigger!"

On that clear summer night, the impact of her words struck him with the full fury of a thunderstorm.

She was finally asleep, nestling in the crook of his arm. Bryson lay awake, contemplating events past. He had known her for less than two months, but already their relationship was both tender and complicated. Things were indeed moving too fast. He felt immensely protective toward her, and what she told him about her visit to the doctor was disturbing. But he wouldn't do anything to influence her decision. It wasn't a question of right or wrong; it was a matter of what was best for her. And only she could make that choice. If she told him tomorrow that she wanted to terminate the pregnancy, he wouldn't interfere. Certainly he had enough data from her tracings after eight weeks of investigation, that he could write a reasonably scientific paper with justifiable conclusions. He had avoided telling her about the "interference" with MEDIC, knowing it would only upset her more. Though inexplicable, it didn't seem to be doing her any harm.

She had been helping him in the lab shortly after her own classes ended. His budget allocated a slot for a graduate research assistant, but she proved more than that. Samantha was a capable administrator and decision maker. She conducted the routine sleep studies on other subjects, freeing Mrs. Rutledge for a backlog of paperwork. And when she mastered the intricacies of EEG recording and reading, her assistance proved invaluable. The only tracings she didn't review with him each morning were her own, and those were the rules. She already knew more than many doctors.

He now was genuinely worried about her. She concerned him with her insistence on exercising, with her adamance about consuming a diet of almost pure protein. The obscure references she quoted were forced and mechanical, as if she were being compelled to do what she did without real conviction. And her story about the baby's alarming rate of growth scared the wits out of him, more than he dared admit to her. He closed his eyes in meditation.

Earlier, when they returned to the room from the beach, Bryson struggled to remain calm. She was edging toward hysteria. In her need for comfort, he had to be her consolation.

"The baby's head is always bigger than the body at this stage of the game," he reassured her.

"No, there's something wrong, I know there is! Please don't patronize me, Jon! I'm so worried, I don't know what to do. Why won't the doctor tell me the truth?"

She was near tears. Again he held her by the shoulders, pulling her close, smoothing her hair with his hands.

"Sam, honey, don't let your imagination run away with you. You're taking a grain of information and building it into a haunted sand castle."

"But suppose the baby has an abnormal head, or a brain defect, then what? Suppose it's hydrocephalic? I'm sure the doctor knows something is wrong and just won't tell me because he thinks I'll break down and cry. Well, I am going to cry!" she said, beginning to sob again. "I can't help it, Jon. I'm so scared!"

He held her tight until her trembling ceased.

"Shit, Sam, you're going to suppose yourself into a nervous wreck. Look, we use sonography in neurology, too. Any of those tests have a certain range of error. The calibration in the damn machine might be off."

"So what should I do?"

"First, stop worrying. There's nothing wrong with your pregnancy. And then, at the very least, have the damn test repeated. Or get a second opinion. Any doctor can make a mistake.

She placed one of his hands on the swell in her abdomen. "Tell me the truth: does that feel like a four-month pregnancy, or five?"

"I had two months of obstetrics over ten years ago. I can't even tell if you're pregnant."

"What do you think that is down there? A cantaloupe?"

"I'm not in the vegetable business, either."

"Some doctor."

He put his arms around her. "The best you ever had."

The struggle to unravel the mystery of what was happening with Samantha was taking its toll on him. He was losing his objectivity. Rosie was right: he *had* proved what he intended when he determined that the fetus dreamed.

For all intents and purposes, he could stop Sam's sleep studies right then and there. He had enough data to be able to write an impressive and eloquent paper on his findings, a treatise that would keep him in grant money for the next decade.

But the bizarre things happening to Samantha vitally concerned him. He had no reason to suspect that continuation of her sleep sessions would have any effect on her symptoms and unusual behavior. Perhaps keeping her in the studies would eventually have the opposite effect, by at least allowing him to start asking the right questions about what was happening to her, if not supplying the answers.

Bryson eased his arm out from underneath Samantha's neck. It was time to sleep; he had done enough worrying for one night. He gazed at her one last time before closing his eyes. The immense protectiveness he felt for her transcended science and logic. His concern was almost paternalistic, so deeply did he care for her. Where, he thought, is the impartial scientist now?

What Samantha needed most was comfort and reassurance, not speculative conjecture. He determined to be there when she cried out to him, to offer his arm for support, if not his heart. Sleep slowly began to overtake him. To hell with worrying, he thought. He and Samantha had two days left in their vacation. He would damn well show her the best two days of her life.

12

Bryson wore his tan unceremoniously, without ostentation or display. The seaside bronzing of his skin came naturally, as if it were a casual accompaniment, just as if one might offhandedly match a suit to a necktie. Mrs. Rutledge smiled warmly upon his return to the lab, at his open-air good looks, a mother's pride in her son.

They made small talk, over coffee. She inquired about his week at the beach; he about the workings of the lab in his absence. Bryson had the impression there was something she was withholding. Not unexpectedly, then, when he had finished his coffee and was fully settled in, Mrs. Rutledge continued talking.

"You couldn't have departed at a better time for you, nor a worse one for me," she lamented. "The day you left for the beach, all hell broke loose."

"Something serious?"

"Bad enough. You hadn't been gone ten minutes when I received a call from the supervisor in the computer center, a Mr. Roberts. He was furious. He said that this time you had gone too far, and demanded to speak with you. I don't think he believed me when I told him you were gone for the week. He called every day. The best I could do was promise you'd phone him when you returned."

"Did he say what he wanted?"

"Not specifically. He made vague references to more computer malfunctions. I got the impression he feels none too kindly toward us or the lab."

"To say the least. What a welcome home," he said, picking up the phone. "Let's see what he has on his mind."

Roberts was away from his station. Bryson spoke with Pattner.

"You trying to get me fired, Doc?"

"Just bring me up to date, Mr. Pattner. What happened last Monday?"

"A week ago, we got our first clue about what's causing the interference I mentioned to you."

"What?"

"Most of that interference occurred when you did your afternoon sleep study, the one at four o'clock. Well, the Friday before last—must have been just before you left for vacation—it looked like all the computer units were throwing their circuitry somewhere outside of our center."

"You mentioned 'circuitry' once before. What are you driving at?"

"I'm not really sure. It appeared that MEDIC was feeding bits and pieces of information to some remote area, a kind of transmission of data. We discovered that the transmissions were the basis of the interference we were experiencing. There was no specific pattern to it. But some of the units seemed to be emptying their entire memory banks."

Strange, thought Bryson. A computer, no matter how sophisticated, shouldn't malfunction that way.

"I still don't see what that's got to do with me."

"Well, we spent the whole weekend trying to determine the direction of the transmissions. We figured it out last Monday morning. MEDIC was funneling its circuits and memory banks directly toward your lab."

Bryson laughed, somewhat uneasily. "You can't be serious."

"But I am. Roberts was fit to be tied. He was ready to report you to Data Processing. The only thing that stopped him was that the interference didn't recur at all last week, while you were gone. I wish I could explain it, but it looks like we're sending power and input into your lab. Make any sense to you, Doctor?"

"What kind of input?"

"Electrical."

"That's impossible. I don't have any high-powered equipment here that could siphon off voltage."

"Well, come argue with my meters, then. The dials said that MEDIC was sending you power."

Imbecile, thought Bryson. He disliked having to explain someone's job to him. "Mr. Pattner, before I became a doctor, I was in the computer field. The way we worked was very simple. The people who wanted answers gave background data to computer programmers. The programmers took that information and devised a computer program. The program was then fed into the computer, which analyzed the data and gave a response. Everything worked in a precise, orderly sequence, on separate one-way streets. The programmer questioned the computer, the computer gave a reply. There was no give and take, no simultaneous interchange, no funneling of power from one place to another. Are you trying to tell me that things have changed so drastically in the last thirteen years?"

"They sure have, Doc. Maybe not in the rest of the country, but MEDIC's different. This computer was designed to work on a two-way street."

"How?"

"By the way it was built. The computers you worked with were in one room. The difference with MEDIC is that it's spread out all over the place. It's got thousands of terminals, all across the hospital and university. Every one of those consoles, like the terminal you're sitting at, can transmit data to MEDIC."

"But they can't drain anything off MEDIC, for Chrissake!"

"I'm sorry, Doc, but you're wrong. MEDIC was constructed toward a goal of making each terminal its own computer substation. That's still some years away, but the wiring is already laid. Once it's in place, MEDIC will send as well as receive."

"You mean it has transmission capability?"

"Like I said, Doc, the wiring's there. The input module that links you to MEDIC could just as easily be an output module. So if my meters say that we're sending power to your sector, it's because we are."

"That still doesn't make sense. There isn't anything here to use that much electricity."

"Well, maybe it's not exactly electrical power."

"That's what you just said."

"I know, but all I can really tell from the meters is that MEDIC is using electricity to transmit into your area. I kind of assumed it was electrical. I suppose it could be transmitting something else."

"Like what?"

"I can't help you there. But you remember the other day, when we had the shut-down? We had an inkling something might be happening with the memory banks then."

"Go on."

"Maybe it's got something to do with that."

"You have a vivid imagination, Mr. Pattner."

"Could be. But after we finally figured it out, the meters

indicated that unit nine had tripped its memory banks, and it headed right into your lab."

"What's unit nine?"

"A through D."

"Better run that by me again."

"Unit nine houses letters A through D. You see, MEDIC's a library. It stores all the world's medical knowledge alphabetically. So whether or not you were ready for it, anything medical that's spelled with an A, B, C, or D, was going across those wires toward you."

The picture was starting to take shape, the gray areas becoming clearer.

"Listen," Bryson said, "if I start another sleep study, can you get a handle on the transmissions?"

"How do you mean?"

"I mean, can you tell what it's transmitting?"

"No. The only way we could tell is if it gave a printout at the same time. And it wouldn't."

"Can't you tap into the cables leading from MEDIC to my lab?"

"Shit, we'd get electrocuted. The only other thing you could try would be the same thing I mentioned once before, when we talked about the one-word printouts: have Freud do an analysis."

"And you can't, because of Roberts."

"That's it in a nutshell, Doctor."

Mrs. Rutledge watched his face as he thanked Pattner and rang off.

"What's wrong?" she asked.

"Did I say something was wrong?"

Bryson folded his arms across his chest and tried to put his thoughts into words. The programmer's disturbing information seemed to jibe with what was happening to Samantha. It would help him to try to express what he was thinking.

"Rosie, sit down for a moment while I do some pacing. Pattner may not know it, but I believe he's just explained something relating to Samantha. Before I took my vacation, all we knew was that the fetus was probably dreaming. It was also sending impulses to the computer, and there was some sort of interference with MEDIC. Well, it seems to me that this business of Samantha assuming a fetal position—when the EEG pen stops writing—has something to do with data the computer's transmitting to her."

Mrs. Rutledge listened intently while Bryson explained what Pattner had said about MEDIC being a two-way street, about the transmission of power, and about the bizarre drainage of the memory banks.

"It appears, then," he continued, "that the 'interference' is a kind of data transmission. I can't precisely explain the memory bank connection, if there is one. Of course, I can speculate all I want."

"Give me a for-instance."

"Okay. For instance, maybe a run-through of the memory tapes somehow energizes the computer, and heightens the quality of the fetal signal, making it more interpretable."

"That doesn't explain the transmissions."

Bryson shrugged. "Right. I'm just thinking out loud. For-instance number two: transmission of the memory data into my console elicits more fetal signals."

"What about number three?" said Mrs. Rutledge, with an edge to her voice.

"Number three?"

"That the computer is emptying its memory banks into

Samantha, and the process is having a physical effect on her."

He shook his head. "How long have I known you, Rosie? Two years?"

"Two years, July first."

"Damn. It bothers me that you can read my mind in such a short time."

"Just instinct."

"Whatever it is, you're right. I think what you just said might be happening. But if it is, our hypothesis makes two assumptions. First, that the computer has some kind of ability to take simple EEG wires and electrodes and convert them to miniature transmitters. And second, that MEDIC must have some reason for transmitting all that information. Any ideas?"

"Isn't that a little far-fetched, assigning motivation to a machine?"

"To an ordinary computer, yes. But remember what the programmers said: this computer almost thinks."

"Okay. Maybe it's in love, and this is electronic hand holding."

"Christ, Rosie, give me a break. I'm being serious."

"So am I. She is rather attractive."

"How would MEDIC know that?"

"Well, as long as you're going to give it so much credit, perhaps the computer can extract information from a subject's brain waves that we never thought possible. Physical characteristics, for example. Or the fact that Samantha's pregnant."

"I never thought of that," Bryson reflected. "But I can't buy the love bit. If what you say is so—then this computer does think."

And maybe even talks, he thought to himself.

"What would it take for Mr. Roberts to be persuaded to let us use the Freud Program?"

"I think he'd rather cut me off first. He doesn't want any of our meddling."

Mrs. Rutledge cleared away their cups while she thought about his answer. "Why don't you construct your own computer analysis?" she asked.

"I have no access to MEDIC, other than from this lab."

"But from your training, you know how to program. If, as Pattner said, each terminal is a future computer substation, and the input modules can receive—well, you have friends in the computer business. What's to stop you from getting your own little computer, devising your own program for data analysis, and hooking it up right here on our console?"

She was right. There was nothing stopping him. He could easily obtain one of the more sophisticated portable models, tap into the circuits, and analyze the content of the two-way transmissions. He would have to circumvent the computer center, which would undoubtedly object to an intrusion into its territory. But from an engineering standpoint, it would be a piece of cake.

13

The minicomputer was a marvel of electronic wizardry and mechanical miniaturization. It was equally spectacular in its simplicity. A product of advances in quartz and gold microcircuitry, the entire unit was twelve inches high and one yard wide, with a separate typewriter console for programming. It had arrived on Thursday evening, not long after Bryson contacted an old friend at I.B.M. Mrs. Rutledge had it uncarted, stored in a supply closet next to the EEG machine.

The timing was perfect. Samantha had been asked to substitute-teach for summer school biology class—something she had hoped to do to make more money. The following morning, she had been called, and Bryson went to work tapping into the line connecting MEDIC to the sleep lab. He spliced through the main cable to uncover the interior color-coded wires. Their sequence was intricate, but after several hours he achieved a satisfactory connection. He punched a hole in the EEG console and inserted the minicomputer's adapter. Whenever he wanted to monitor the line, he merely had to plug in a jack.

Samantha had access to the supply closet but little reason to enter it. It housed paper goods and secretarial paraphernalia that fell under the domain of Mrs. Rutledge. Nevertheless, Bryson hid the computer on a movable metal cart under several cartons of EEG paper, unseen by the casual inspector. Late that afternoon, after Samantha had finished her sleep period, Bryson turned off the lights and locked the lab for the weekend. He would devise a simple computer program and make final adjustments on the machine on Monday.

On Monday morning Samantha was back at work conducting sleep studies. The Somnapar study, her other project, was nearing completion after nine months. Two hundred eight-hour EEG patterns had been obtained, along with MEDIC's analysis of each. In one hundred cases, the subject was given a placebo; in the others, Somnapar. Since the study had been double blind, no one would know what each subject had been given until the termination of the study. Then the code would be broken and the results tabulated. It would take Samantha several weeks to compile the data.

Bryson spent the afternoon in Jubilee's medical library. By three P.M., he had devised a basic computer program that he would try out at Samantha's next sleep period. The program was simple. It instructed the computer to monitor both outgoing EEG signals and any input from the other direction. Bryson also had it disregard Samantha's background brainwave static, making it concentrate on fetal impulses only. Known EEG waveforms were fed in for computerized comparison to the fetal signal. Bryson wasn't interested in the fetus' demonstrated EEG activity, but rather in the ways it differed from known patterns. He also wanted to discover if there was any scheme or format to what appeared to be strong but random oscillations.

As for the transmissions from MEDIC, his instructions to the minicomputer were purely analytical. The first thing the computer would do would be to assess the quality of MEDIC's signals. Were the transmissions purely a flow of electrical impulses? And if they were, what was their pattern, if any?

Shortly before four, Bryson returned to the lab. Samantha was about to begin a sleep period. Her greeting to Bryson was casual, perfunctory. Lately, she seemed obsessed with her naps. Even while they were at the beach, she would nap daily. During an otherwise idyllic week of vacation, she was irritable in the afternoons, but was unable to tell him why. Now, her agitation ceased. It was as if she was glad to be back sleeping in the lab, back to her daily afternoon symbiosis with the EEG.

As was her custom, Samantha was asleep in minutes. Bryson wheeled the minicomputer's cart from the supply closet and plugged its jack into the console.

"Here goes nothin', Rosie."

Abruptly, the EEG pen stopped. Samantha lay still in the sleep room, undisturbed. Mrs. Rutledge and Bryson looked at one another, then back at the machines. In a few minutes the pen started charting again. The printout was at first a small oscillation, a blip similar to the one on Samantha's original tracings. The markings were tentative, those of a wary boxer appraising his opponent. In increments they became stronger, darker. Soon they were the robust fetal oscillations to which he was accustomed.

"What do you think that pause was about?" he asked.

"Maybe it knows we're eavesdropping. This *is* like a wiretap."

"C'mon! It's a machine. I can't give a machine that much credit. Let's see what we can turn up."

Their computer was strangely silent. The transmissions to and from MEDIC resumed their normal pace, but except for operating lights that signaled the minicomputer was working, there was little in the way of sound or noise to indicate that anything was happening. It offered only an occasional click, a momentary metallic shifting of gears.

Samantha's two-hour sleep period was nearly over. Bryson wasn't even sure the machine was functioning.

He pressed a button marked "data analysis." A short digital printout scudded out of the computer. Bryson tore it off and read it to Mrs. Rutledge.

" 'Probable coded transmission. Insufficient data.' Shit."

"What's a coded transmission?"

"I don't know," he said, looking through the mirrored glass at Samantha. "She's getting up. Let's save it for tomorrow."

They tried again the next afternoon. This time there was no slow-down when they plugged the computer into the console. The minicircuits seemed slightly more active, but after another two hours of analysis, its printout was the same.

"Maybe you have to give it more to go on," said Mrs. Rutledge.

"More what?"

"Expand its computer program. The program you gave it might not have enough parameters to which it can compare the transmissions."

"I don't know what to add. It's already programmed to detect known physical signals—things like radiation, electricity, tactile vibration, sound and radio waves. The least I expected was for it to tell me what kind of stuff the transmissions were made of."

"You said that this is an experimental, advanced design. Perhaps it's gone beyond that. Could it have already determined the physical nature of the signals, and be trying to decipher them?"

"You mean, is it answering more than I've asked of it?"

"Yes. Maybe it's some kind of code?"

Bryson went back to the library that evening. There were

thousands of codes in existence, all based on different formulae. There was, however, one kind of code which seemed universal. Based on a mathematical sequence of numbers, it was the code used by NASA in its deep space transmissions, carrying earth's location and a message of peace to other possible life forms. Bryson extracted its mathematical elements and altered his computer program to include them.

The result was immediate. The following afternoon, no sooner had they attached the computer to the console, than its printout began.

Bryson beamed and rubbed his hands together excitedly. "Pay dirt," he said, and examined the paper which rapidly spilled out of the computer. Mrs. Rutledge watched over his shoulder.

It was like ticker tape. From the computer came an unending stream of numbers. The non-stop numerical phraseology mirrored the fetal EEG signals, speeding up when EEG activity peaked, slowing when it waned. Equally important to Bryson was the continued flow of numbers on the printout at a time when the EEG pen stopped charting.

These numbers clearly were the reverse transmissions from MEDIC.

"You're a genius, Rosie," he said. "Sam's alphabet soup is a numbers game."

She looked at him blankly. "If I'm so smart, why can't I make any sense out of this gibberish?"

"Because of the code. Each number stands for something, say a letter. Or a group of letters, maybe a phrase. On your suggestion, I asked the computer to figure out if a code existed. The computer did that; these numbers are the substance of the code. Now all I have to do is ask the computer to break the code, to convert the numerals into letters and words. I'll reprogram it with those instructions tonight."

The final adjustments would be simple. The hard part had been to verify that an interchange was occurring. This achieved, the rest was child's play. It would take him less than an hour to insert the remaining instructions.

"You know, Rosie, sometimes I think you're telepathic," he smiled, pleased that she understood him so well. "I bet you can read my mind."

Mrs. Rutledge didn't answer. She silently wondered if he shared her concern. She stared through the mirrored glass at the sleeping curled-up form of Samantha, who clutched more tightly than ever to the electrode attached to her abdomen.

He wasn't sleepy. His mind was digesting and processing the day's information when it should have been counting sheep. Bryson got out of bed and walked naked through the unlit condominium. He needed diversion. He closed the blinds and switched on a desktop lamp. He leafed through the stack of medical journals, then brushed them aside. Serious study was impossible. He then found a paperback thriller and lay down on the couch. Science fiction had been his literary passion for years, but after several pages of time-warping through distant nebulae, he knew he couldn't concentrate. He dropped the book on the carpet with a sigh, drumming his fingers on his chest. What he needed was something light and effortless to numb his mind.

He uncorked a bottle of California Zinfandel and sat in front of his TV, turning on his home video computer. The apparatus was expensive, but he had had to buy the entire game just to play the one cassette that interested him: backgammon. He sipped the smooth wine and worked the hand controller. In less than an hour, he had won four games out of five and nearly finished the bottle of wine. He yawned, turning off the set; the Zinfandel and the video game were just what the doctor ordered. He switched off the lamp and returned to bed.

Tired now, in his mind Bryson re-enacted the events of the preceding two months since Samantha had first entered the sleep research lab. From the outset there had been the suggestion of something strange and incomprehensible. Nothing was clear cut; it was the bizarre nuances, the annoying innuendos of the unseen which made him dig further. His greatest discovery had been the suspicion, then the confirmation, that fetuses dream. Without that, the other clues would have been meaningless. The computer malfunction, Samantha's unusual habits and behavior, the still unexplained transmissions from MEDIC— these were all inexorably linked, and would soon lend greater credence to the startling concept that a tiny, unborn child was capable of dreaming.

He had little free time to see Samantha since their return from the beach. She had wanted to be with him but he begged off, claiming other obligations in the clinic. In truth he longed to see her too. Telling her about the transmissions seemed pointless at this time, since he hadn't discovered their content or intention. Yet, concerned though he was, he began to feel cautious optimism. The potential for scientific discovery was now even greater than before. But until his computer unraveled the final thread of the mystery, Bryson had to continue his work, which left

him no opportunity to be with Samantha. Comforted by
the thought of her, he finally fell asleep.

The next day, he and Mrs. Rutledge hovered nervously
over the machine, as Samantha began her sleep period.
Had he been expecting too much? The computer was,
after all, merely a mechanical contrivance, albeit a sophisticated one. They watched the quiet background of
Samantha's brainwaves register on the EEG, and the sudden vibrant superimposition of fetal signals. At once the
minicomputer began its printout. Paper spilled rapidly out
of its terminal, flowing in serpentine fashion onto the floor.
Bryson picked it up, scanning the paper as he pulled it
through his fingers. His eyes widened in amazement.

The numbers were gone. Letters took their place, back
to back, without spacing, forcing the words into a continuous run-on sentence.

beginletterwcomputeuterinearteryglucoseconcentrati
onwithvariablematernalcarbohydrateloadsclarifyfetalbili
arymetabolismunderconditionsmaternalstresscanmutag
eniceffectultrasound. . . .

The lettering was precise. It speeded up when the
EEG impulses were strongest and slowed when their amplitude decreased, but never stopped. The run-on sentence
was thousands of words long before Bryson paused to look
up, astonishment rendering him speechless. He slumped
into a chair, shaking his head with wondrous slowness and
anticipation, as if he were about to open an envelope he
suspected contained a large personal check.

"This isn't a dream at all," he said, his voice rising with

a lilting, musical quality. "The damn thing's communicating!"

His words mesmerized Mrs. Rutledge. She stood stock-still, not daring to move, to breathe. She felt flushed. Beads of perspiration broke out on her forehead. Slowly she allowed herself to inhale. She ventured a glance at Bryson. He too was sweating. Their eyes locked in bewilderment, the riveting gaze of those filled with awe.

"The baby's communicating with MEDIC?" she asked.

"See for yourself," he said, his trembling hand gesturing at the reams of paper on the floor.

"Just look. It's asking questions to its teacher: *compute . . . clarify . . . can. . . .*"

"My God, it's not possible."

"It's not only possible, it's happening right in front of our eyes!" His words sounded attenuated, stretched thin in enchanted disbelief. He had opened the envelope, and it contained a million dollars.

They watched motionless as the paper on the floor piled into a growing heap. It continued for several more minutes, slowed, then stopped. At the same time the EEG pen ceased writing. They waited.

"MEDIC's turn?" Mrs. Rutledge whispered.

Bryson nodded. Suddenly the printout resumed. Simultaneously, through the glass, they saw Samantha curl up in her fetal pose. The paper spilled out at a furious rate, three times its previous pace. Bryson allowed it to fall awhile, then reached for it tentatively.

He unfurled the paper between his fingers, glancing at every hundredth word: *waage . . . waddle . . . wangensteen . . . wart . . . wound. . . .*

"I don't believe it," he said.

Each word, beginning with the letter "w" and in alphabetical order, carried an explanation behind it. Bryson raced through reams of paper until he found the end of the "w"s. The interminable run-on sentence continued:

uterinearteryglucoseconcentrationdirectlyproportional
toingestedcarbohydrateloadconcentrationvarieswithper
ipheralinsulinsecretionmaximalbenefitforfetalgrowthoc
curswithingestedloadof. . . .

Bryson tossed the paper to the floor and smacked himself in the forehead. He grew suddenly animated, an engine roaring to life.

"Dummy! All the time I thought the transmissions were between MEDIC and Samantha! It was so obvious. How could I miss it? They as much as told me so, with 'Floating' and 'Commence Dialogue.' That was the very beginning—when MEDIC and the fetus first made contact. Don't you see it, Rosie?"

"I'm not sure." She hesitated.

"The baby's talking to the computer! They're having a regular, goddamn conversation. MEDIC's transmitting information through Samantha to the baby. Incredible!"

"It doesn't seem like such a regular conversation to me."

"No. It's beyond that. Do you remember the business of MEDIC emptying its memory banks?"

"Of course. You said you didn't know what to make of it."

"Well, that's exactly what's happening! For some reason, the computer is feeding all of its knowledge to the fetus. In this case," he said, pointing to the printout, "the baby asked it to feed it the memory bank housing the letter 'w.' And right here," he gestured again, "MEDIC replied, with all these 'w' words: *waddle, wart,* and all that. What's more, if the kid doesn't understand something, it asks the computer questions—*compute, clarify, can.* Unbelievable!"

He arose, agitated, pacing. An easy smile spread across his face. The shock of incredulity was gone; in its place, enthusiasm. The discovery was far beyond his expectations.

"Don't you see what we have here? The world's most advanced computer is having a dialogue with an unborn child! The computer supplies information, and the fetus absorbs it. Why, its capacity for knowledge must be unlimited. I can't wait to tell MacFerson. That baby probably knows more about medicine than the thousand top scientists and physicians in the world. We're witnessing a miracle!"

Her lanky stride carried her beyond the hills at the park's end, into a copse of Chinese elm. Samantha meandered among them, her footstrike as silent as that of the nocturnal creatures that followed the trail by moonlight. She felt at one with the earth. Jogging outdoors on a warm summer day, she was, at once, rootlets of a seedling that suckled in rich, moist earth, and the ripest melon on the vine, its skin stretched so full from basking in the sun that the rind nearly burst forth with lushness. All was right with the world.

She threw her head back, tilting her face skyward. Rays of the sun, peeking through the venetian-like slats of overhead boughs, made her face glitter. Samantha was so relaxed that she ran with eyes half closed. She held the fullness of her abdomen in her palms.

Grow strong, my baby. I will nurture you, protect you. You are the fruit of my body, my flower's sweetest nectar.

She emerged from the thicket, the dirt trail abutting the park's asphalt path. Samantha opened her eyes and plodded homeward. She focused on a church steeple in the distance.

Only pleasant thoughts, she reflected. Don't let your mind wander. If I maintain concentration, if I stay in control, worry cannot intrude. I won't permit it. Don't think, don't think. My child is healthy. For God's sake, Samantha! Control yourself. You must fight it. Concentrate!

She counted each step she took, visualizing the passing numbers, their sequence as numbing to her as sheep to an insomniac. Her eyes narrowed, her vision unwavering. One thousand one, one thousand two . . .

She suddenly stopped running. She turned her head to and fro, searching for the steeple. It was no longer on the horizon. Where . . . ? She looked behind her. It was there in the distance, more than a mile away.

Please, no! her mind cried. I can't have lost touch. I couldn't possibly have run that mile without noticing it, could I? Will someone please tell me how?

From the mental fog of an instant before, her mind now grew ablaze with jumbled thoughts that snapped within her skull like green kindling. *The discoid placenta is developmentally similar to—fetal cardiac output is maximal when—the oxygen saturation of hemoglobin F rises when— . . .*

The cacophony in her brain rose to a deafening crescendo. Samantha closed her eyes, clapped both hands to her ears, and screamed.

"Stop it! I won't let you!"

At once she was off, no longer jogging but sprinting home. She cupped both cheeks with her palms like earmuffs, as slowly, so slowly, the first tear trickled from her eye to her nose. Initially, her chin trembled; but when the crying began, it contorted her face with sobs. Through her tears, she verbally struggled with the litany of her intent.

"I will not let this happen!" she cried. "My baby is fine . . . I will not surrender!"

Samantha tripped on a loose stone and fell to the pavement, skinning her knee. She was up in an instant, fighting to hold back the tears. As she encircled her waist in a cross-armed hug, she looked skyward.

"What have I done? Why is this happening?" she sobbed. "Please, God. I am so terribly scared!"

14

They lunched in the coffee shop.

"I didn't sleep a wink last night," Bryson said.

"You and me both. I think I slept less than an hour," Mrs. Rutledge replied. "After you called, I gave up altogether."

"I know it's complicated. But you have to admit, it's a miracle."

"Yes, I suppose. This is a remarkable breakthrough, in terms of human discovery. But I'm worried about that girl. And don't pretend for an instant," she said, "that you're not worried, too. You told me as much yourself. What's more, I may be getting old, but I'm not blind. I know you care for her. And she cares for you, too, maybe more than you'd like to admit."

"Now wait a minute. You're taking this much too seriously. Samantha's a healthy, pregnant woman. And maybe I do care for her, so what? That's not the issue. The point is, if we can monitor the development of this remarkable child, the whole world will stand to benefit. I'm just as concerned about Sam as you are. I wouldn't let anything hurt her."

She placed her hand on his shoulder affectionately.

"Then why, dear doctor, does she curl up like that during the transmissions? What's this insanity with her confused medical chatter about things she doesn't understand? Her dreams? I believed her explanations at first. But now we know much more. Are you going to tell her?"

"Yes, I am. But I must know the computer's motivation first. MEDIC is an extraordinary machine," he said. "According to Roberts and Pattner, it's almost capable of thinking—making method of madness, changing the confusing into the logical. Months ago, when we first began our sleep studies, but long before Sam was involved, it started to focus on the brainwaves coming from our subjects. But we didn't appreciate what their brainwaves were doing to MEDIC. A machine so nearly human, suddenly barraged with very real, very human impulses, must have tried to understand what was happening. It began hypothesizing, what the programmers call 'unifying freely relating events.' It became so curious about our subjects that it began to function erratically. So they developed the Freud Program. Freud confirmed that its malfunctions and quirks did indeed coincide with our experiments. Are you still following me?"

"So far so good."

"Okay. Enter Samantha. Nobody knew at the time that she was pregnant. But MEDIC caught on pretty quickly. It was being stimulated with a whole new type of signal, fetal brainwaves. It became fascinated with these impulses. Maybe obsessed would be a better word. It focused its entire attention on these brainwaves, and—maybe from that very first day—attempted some sort of preliminary communication."

"Then they really have developed a dialogue."

"Yes. It's been going on a long time. The words 'Floating' and 'Commence Dialogue' came either from the fetus or MEDIC. They were the first acknowledgment of each other's existence."

"So you're suggesting," said Mrs. Rutledge, "that the motivation for this dialogue was a kind of mechanical evolution, a sort of reaching out to an untainted, pristine human brain, an unborn being with whom . . . ." Mrs. Rutledge interrupted herself . . . "whom it can mold into whatever it wants! Doesn't that bother you?"

"Now you're letting your imagination run away with you. MEDIC's not molding the fetus into some kind of monster. There's no diabolical purpose here. It's pure mathematical communication."

"But you said yourself that the baby is already smarter than a thousand doctors. Don't you consider that monstrous? Isn't the child a monstrous wünderkind?"

"Only if it were done intentionally. And it wasn't. When MEDIC feeds its memory banks into this child to establish rapport, it's communicating in the only way it can. The child's inevitable superior mental development is a byproduct of that rapport, not a goal."

It was time to return to the lab. They decided to walk back. The weather was wet, and Bryson suggested a route under Jubilee General's massive concrete verandas. Mrs. Rutledge allowed him to take her elbow and steer their passage. She glimpsed his face as they walked. It bore an expression of fiery determination and enthusiasm. She couldn't help but smile at the sight. Two years before, when she had first taken the job in the lab, Jonathan Bryson had impressed her as a young researcher of great promise and keen skill. But he was unfulfilled. Constantly searching, never satisfied, he completed each successive project with an unmistakable feeling of discontent. He ruminated. Each study had been successfully evaluated, and—because of the quality of his research—usually applauded. But Mrs. Rutledge had the impression that they left him empty, with the feeling of "Is that all there is?"

Now, she thought, his search was over. He had found an avenue of scientific inquiry so fascinating that his interest in it was nothing short of lust.

"Well," said Mrs. Rutledge, "I suppose it sounds logical enough. But there are still two things I don't understand. First, why does the baby keep asking the computer questions? And second, what will happen to Samantha?"

They stopped for a moment under a concrete overhang, looking out across the campus in the distance.

"I think I can answer the first question. At the point they first established communication, the baby's brain was a tabula rasa, a blank slate. It absorbed and stored everything MEDIC fed it. Its brain was becoming an encyclopedia of medical facts. At some point, though, human thought must have begun. The fetus began to use its mind. But unlike you and me who must rely on a comparative smidgen of knowledge and experience, this baby has unlimited resources to draw from as a source of its thoughts. You know the old saying about how the rich get richer? I think the same thing applies here. The baby already has knowledge which is encyclopedic, but it wants more. It knows a great deal about itself, but it wants to know everything. So it asks questions. When we want to learn something, we try adding two and two to make four. This baby adds two million to two million to come up with four million."

"Do you think that explains Samantha's ramblings, the things she says just pop into her head? She must be intercepting some of the data transmitted from MEDIC."

"Precisely. It's inevitable that she's assimilated something. And even though the information is meaningless to her—such as the best way to increase uterine blood flow to enhance fetal growth—it means a great deal to the baby. Do you remember her alphabet dream I mentioned to you?"

"Yes."

"What Sam remembered as an alphabet waterfall was literally a shower of letters and numbers, information that MEDIC transmitted to the fetus using Sam's body as a conduit. That information funneled through her like a waterfall."

They were getting chilled. Bryson escorted Mrs. Rutledge back to the building entrance.

"Do you think the fetus is trying to do what you suggest?"

"Enhance its own growth?"

"Yes," said Mrs. Rutledge.

Bryson shook his head. "I don't know. I admit, it's something that's occurred to me. I'm sure it wants to find out if it can; that's why it asks questions. But what bothers me is that it may be succeeding."

"You're joking!" said Mrs. Rutledge, suppressing a shiver as she stopped in her tracks.

"I was never more serious in my life. And that brings me to the second question you asked—its effect on Sam. If this fetus has learned how to increase its own growth—that would explain why Sam acts so strangely. It would mean that her diet, her exercising, her rest periods—these aren't her own ideas. They're the baby's way of using her body to augment its own development."

"And you say that's not abominable?"

"Oh, Rosie. We can't prove that yet; this is just conjecture. We might be way off base. But if it were correct, which I think is patently impossible, it would raise the possibility of something I'd be very reluctant to consider."

They stood before the elevator. The doors opened, but Mrs. Rutledge didn't go in. She knew what Bryson meant, and she stared back at him, unblinking.

"That we're dealing with an unborn medical genius which has learned how to control its own growth, and has an effect on its mother's behavior . . ." she said, her voice trailing off in a whisper. "You must stop this, then. It could be horrible!"

"Rosie, there's no malice in the child's intent. Her jogging, rest periods, even her dietary changes are probably doing her a world of good. Hurting Samantha would mean the baby was hurting itself."

The elevator door started to close. Bryson opened it again and led Mrs. Rutledge inside, pressing the button for his floor.

"Come on, Rosie," he continued, "we don't know the fetus controls its mother. I told you I thought it was impossible. Sure, if it were true, we would have to stop. But we're both letting our imaginations run wild. We started off with a simple hypothesis and made a quantum leap into the Twilight Zone. I need your help."

They reached their floor and glided through the corridors. Mrs. Rutledge pursed her lips. "What do you want me to do?"

"Help me continue the sleep studies. Keep an eye on Sam's behavior. And help me with the minicomputer."

"For how long?"

"As long as it takes to prove or disprove our theory. It shouldn't take long. If we get nowhere, I'll stop the study. We'll cancel her sleep sessions and return the minicomputer. Finished."

"Maybe we should get some help. What we've discovered so far is so astonishing that it wouldn't diminish your

134   DAVID SHOBIN

recognition. Shouldn't you tell the medical and scientific communities of this incredible phenomenon?"

"Soon. I just need a bit more data. If I'm going to present these findings rationally, they need a solid foundation; my conclusions must be irrefutable."

Mrs. Rutledge unlocked the door to the lab. She put on a lab coat and sighed deeply. She had made her decision.

"All right. But on one condition."

"Name it."

"That you tell Samantha."

He frowned. "Give me one week. We've only just discovered what's happening in the transmissions. I'd like a few more days to study them. But then I'll tell her. I promise."

She shook her head slowly, but then warmed and smiled.

"My downfall. I always give in to young, good-looking guys."

He patted her hand. "What were you like twenty years ago, Rosie?"

"Too much for you to handle, dear Doctor. Okay, have it your way. But only for a week."

The experiments continued. During each sleep period Bryson and Mrs. Rutledge hovered fascinatedly over the computer, like Wall Street analysts. But it didn't take a week for Bryson to discover that what he had thought existed only in Mrs. Rutledge's far-fetched imagination might indeed be occurring. Each session proved more revealing than the previous one. Soon MEDIC had exhausted its memory banks, and the interchange between it and the fetus became a rapid question and answer period, dazzling in its speed. So much information was exchanged that the minicomputer was overloaded, unable to monitor the entire dialogues; it automatically took to excerpting the highlights.

The fetus questioned MEDIC about little-known case reports in obscure medical journals; about the direction of certain research in remote parts of the world. But always the thrust of its questioning was the same: There was no aspect of the mechanics of fetal growth that it ignored. After several days of monitoring, Bryson was convinced. The fetus was totally self-indulgent. It would do anything to increase the quality and rapidity of its mental and physical maturation. And if that meant using its host as a vehicle toward attaining that goal, so be it. To the growing baby, Samantha's body was a funnel, a cornucopia linking it to the outside world until such time as it could survive independently.

On the third day of monitoring, one of the excerpts reported a study from South Africa indicating that amygdalin, or Laetrile, increased the visual acuity of newborn infants. The next morning, Samantha arrived at the lab with a bag full of apricot pits. Throughout the morning, while Samantha reviewed her data on Somnapar, she chewed on them. She was a squirrel gnawing an acorn, holding the pit in her fingers and nibbling into its core, spitting out inedible pieces. On a hunch, when she left, Bryson looked up the constituents in apricot pits. They were one of the greatest natural sources of amygdalin.

It was time to tell Samantha.

It was early August, and they dressed casually for the drive to Richmond. Bryson had placed the sun roof in the trunk, and a warm breeze blew through the sports car. Samantha's hair billowed in the wind. They left the lab immediately after a sleep period, hoping to arrive at Charlie's

Place for their eight o'clock dinner reservation. It was the first evening they would spend together since returning from their week at the beach. They were silent during the drive, the hum of the motor and rush of the wind discouraging conversation.

They dined on steamed crabs and beer, Charlie's Place being the only restaurant outside of the Chesapeake Bay area that knew how to steam and season the crustaceans properly. They finished the first pitcher of draft, and ordered another.

"I shouldn't have more," she said. "The occurrence of birth defects is directly related to the degree of alcohol consumption."

"Do you know why you're saying that, Sam?"

She looked at him blankly. "Sure. Because it's true."

"Yes, it's true. But how do you know it's true?"

"I read the papers."

He was fidgety, pausing to crack a crab claw, searching for the right way to begin his explanation. After collecting his thoughts, he asked her to stop eating and pay attention.

"What I'm going to tell you is complicated," he began. "In some ways, it will be hard to believe. But everything I say is true."

"What's the big mystery?"

"It has to do with the results of your sleep studies. I've been evaluating them for over two months, and I finally have some results. You've been kind enough not to press me for information about your sleep studies. But now that I know the score, I owe you an explanation."

"Okay. Explain."

"When Mrs. Rutledge and I first started evaluating your

EEG patterns, we were concerned with whether or not your baby had REM activity. I told you that much. You were pretty skeptical but agreed to go along with the project. The whole purpose, if you remember, was to develop a standardized early fetal EEG terminology as a basis for experimental drug research comparison."

"I remember."

"We found out fairly early that your baby does indeed have REM activity, but of an unusual sort. After weeks of evaluation, the computer concluded that the baby has numerous types of atypical, unspecified REM patterns. So we were able to prove that the fetus has abundant cerebral activity, but nothing that followed a set pattern which could be standardized. But there was something else, something strange."

"Now you're scaring me."

"I'm sorry, Sam, I'm trying not to. But hear me out and I think you'll understand. We discovered, early on, that while you were sleeping, there was some sort of interchange between the lab and the computer. It was a kind of give and take. The fetus would transmit its unusual EEG impulses to MEDIC, and in return MEDIC would transmit something back to the fetus. At first we thought the transmission was going from MEDIC to you, because you acted strangely when it occurred. You would curl up in a fetal position. But later, we concluded that your behavior was a kind of protective reflex. The information was going to the baby."

"What information?"

He waved his hand patiently. "Hold on, I'll get to that. When we were at the beach, you told me about the thoughts which seemed to pop into your head, things you knew which you had no reason to know. And you were right. I laughed it off then, but the fact is, there was no way you should have known that stuff."

"And now you know the way?"

He took a deep breath before continuing.

"Yes. It may sound crazy, but this is it: your baby and the computer are having a conversation."

Samantha looked at him as if he were insane. She chuckled. But she saw that he was serious and stopped laughing.

"Jon, tell me that you're pulling my leg."

"I'm not. Every time you sleep in the lab, your baby and MEDIC are having a dialogue. Basically, the fetus asks the computer questions, and the computer supplies the answers. And more. As far as we can determine, your baby has become a storehouse of medical knowledge. It knows everything from physiology to therapeutics. But what it seems to want to know most is how to grow faster, bigger, and stronger. Most of its questions to the computer have to do with fetal growth and development. And indirectly, that explains why you're acting the way you are."

Stunned, she sat back in her chair and said evenly, "I don't understand what you're talking about."

"This is how it happens: when thoughts pop into your mind, when you exercise, when you alter your diet, you're doing things that the baby wants you to do. Apparently these activities foster its development."

"That's ridiculous. I do those things because I want to, because they make me and my pregnancy healthier. There's no little voice inside," she said, pointing to her abdomen, "saying, 'Hey Mom, sprint the next hundred yards.' These are things I do because they're best for me."

"And how do you know that?"

She paused. "I don't know. I just do. You said yourself that I probably picked it up in one of my courses."

He looked at her plate. "Why did you eat just the claw meat, and not the back fin?"

"Because the ratio of dietary D.N.A. to R.N.A. in the blue crab species is highest—" and then she caught herself, stopping in the middle of her automatic catechism, as one hand flew to her open mouth in shock. He put his hand on hers.

"You didn't learn that in any course, Sam. That's the type of information MEDIC gives the baby. It's the baby that's interested in your diet, not you. It's the baby that wants you to jog, to nap."

A moment before, she had been simply scared. Now she was utterly horrified.

"You mean I have no autonomy, no freedom of choice? I act the way I do because this thing inside tells me to?"

"In some ways, yes. Some of it you pick up indirectly, because your body is the vehicle through which the dialogue occurs. Your sleeping brain eavesdrops, and inevitably intercepts bits and pieces of information. These are the thoughts that pop into your head. But as for the rest of it, you do much of what you do because your baby tells you to."

"I don't believe it. How did you find all this out?"

"That's not important. But it's true. I wouldn't make it all up. There's so much we don't understand about emotions and the unborn, about the psychological interactions between baby and mother. But we do know, as I once told you, that the fetus reacts to physical stimuli, such as loud noises, or to soothing music. And it probably reacts to the mother's emotional state as well. For instance, there's a relationship between the mother's psychological well-being during pregnancy and general restlessness in newborn infants. Babies of highly anxious mothers cry more during the early weeks of life, particularly before feeding. Given that fact, what's to say that the baby's emotional state can't affect its mother—that fetal feelings don't affect its mother's reactions?"

"There's a helluva difference between actions and reactions. Let's say that I accept your premise that the baby's emotional state, if you want to call it that, can make me react in a certain fashion. That's a far cry from the baby forcing its mother to act a certain way."

"I'm not so sure, Sam."

Samantha was aghast. Her fingers had begun to quiver, and she held tightly to her fork to keep it from falling. "You're saying that this baby could make me slit my wrists if it wanted to, or have me jump off a cliff? God, do you have any idea how horrible what you're saying is?"

"Don't get upset, Sam."

"Upset?" she said, her voice rising shrilly. The people at the neighboring tables looked their way. "I shouldn't get upset? Did you think this news would make me happy?"

"Nothing in the fetus' dialogue with the computer indicates that it would want to harm you in any way. It wouldn't make sense. Harming you would harm it. That would be self-destructive."

She concentrated on his words, running her fingers through her hair.

"Do you realize what this is doing to me, Jon? And how could the baby be doing it? I'm not some kind of marionette that jumps when the puppeteer pulls the strings!"

"It's always harder to explain why something occurs than to simply note that it happens," he said. "Obviously the fetus doesn't interact with you on a conscious level. If it did, you'd be aware of it. When it controls your behavior, it must do it subconsciously. And probably through your autonomic nervous system, the part that's not under voluntary control. It may be doing it hormonally. Are you familiar with autoregulation, and the mechanism of hormone action?"

"At this point I'm not familiar with anything."

"If this baby is the medical whiz kid I think it is, it knows everything about hormone effects. It knows the action of various hormones and how they elicit a given response in your body. And in your developing pregnancy it has its own separate, abundant supply of hormonal substances peculiar to the fetus, the membranes, and the afterbirth—all kinds of steroids, catecholamines, and prostaglandins. If it chose to secrete some of these preferentially into your blood stream in a given ratio, it could regulate almost all of your biologic functions. And perhaps alter your thinking, too. Why, it could raise or lower the blood pressure in your brain, completely alter your cardiac output; modify the functioning of your muscles, or—"

Samantha burst out crying. She pulled her hand away from his, knocking silverware to the floor. Her shoulders sagged, and she turned her body away from him, sobbing into the wall. In the excitement of his explanation, he was blind to the effect it was having on her. Everyone in the restaurant was staring at them.

She spoke while she cried. "I suppose these aren't real tears," she said. "The baby's hormones are making my eyes water. And you act like this is some kind of great scientific accomplishment," she cried. "Well do you know how I feel? I feel shitty, that's how. Don't you have any idea what this means to me? It means that my baby's a freak. Or that I'm a freak, some kind of cheap, goddamn robot; that I have no control over what happens to me. Doesn't that bother you? Don't you even care?"

"Of course I care. If I didn't care I wouldn't have told this to you."

Her eyes were red, and she stammered through her sobs. "Care, for God's sake? We had a beautiful time at the beach, and then when we got back, you wouldn't even talk to me. You acted like . . . Every night I sat in my apartment, wondering what I did wrong, what I did to make you hate me. I love you, don't you know that? And then you finally ask me out to dinner. . . . We could be together again. And what do you tell me? Not 'Samantha, I'm sorry I couldn't see you, because I was working.' That's what I expected you to say. I was prepared for that. But instead you announce, 'Great news! I've just discovered that you're a robot, a walking zombie!' "

She was sobbing loudly, and couples at other tables turned to watch them. Again, he reached for her. "Sam—"

She jerked her hand away. "Don't touch me! I'm a freak, remember?"

"You're not, you don't understand. If you'd just—"

"Go to hell," she shouted, and stormed away from the table.

He threw two twenties onto the tablecloth and followed her into the parking lot. She was sitting on the front fender of the car, hunched over, wiping her eyes.

"Let's go, Sam."

"I'm not going anywhere."

"Please get in the car."

"What're you gonna do, macho man, throw me inside?"

"It's a long walk back. If I promise to keep my mouth shut, will you come?"

She got in.

They drove in silence for an hour. Her crying had stopped, and she gazed through red eyes at the passing countryside.

"Just drop me off at my apartment."

"Is that what you want?"

"It's what I want."

"I'd like to be with you tonight, Sam."

She didn't respond.

He continued. "I didn't drive all the way to Richmond just to lay this news on you. I could have given you the results of the study back on campus. But I thought an evening out would do us both good. These past few weeks haven't been easy for me, either."

"Cut the sincere routine. You're so full of crap."

"Maybe, but it's true. I wanted to tell you what was going on for a long time. But I couldn't, until now."

"No one was stopping you."

"No one but me. It's not that I'm caught up in self-love and scientific admiration. I wasn't using you as a guinea pig for the advancement of medical research. It's just that I couldn't let you know results until I had them. And now I do, so I told you. But I didn't last week, or last month. How would you feel if I told you that I think your baby dreams, or that I think it's communicating with the computer and might be affecting your behavior, but I wasn't sure?"

"A hell of a lot better than I feel now."

"I doubt that. You would have been just as uncertain as I was, and just as eager to solve the riddle. Especially because it involves your baby and your body. Don't you see, that's why I had to wait. It wouldn't have been fair to tell you half an answer too early."

"You're all heart, Jon. And what do you expect me to do now? I feel like I'm diseased. You tell me I'm carrying some kind of super baby that just happens to be able to tell me what to think and how to act. Am I supposed to be thrilled? I wouldn't be surprised if you expected me to keep coming to the lab every day, so junior here can keep getting pumped full of MEDIC's mega-thoughts."

"That I'll leave up to you."

"You must be nuts! Give this kid any more mental juice, and its damn brain would pop out of its little skull, not to mention that it would probably have me doing somersaults after I ran the marathon. The way you say the baby's developing, I wouldn't be surprised if it crawled down my legs any day now, and said, 'Thanks for the ride, Mom. You've got a spiffy uterus.' "

He laughed in spite of himself.

"It's not funny!" she shouted. But in a moment she too broke down and smiled. "Well, maybe it does have a light side. But don't think for a minute that I'm doing another sleep study."

"To be honest, I didn't think you'd want to."

"So why did you say you'd leave it up to me?"

"Because if you did want to continue, I don't think the study would hurt you. Not physically, anyway. And at the rate things are going, you'd be the only person in history to give birth to a college graduate, even though I'll bet it'll be the same as any other newborn. But the emotional side is a whole different ball game."

"Damn right it is. I may be healthy in body, but right now I'm a mental leper. I'd like to continue the Somnapar project, if that's okay with you. And I'm still interested in neurophysiology. And the answer to your question is yes."

"What question?"

"The one that asked if I still wanted to spend the night with you. But first thing in the morning, I'm going to my doctor."

"Second thoughts again?"

"No. Decisions."

It was twelve-thirty A.M by the luminous dial of Bryson's bedside clock. He slept on his stomach, breathing inaudibly, the only sound the humming of the window air conditioner. Samantha rolled away from him and got out of bed. His naked body was covered to the waist with a white sheet.

She gazed at him dispassionately. Such a bastard, she thought. Nothing meant more to him than his research. He had lied to her before and would lie again. There was no reason to believe him now. The business about the baby controlling her was sheer nonsense, a fabrication. It was a seed planted by him to drive a wedge between her and the baby, to sow doubt in her mind. But he was wrong. She wanted the baby more than ever. There was an inseparable bond between them, one he could never tear apart with his falsehood and duplicity.

And later she had given herself to him. Not willingly. Not with passion or desire. He forced himself upon her. His assault was cruel, coarse. He hurt her. As he slammed himself into her, over and over again, she stared at the ceiling. She was afraid he might injure the baby by his roughness. Emotion welled inside her. He was brutal, disgusting. It seemed like an eternity before he rolled off her, sweating repulsively. She lay still. Soon he had fallen asleep.

She waited an hour, unmoving. He rolled over several

times in his sleep before finding a comfortable position on his stomach. Only then dared she move from the bed.

Her head ached. The pain burned between her temples, a fiery poker piercing her skull. And all because of him. He revolted her, made her sick. The pain worsened. Her head throbbed. He should be the one to suffer, not her.

She walked quietly into the living room and sat before the hearth, holding her head. An iron rod was on the mantel facing her, next to the cinder sweep. The pain was now so intense she could hardly see. It was his fault. The bastard. She picked up the iron rod.

The pain was blinding. She could barely see where she walked. Even tiptoeing was an effort; each step pounded in her brain. As quietly as possible, she made her way back to the bedroom, carrying the rod at her waist.

She crept to his side of the bed. He started snoring loudly, grunting. The pig. She raised the rod over her head, gripping it tightly in both hands. The pain raged behind her eyes. You're killing me, she thought. She had to end it. Do it now.

With all her might she slammed the rod into his skull. Its tip drove into the bone behind his right ear. Bits of hair and skin flew into the air. He started moving. She screamed. She raised the rod again. He struggled to all fours on the mattress, snorting against the blood pouring out of his nose onto the sheets. She shrieked at him and hit him again. He was coming toward her now. The tapping began on her cheek. She struck him again, again. His hands were at her throat. The tapping on her cheeks was stronger, faster. She was choking, she couldn't breathe, please stop. . . .

"Stop, stop," she moaned.

Bryson slapped her on both cheeks, trying to wake her.

Samantha stopped screaming, and her lids fluttered open. She stared at him distantly, her vision foggy. Then she saw him again and her eyes opened wide in shock. He tapped her again on the cheek.

"You're dreaming, Sam. Sam? Are you awake?"

A small gasp escaped her, a whisper of breath. She felt her chin start to quiver. "Oh, no," she said, her voice a high-pitched cat sound, the tears welling in her sockets. "Why?" she said, choking. She turned her face away from him and buried it in the pillow. The linen became wet with her tears. His hand was warm and gentle on her shoulder.

"Why, God?" she said. "Why did this happen to me?"

15

Samantha called her obstetrician the next morning, a Monday. She told his receptionist that it was an emergency, and she managed to extract an early afternoon appointment. When she saw the doctor in his consultation room, Samantha said she had decided to have an abortion. It wasn't a rash decision, she said; and if it was all right with the doctor, she preferred not to discuss the reasons for her change of heart. And she wanted it done as soon as he could arrange it.

Her obstetrician was perplexed. A pleasant, balding, rotund man in his mid-forties, he had been caught up in Samantha's early enthusiasm for the pregnancy. She had seemed sincere in her motivation to be a working mother. They discussed the fact that she wasn't married. He was impressed with her sincerity, with her desire to do what was best for her baby and not complicate her life with an unhappy marriage. And she was no deadbeat. She paid her monthly bill toward the balance of his fee promptly. Her sudden decision to terminate the pregnancy was confusing. Still, if that's the way she wanted it, that was what he would do. An abortion at this stage of pregnancy, almost five months, was distasteful. But he had long since stopped imposing his own prejudices, his code of ethics and morality, on his patients. The law of the land allowed him to skirt the issue and simply conform to his patients' desires. His only criterion was that the patient had thought things out, and wasn't acting impulsively or from psychological imbalance. In that respect, Samantha appeared perfectly stable.

In the examining room, he was more confused still. Samantha simply had to be off on her dates. The size of her pregnancy once again indicated a pregnancy even more advanced than his ultrasound suggested, a size very near the legal limit for pregnancy termination. It would be a good idea for them both to be done with it as quickly as possible.

Samantha dressed and returned to the consultation room. There the doctor explained the various methods available for late pregnancy terminations. Each had inherent risks and advantages. The method he thought best for her involved a short hospitalization, with injection of a substance abdominally, through the wall of her uterus and into the amniotic fluid surrounding the baby. After an interval of some hours, labor would ensue, and in due course Samantha would deliver a stillborn fetus. She would be sedated throughout labor. Ideally, the whole thing wouldn't take much longer than a day, and Samantha would be discharged when she'd recovered from the sedation. He had surgery the following morning, but if she wanted, he could inject her uterus before he began his morning cases. Could she be ready on such short notice?

Samantha said resolutely that she could. The doctor called in his receptionist to make the necessary arrangements and bade Samantha good day. He would see her the next morning. In the outer office, the receptionist had several forms for Samantha to sign. Then she phoned the hospital and booked Samantha's case. There followed a discussion of the bill, much of which had already been paid, the fee for an abortion being less than that for a delivery. The balance of her account amounted to one hundred dollars, for which she would be billed.

Samantha went directly from the doctor's office to hospital admitting. She signed the appropriate consent and pre-registration forms, as well as several insurance papers which would enable the hospital to get paid. Next she was directed to the lab. Blood and urine specimens were taken, and a chest x ray was made. With an admonition not to drink or eat anything after nine P.M., Samantha was instructed to return to the admitting office the following morning at six A.M.

She decided to stroll home from the hospital. It was the height of summer, a sultry afternoon. An impulse beckoned her to jog the several miles back to her apartment. But then she realized that was ridiculous. There would be no more jogging. No more dietary extremes, exercise binges, bizarre thoughts coming to mind. Soon it would be all over.

She had come full circle. It might have been better for her if she had never become pregnant. But then she would have never, in all likelihood, have met Jonathan Bryson. She would never have had a chance to grow as emotionally captivated with another person as she had become. She loved him totally. Their relationship held the unspoken promise of a life together, of shared goals and ambitions, of working side by side, of a merging of careers into one wonderful, combined, professional effort, supported by mutual trust and solid emotional underpinnings, unencumbered by the constant intrusion of someone else's child.

She wondered at her lack of regret. There was no remorse, no sense of guilt. She had lain awake after her nightmare, sorting out her feelings. What had begun as a fervent hope early in pregnancy had turned into a hideous joke. She had stopped making plans for the baby long ago. She should have known then that something was wrong. Instead of hope, her waking thoughts were filled with continuous dread. Of a uterus larger than expected, perhaps housing a defective child. Of worrying about the proper diet, the exact caloric expenditure, the right amount of exercise. And below the surface of her consciousness, the swirling undercurrent of rigid obsessions, strange thoughts, compulsions, their incessant nature nearly drowning her.

She sat on a bench and let the sun soak into her skin. The problems of the past few months would soon evaporate. Jerry was gone, and good riddance. Strange. If he knew what was about to happen, he would probably offer to drive her home from the hospital. But she hadn't heard from Jerry since she told him she was pregnant—no call, no letter. Just as well. Since Bryson had entered her life, she had almost forgotten him completely.

The nightmares had nearly driven her to the doctor earlier. They were uncontrollable and incomprehensible, a frightening barrage of nausea and evil. In the back of her mind she was ignoring them, hoping that they were a stage which, once passed through, would never reappear. But they didn't let her alone. And the final straw had been Bryson's revelation about the computer dialogues. She was the shell in which an unknown creature was growing. It was no longer her baby. It was her master.

Samantha stretched in the sunlight and sighed, and continued with her walk. It was almost behind her now. Some slight discomfort lay ahead, perhaps, but nothing she wouldn't be able to endure. She hoped it wouldn't take long. She wanted to be free of her burden. On balance everything was working out for the best. She was healthy. She was strong. And she was in love.

It was four o'clock when she reached her apartment. She called Bryson.

"I saw the doctor and made all the arrangements," she said. "I enter the hospital early tomorrow morning."

"You're going through with it, then?"

"Yes."

He hesitated. "Are you sure?"

"I'm sure."

"How long will it take?"

She explained the procedure. "He'll give me the injection a little before eight in the morning. After that I have to wait. I might have to stay overnight. But I shouldn't be home later than the following afternoon."

"Is it safe?"

"I guess so. You should know better than me."

"It's a little out of my line. But I meant, is it safe for you to leave so early?"

"Jon, I want this over and done with already. I'd do it today if the doctor could arrange it. Believe me, as soon as the anesthesia wears off, I'm leaving."

"Why don't you have the nurses call me when it's over? I'll pick you up."

"Okay. I already gave them your name as next of kin."

"For God's sake, don't be so morbid. Women have these every day. A piece of cake."

"For you, maybe. I just didn't want them to contact my parents for something."

"Oh." He paused. "Sam?"

"What?"

"You worried?"

"Yes. A little."

"Don't be. I'll be checking on you all the time. And, Sam?"

"What now?" she said, exasperated.

"I love you."

He hung up the phone. She cradled the receiver in her hands, hearing his words over and over in her mind, until a shrill whine from the earpiece signaled that she must hang up, too. She felt a warm, comforting glow expand within her, bringing with it a sense of peace and contentment she hadn't known before.

The following morning, Samantha reached the hospital shortly before six and went directly to the admitting office. Although it was early, the hospital was bustling with activity. The lobby was filled with patients awaiting admission. Stretchers were being pushed from one corridor to another. Samantha went to the admitting desk and signed in. The admitting officer strapped a plastic I.D. bracelet to her wrist. Then she told Samantha to take a seat until her room was ready.

It wasn't long before a ward clerk entered the lobby and called out her name. They took the elevator to the fourth floor, and the clerk led the way to Samantha's semiprivate room. The room had two beds, a cramped bathroom with a narrow commode and stall shower, and a small closet. The clerk drew a curtain to separate the beds. She handed Samantha the white starched hospital gown that lay on the pillow, and told her to put it on with the strings tied in the back. Then she told Samantha to store her clothes in the closet and wait for the floor nurse.

The nurse entered five minutes later, pushing a portable blood pressure machine. She said hello and asked Samantha to make herself comfortable. While Samantha stretched out on the bed, the nurse asked a series of questions, taking notes on a nursing admission form. What was the purpose of Samantha's visit to the hospital? She said, smiling constantly, that she knew anyway, but she had to have the patient state it in her own words. It would take only a few minutes. Did Samantha have any allergies? Had she been previously hospitalized, were there any major illnesses, what was the state of her bowel function? Soon the questionnaire was complete. The nurse took Samantha's blood pressure, temperature, and pulse. Pronouncing her vital signs normal, the nurse left and told her to relax until the doctor was ready.

She propped up her pillow, leaned back, and looked out the window. It was a clear, bright, summer morning. Later the heat would grow oppressive. In the distance, Samantha watched a young mother push her infant across campus in a baby carriage. The child began to cry. Samantha narrowed her gaze. A sudden tension in the back of her neck tugged at her brain. The mother picked up her child, cuddling it, caressing its face. It was a tender scene.

Samantha was comforted by it.

She looked away now. There was a trembling in her abdomen, a fluttering of life. She placed her hands just below her navel, on top of her gown. Tiny kicks tapped against her fingertips. It was a warm, endearing sensation. The tension in her neck was gone. Samantha smiled and closed her eyes. She began to hum a lullaby.

It was a soft, lilting melody. In a few moments she opened her eyes and peered through the window again. She couldn't see well; her vision was glazed. She wondered if the young mother was still there. No matter. That was where Samantha belonged: outdoors.

Visions of cradles filled her mind. She pictured herself

in the park, softly rocking her baby, humming the lullaby her mother used to sing.

She untied her gown and folded it neatly on the bed. Soon she was dressed in her street clothes and slipped out of her room. The hospital corridor was alive with activity, but no one noticed her pass down the hall toward the elevator. The doors swung open. She pressed the button for the lobby. Two minutes later she left through the hospital's main entrance.

What in the world was I doing in there? she wondered. It was rhetorical conjecture, demanding no answer. The important thing was that, regardless of what had possessed her to enter the hospital, she was now free. Samantha practically skipped back to her apartment. Once inside she donned her running gear. Within minutes she was in the park, on the first leg of a twelve-mile run.

Hours later, Bryson was returning from neurology clinic when Samantha sauntered toward him outside the sleep lab. He smiled and embraced her, kissing her cheek.

"That didn't take long," he said. "I wouldn't have thought you'd be finished so soon. Why didn't you call me?"

She pulled away from his hug and entered the lab. Bryson frowned. He followed her inside, his smile gone.

"What's wrong, Sam?" he asked. "Did everything go all right?"

"I didn't have it."

"You *what?*" he said, looking at her abdomen for the first time.

"I couldn't go through with it." She busied herself with papers on the desk top.

Bryson was flabbergasted. Of all possible eventualities

from that morning's events, this was one he had not anticipated.

"What happened? You seemed so sure."

"I guess I wasn't, after all. I changed my mind."

"I don't get it. Yesterday you seemed so determined."

"That was yesterday. Today I realized I was doing the wrong thing."

"You didn't go to the hospital, then?"

"Yes, I did. But after I was admitted, what I was doing there suddenly dawned on me. I was actually going to kill my baby! Can you believe that? What ever got into me?"

"Sam . . . I thought . . ." He stopped, at a loss for words. Something was definitely wrong. He felt as though he were listening to a symphony played by incompetents: all the notes were flat. Mrs. Rutledge was now at his side. They exchanged worried glances.

"Samantha," said Mrs. Rutledge, "you're not frightened about the baby any more?"

Samantha looked up and grinned.

"There's nothing wrong with the baby. It's a normal, healthy child. Someone must have made a mistake."

"But we discussed . . ."

"There is *nothing* the matter with my baby."

Bryson pulled over a chair and sat beside her. He took her hands in his and rubbed them softly.

"Maybe I'm not phrasing it right," he began. "Is there something I should know, or something you want to tell me?"

She arched her eyebrows and looked at him dumbly. Then she shrugged and returned to her paperwork. Bryson grew annoyed.

"Sam, look at me, dammit! I am trying to help you. I care about you. The other night in Richmond, you were worried out of your mind. You couldn't believe that the baby could control your behavior. You said you felt like a puppet, and that the feeling was horrible. All right, I admit I misunderstood. I never realized it would affect you that way. I guess I didn't appreciate the impact of the nightmares, of your exercising, of the information that popped into your head— until that night. But if you were so determined to have an abortion, why didn't you?"

"Does it matter?"

"You're damn right it does!"

She thought about her answer a long while before replying. She looked up from the papers and smiled at him. "It was you, Jon. You talked me out of it."

"What?" he exclaimed in astonishment.

"It came to me in the hospital, lying in bed waiting for the nurse. Everything you had said was true. There was never anything wrong with the baby: it was all in my imagination. The dreams, the facts I know—I must have learned about them in one of my courses. You told me that. Also, emotional changes are perfectly normal in pregnant women. Most important of all, you convinced me that the baby could never bring me bodily harm. You said it yourself: that would be self-destructive, wouldn't it?"

Her expression was smugly complacent. Bryson knew that she truly believed everything she said. Gone were her fears and apprehensions; or, if not gone, somehow submerged, perfectly concealed. Bryson released her hands and withdrew. He retreated into a corner of the lab where Mrs. Rutledge had been waiting.

"I can't believe it," he whispered. "She's parroting everything I told her. It's a reversal of roles, with Samantha the perfect mimic. I don't like it, Rosie. Her resolve is gone."

"What are you going to do?"

"I'm going to call her doctor and find out what happened."

After Samantha had left, he spoke with Dr. Pritchard. The obstetrician was courteous and attentive. He informed Bryson that Samantha had been formally admitted to the hospital. While an orderly was preparing her stretcher, Samantha apparently got dressed and slipped out of the building unnoticed. He assumed she had simply changed her mind. The obstetrician had seen it many times before. There was no attempt to locate her and talk her into going ahead with the procedure. Such attempts would carry inherent coercive elements which were medically and morally unjustifiable. Some patients returned again, others chose to proceed with the pregnancy. The degree of ambivalence demonstrated by Samantha often indicated underlying psychological difficulties.

Bryson thanked Dr. Pritchard and repeated the discussion to Mrs. Rutledge.

"I suppose I'd draw the same conclusion," said Bryson. "He thinks Sam is flaky."

"You wouldn't consider telling him about the dialogues?"

"No. It's enough that he thinks Sam is a bit off. I wouldn't want him to presume the same about me. Anyway, he knows no more about sleep studies than I do about Pap smears. What's more, it's a bit academic now, wouldn't you say?"

"Why? What's to stop her—" Mrs. Rutledge began, ending in mid-sentence when she caught his implication.

"Right, Rosie. This has to be the end of Sam's sleep periods. If we discontinue the studies, we interrupt communication between MEDIC and the fetus. As a result, what little control the fetus exerts over Samantha will probably disappear."

"You don't mind having an unfinished research project?"

"Oh, a little, I suppose. I can still submit my conclusions at the fall conference. But Sam means more to me than the end results of this study. I still maintain no physical harm would have come to her. But the ways the baby affected her behavior extract an emotional price. And that's enough for me."

The following morning, when Samantha arrived at the lab for her work with the other sleep volunteers, she appeared outwardly calm. She acted almost normally, although there was a nuance of mechanical uneasiness to her movements. At four P.M., she asked Bryson to resume her sleep period.

"What for, Sam? The study is over."

"It calms me. I feel soothed, more relaxed afterward."

As politely as possible, Bryson forbade it. Samantha was mildly agitated by his decision. He knew that this was going to be a difficult period for her, a time of transition.

To facilitate Samantha's return to normal, Bryson and Mrs. Rutledge agreed to spend as much time with her as possible, to draw her out, to help her verbalize her feelings. They took her to breakfast and lunch. They discussed the details of the lab's other projects thoroughly. And Bryson spent most of his evenings and some nights at her apartment.

It was when they were alone that he noticed a definite change in her. She volunteered little of herself, and consequently they talked less. What conversation there was, he initiated. In contrast to their earlier manner of speaking —long hours of playful interchange—Samantha's replies were now terse persiflage. But when they made love, the change in her was most profound. Previously, Samantha had been carefree, giving, and tender. Now their sexual encounters had overtones of artifice. She appeared to be going through the motions. Fearing that he might be forcing her, Bryson stopped his sexual pursuit. But Samantha would have none of it. When she sensed that he was unwilling to be the aggressor, she initiated their sexual activities. It seemed to Bryson that she wanted coupling, not lovemaking. What had been amorous interludes became simple fornication. She mechanically returned his kisses with a perfunctory hug.

In the lab, Mrs. Rutledge noted similar changes. Samantha appeared to become progressively more withdrawn. Their cajoling was having little effect. Each afternoon Samantha asked to have a sleep session; and when Bryson refused, she grew increasingly anxious. By the end of the week, she was openly hostile. Although they did their best to mollify her, their attempts fell on deaf ears. Samantha was getting worse rather than better. Bryson and Mrs. Rutledge were baffled.

He spent the entire weekend with her. Bryson reasoned with her, appealing to her logic and sensibility. Each time they occurred, Bryson pointed out the peculiarities which persisted in Samantha's behavior—the information which continued to pop into her head, the unusual speech patterns, the insistence on her faddish diet and exercise. They were manifestations of the fetus' will, he explained.

"I've been watching you for five minutes," he said, leaning against her apartment's wall, "timing your respiration. Normal pregnant women breathe faster than nonpregnant women. But not you. You take five or six deep breaths per minute. It's the baby, Sam—the baby wants you to breathe like that for some reason. What you're doing isn't normal even for trained athletes."

"Then I guess I'm healthier than they are," she casually replied. "The optimal partial pressure of oxygen and carbon dioxide is attained better by controlled deep breathing than by the normal hyperventilation of pregnancy."

"You see, you see!" He gestured with his hand. "That kind of 'baby talk' is what the fetus wants, not you."

She ignored him and walked to the refrigerator. Bryson was encouraged. At least she hadn't snapped at him with the kind of open hostility she showed so often. He followed her into the kitchenette, continuing his explanation. She opened the refrigerator door.

"Now what shall I eat," she said to herself, as if he weren't there.

At other times Samantha listened patiently. He felt that, at any moment, the weight of his precise logic would break through, and that Samantha would agree, "Yes, I see it now." But the persuasive element was not strong enough. Samantha simply was not convinced.

It was Sunday night. The distant church bell tolled twelve. In nine hours Bryson would be back in the lab. He lay beside Samantha, unable to sleep. He thought her asleep, but the faint rustling of her hand under the sheet proved otherwise. Her palm whisked across his thighs, encircling his penis. He turned on his side and slipped his hand under her head and around her shoulders. He kissed her neck. Samantha's legs parted, and she lifted the one nearest him. They came together scissors-like. She guided him into her.

How wet she was, he thought. Even without foreplay she was fully prepared for him, her arousal total. Bryson found the swift transition from flaccidity to firmness terribly exciting, and he glided within her slippery tightness. He nuzzled her breasts, and rubbed the ball of his thumb rhythmically against her nipples.

To Bryson, making love to a pregnant woman was a fascinating study in geometric agronomy: angles and curves abounded, and everywhere was lush, rounded ripeness. The swell of Samantha's abdomen rippled softly up and down, wind across a wheat field. Her pink areolae, growing slightly browner with each passing month, were wide and distended. Most curious was the jiggling, jelly-like movement of her full breasts. As their bodies undulated, Samantha's breasts bounced individually to opposite sides of her chest, and then rebounded quickly to its center, a rhythmic to and fro, like the vigorous hands of a symphony conductor.

Once spent, Samantha fell asleep quickly. Bryson pressed his cheek to hers, and he held her tightly. Then he closed his eyes and dozed off.

He was awakened by the distant sound of clicking. He turned to Samantha. She was still asleep, yet she was shivering perceptibly. He touched her skin; it was ice cold. Her teeth were chattering. There was something strange about the sound. It wasn't the typical staccato chatter of someone chilled, but had a pattern to it. Her teeth would click rhythmically, stop, and then begin again.

He got out of bed and found a heavy blanket in the closet. Samantha was naked, having discarded her clothes before making love. He covered her with the sheet and blankets. In the process, his hand grazed her abdomen, and he jumped back, astonished. Her lower abdomen was burning. The skin over her uterus was fiery hot, in stark contrast to the pallor and chill in the rest of her body. He tucked the blankets around her snugly.

Bryson sat on the edge of the bed, watching her in amazement. Somehow her body's blood had diverted itself to her uterus, increasing its metabolism and heat. In compensation, the temperature in the rest of her body automatically lowered.

How had she done that? Certainly, it didn't just happen. Body temperature was supposed to be involuntary. But Bryson realized that she hadn't done it voluntarily. Here was clear evidence of the fetus at work, the change in Samantha's body temperature another manifestation of the way it controlled her. Frightened, he shook her awake.

"Sam! Sam, honey, listen to me!" He grasped both her shivering cheeks with the fingers of one hand, steadying her face, forcing her to look at him. His other hand found hers and slid it onto her abdomen.

"Listen to me Sam, please. Are you awake? Feel that, Sam. Feel it."

She was awakening slowly, but the sudden realization of what he was showing her made Samantha fully alert.

"Look at you," he continued. "See yourself as I do. You're shivering half to death, but your uterus is burning up! Can you feel it, Sam? Do you understand what I'm saying?"

She understood. The shock he had been looking for, the

awareness of reality, registered in the expression on her face. She withdrew her hand from her belly, and uttered an "ah," a whimpering, whelp-like sound that arose from the back of her throat. The reality was terrifying.

"The baby's doing that, Samantha. The baby can control the warmth and blood flow to your uterus the same way it controls your outward behavior. This is what Rosie and I have been trying to tell you. This is no typical emotional change of pregnancy. This is the fetus showing you, more graphically than I could ever explain, that you're no longer yourself. It can control you, Sam."

Tears filled her eyes. Her shivering ceased, and the chill was gone. Her abdomen grew cooler, and soon her skin had started to warm.

"Why does it do that to me?" she murmured, the sound of defeat.

"I don't know, Sam. We just know that it does. When the baby's in control, you're not. You lose touch with reality."

Samantha started crying, sobbing softly into the pillow.

"Tell me it's not true, Jon." she cried. "Please tell me my own baby wouldn't do this to me."

"It does, Sam. You saw for yourself. You've got to believe me."

He held her tightly. Her body was shaking again, but this time with anguish rather than cold.

"No, no," she stammered. "I promised myself I wouldn't let it happen. How could it be?"

"It wasn't you. It wasn't your choice."

"I'm so confused. I have to lose it, don't I?"

He kissed away her tears. "First you had to know, to understand for yourself."

"Oh God, I need you, Jon. Please help me. Hold me."

"I will, Sam. I will."

It was a long time before her quivering ceased. He hugged her close. Slowly they fell asleep, arms and legs entwined.

16

She was firm in her decision, her resolve strong. Dr. Pritchard had made arrangements for her to re-enter the hospital the next morning, she said. The doctor didn't seem surprised that she had called. She had the impression that he expected to hear from her.

Her explanation was a catharsis. Samantha felt drained when she finished. Bryson was moved; he put his arms around her in consolation. She was doing the right thing, he said. Samantha pulled away; she didn't want to be coddled. But she kissed him on the cheek, warmed that he understood. Her decision was now irrevocable.

Bryson offered to spend the evening with her, but Samantha insisted she wanted to get a good night's sleep. Would she be all right? Samantha assured him that she would. Her conviction about her ability to proceed with the abortion was absolute. Bryson wanted to drive her to the hospital in the morning, but she demurred. Her actions, like her decision, were to be hers alone.

She walked home contentedly. Her stomach had settled; she even had an appetite. A week before, she had been on the same threshold. Then, her decision had been reactionary, an impulsive reflex to what Bryson had told her about the baby. Now it was fully thought out. She had struggled, and she had conquered. She would surrender her will to no one. She loved Bryson more than ever for letting her make the choice. Soon she was back at her apartment again.

Jon and me, she thought. It had a nice sound to it. She could hardly believe that it was really happening. She wished that he were there right then, wanting him more than ever.

Samantha took a bottle of Beaujolais from her wooden wine rack and uncorked it. It was time to celebrate. The effect of alcohol on her pregnancy no longer concerned her. She poured herself a glassful and took a long draught. It was mellow, satisfying.

Her apartment was sunny and warm. She lowered the shades and turned on the air conditioner. She unbuttoned her blouse and wiggled out of her jeans, leaving her clothes in a pile on the floor. To hell with the wash. Right now she wanted to relax and unwind.

She finished her first glass of wine and poured herself another. The wine made her languorous. She turned on the tub water and drew herself a cool bath. While the tub was filling, she gazed at her reflection in the mirror.

A slight tan remained from her week at the beach one month ago. Samantha was proud of her figure. Her flesh was firm, the muscles toned. She cupped both her breasts, weighing each in her palm. The nipples hardened. Her breasts had no sag or bounce, standing straight and erect. A shiver ran through her; she pursed her lips and sucked in breath. She put her hand on her pubis, below the swell of her abdomen, and rubbed the mons with her fingertips. With the flat of her other palm she made small circles against her breasts, flicking at the nipples with her thumb.

You feel so good, Jon, she thought.

She turned off the water and climbed into the tub. She poured bath oil into the water and lathered herself until her skin was slick. She lay on her back, head tilted against the rear of the tub, knees apart. The water came up to her neck. Her nipples bobbed through the surface, firm, pink buoys in an oily sea. She took a bar of soap and let her knees flop wide, resting on the side walls of the tub. She slid the soap against her vagina, rubbing it slowly up and down. Her lids fluttered closed. God you feel good.

The wave of nausea that passed over her was sudden, unexpected. Her head jolted upright. She dropped the soap and gripped the sides of the tub to keep from sliding. She started retching uncontrollably. A strong upward spasm forced vomit into her throat, filling her mouth. Her hand went to her lips, too late. Emesis gushed from her mouth, spurting through her fingers. It splashed into the water at chest level, dribbling into the cleft between her bosom. Her larynx went into spasm, and she coughed and gagged without breathing, white-faced. A wheezing spray of vomit splattered against the white-tiled wall. The water in the tub turned a foul, muddy brown, a discolored mixture of wine and rancid bile. Samantha was ashen, hunched forward, spilling her guts into the bath water until her stomach emptied and she found herself soaking in a cooling, sour pool of intestinal contents.

The heaving ceased. She barely had strength to trip the bath stopper with her toe. The foul water slowly swirled down the drain. She could breathe again, and inhaled in quivering, spastic jerks. The last of the water drained away, leaving flecks of vomit and particles of undigested food in its trail. Her skin chilled quickly. Samantha started shaking. She sank to the bottom of the tub and lay on her side, pale and trembling.

Strength returned slowly. It was half an hour before her color returned and she was able to pull herself up to a sitting position. She turned on the water and adjusted the flow until it was strong and hot. Water swirled around her knees. She kept the latch open and cleaned the mess around her, pushing putrid smatterings toward the drain. Wobbly-legged, she pulled herself up farther, and turned on the shower. She directed its jet onto the wall and rinsed the tile. Finally she put her head under the stinging stream and steeped in the spray.

When she finished she dried herself and slumped onto the toilet seat. Her head sagged. She leaned over and opened the cabinet under the sink, searching for a spray can or air freshener. She held the button down until the can was empty. The room smelled of stale, sour roses.

She couldn't think straight. Head bowed, she put on a robe and shuffled from the bathroom. She lay on the couch, shielding her eyes with an arm slung across her head. It had to be the wine, she thought. A spoiled vintage.

Her muscles were exhausted from the isometric straining of her nausea. Spent, Samantha waited for strength to return. She could barely move. The breeze from the air conditioner reached her, its coolness wonderful on her forehead. She was relaxed now, and her mind began drifting.

She was nearly asleep when the back of her head started hammering with crushing pain. It rocketed to the top of her scalp, her brain steaming with pressure. Again she bolted upright, wide-eyed. Her hands went reflexively to her temples, and her mouth jerked open, lips drawn tight past teeth bared in an agonizing grimace. The pressure was intense, and she thought her head was swelling. She closed her eyes firmly and pressed inward with her palms. Her skull seemed ready to explode. The noise that rose from her throat was involuntary, a high-pitched, moaning whine.

She held her head and wailed, paralyzed by the intensity of the pain.

Please let me wake up, she thought. But then she knew it was no dream. She staggered to her feet, sliding toward the phone, still crying, toward help. She imagined that if she released her temples, her brain would disintegrate into a million pieces. Her vision was blurry. The horrible pressure behind her eyes expanded forward, and she thought her irises would pop from their scleras like flounder eyes. She tried to get to the phone but something was pushing her down. She felt a weight on her shoulders. Her knees buckled, and her chin was pulled down as if by an anchor. She sagged to the carpet, spinning dizzily from noise, pressure, and pain until she fainted.

It was dark when she awoke. The pain was gone. Unsteadily she sat up and looked at the clock by the telephone. It was two o'clock in the morning.

My God, she thought. I've been out for ten hours. Then she saw the broken lamp on the floor.

Startled, she got up and looked around the room. She walked toward a light switch and tripped over a chair that lay on its side. She reached the wall, found the switch, and flipped it on. The room was a shambles. Paintings lay on the floor, their frames broken, glass strewn across the carpet. Her desk had been turned upside down, the contents of its drawers emptied. Furniture and books were scattered about everywhere.

She went quickly to the door. It was locked, bolted, as she had left it when she returned earlier in the day. She made a quick search of the apartment. The windows were intact, with no sign of forced entry. Then how . . . ? She was suddenly very frightened. She had to talk to Jon. He would be asleep, but she had to wake him. Nearing the phone, she stubbed her toe on an ashtray. When she bent down to retrieve it, she saw the torn paper. Scattered around the ashtray were tattered photos and shreds of film.

Samantha knelt down and examined them. They were the pictures she had taken with Jon, photos of their week spent together. Most of them were ripped to pieces, photographic shreds of memory, torn apart. The heavy ashtray was broken in two. Under its halves, her favorite picture of Jon had been pounded into pulp of kaleidoscopic Kodacolor. Drops of blood were on the rug around it, and a crimson smear was dried on the glass. Hurriedly she brushed it aside and returned to the phone.

She picked up the receiver and stopped, terrified. She stared at her hand as it held the phone. Across the knuckles was a smooth cut, a neat, sharp laceration, dried rivulets of blood running down to her fingertips. She glanced quickly at the ashtray and then back at her hand. Oh, no, she thought. Her hand started trembling. She put down the receiver.

It was then that she became aware of the baby. It kicked softly at first, and then progressively harder. Its pounding was defiant. Samantha sank to the rug in front of the telephone. She started to touch her belly, but pulled her hands away quickly, too mortified to touch. Her entire abdomen thudded.

She couldn't move. Her body wouldn't function; only her mind continued to work. She could neither believe nor comprehend what she had done. Her apartment was wrecked. Her possessions were torn apart. Pictures of the man she loved were crushed and ripped.

The baby's kicking was incessant, triumphant. She knew she wasn't responsible. She fully understood what Jon had said about the baby. She started to cry.

"Why are you doing this to me?" she cried. "Why am I being punished?"

The baby kicked vigorously, punching, thudding. Samantha cried softly, not daring to move. She tried not to think about what was happening. She wanted to make her mind blank. For the first time in her life, she watched the sweeping second hand of the clock, counting the seconds, obscuring all thought by mentally marking time.

The luminous dial mesmerized her. Hours passed. She kept perfectly still, trying to ignore the fetal movements, her mind vaguely aware of better visibility as dawn lightened the outside sky. The hour hand reached five.

The phone rang. Samantha was distracted; she debated answering it. Three rings; four. Perceptibly, the baby's movements slowed. Seven rings now. The movements ceased entirely. With audible relief, she reached for the phone.

"Hello?"

"Sam, it's me. I have to dash over to the hospital. But since I'm awake, I wanted to make sure you were awake too. I don't want you to be late."

"Oh, Jon!" she cried, her voice cracking under the strain. "I've had such a horrible night."

"That's natural, Sam. Look, I have to go. There's an emergency on the ward. Catch you later. Bye."

"Jon, wait!" she said, too late. He had hung up.

Samantha replaced the receiver, waiting for the movements to start again. She looked at the clock. One minute passed. And soon five more, and still the fetus was silent. She placed her hand on her uterus to feel for activity.

There was none. Samantha snapped out of her daze. She arose and raised the shades, flooding the room with early morning sunlight.

She went to her closet and dressed hurriedly. The clean-up could wait. Once she got to the hospital, she would be safe. Neither pain nor nausea could stop her after she was admitted. They told her not to bring any valuables. She briefly considered packing a small overnight case and decided against it. She wouldn't be staying long. She dressed casually and threw her toothbrush and a few dollars into an empty purse. Her keys were in the kitchenette under a pile of books. She pocketed them and, with a sorrowful last look at her overturned possessions, left the apartment and locked the door behind her.

The admitting procedure was identical to that of seven days before, except this time it seemed to take forever. Again, a clerk escorted her upstairs when her room was ready. An obese, elderly woman occupied the bed nearest the door. She snored loudly, seemingly undisturbed by the tubes protruding from her various orifices.

At seven-fifteen, a medication nurse came in, announcing that the operating room had called for Samantha. She asked her to empty her bladder, after which she gave her an injection of a sedative. A green-gowned orderly wheeled a stretcher into the room. He and the nurse helped Samantha who slid hurriedly onto it. The nurse said goodbye, and Samantha was whisked into the corridor.

They stopped by a large treatment room at the end of the hall. The orderly explained that it wasn't really an operating room, but rather a special area reserved for cases like hers. He pushed open the swinging doors and transferred the stretcher to the circulating-room nurse inside. Samantha felt like parcel post, a package that changed hands many times en route to its destination. The circulating nurse, dressed in scrub greens, was already capped and masked. She said hello and asked Samantha how she was feeling. Samantha replied that she was a little woozy, but she was anxious to get started. The nurse nodded toward an adjacent observation window. Though her vision was blurry, Samantha recognized her doctor lathering up at a scrub sink.

Samantha slid off the stretcher onto an adjustable operating table. The nurse pushed the stretcher aside and flipped on a bright overhead spotlight. She aimed it at Samantha's abdomen. Samantha's knees were secured with a strap. A young doctor entered through the rear door and perfunctorily asked Samantha to put out her left arm. Samantha asked him who he was. He was the anesthesia resident, he said curtly, and was just there to start an IV. He strapped a rubber tourniquet to her arm and inserted intravenous tubing into a vein. He was quick, proficient. He taped down the plastic tubing, adjusted the rate of flow and left, just as the scrub doors opened.

Her obstetrician backed into the room to avoid touching the door with his clean, wet hands. His arms were extended in front of him, bent at the elbows. Water dripped from his forearms onto the floor.

"How're you doing?" he asked, looking at Samantha. She nodded an unspoken hello, praying that he would get on with it.

"Good morning, Dr. Pritchard," said the nurse. She handed him a sterile towel. He dried his arms and donned a scrub gown which the nurse held open in front of him. Then she tied its straps in the back. He walked over to the instrument stand and put on a pair of white latex gloves.

"Get any sleep last night?" he asked.

"Some."

"Good. This won't take very long. First the nurse is going to prep your belly."

The nurse lifted Samantha's gown and folded it just below her breasts. A sterile sheet covered the lower half of her body, from the pubic hair downward. The gentle curve of Samantha's uterus was exposed between the two linen boundaries.

"Cold, hon," said the nurse. She lathered Samantha's abdomen with an antiseptic solution that soon bubbled yellow. After a few minutes of washing, she sponged off the suds with a dry, sterile, cloth towel. Then she sprayed the area with brown liquid iodine, expressing the squirts from a plastic squeeze-container that resembled a plant mister.

"All right, we're ready to start," said the doctor. "I'll explain everything as I go along, Miss Kirstin, so I don't catch you by surprise."

"Fine," said Samantha, aware of the pain starting in her head. "Could you hurry? I'm not feeling very well."

The doctor wheeled over the instrument table. "First I'm going to cover you with some towels." He lay four of them in a square, leaving a rectangular portal of skin exposed. The baby was suddenly active. Samantha protectively closed her eyes against the mounting pressure in her skull. Please hurry, she thought.

Her doctor noted the fetal movements.

"Active little fellow," he said, to no one in particular. He placed his gloved hands on her abdomen and palpated her uterus.

"Did she void?" he asked the nurse.

"Yes, Doctor."

"Hmmm. This is a nice size uterus. Okay. Give me

some two percent lidocaine and a little twenty-five gauge
needle."

"Already on your tray, Doctor."

"Yes, all right. Is the PG drawn up?"

"Forty milligrams."

"Okay. Now, Miss Kirstin, I'm going to numb your
belly." He picked up a syringe filled with local anesthetic.
"You'll feel a little pinprick, there," he said, injecting the
anesthetic just below her umbilicus, "and maybe a burning sensation. Good. How're you feeling?"

"It hurts," said Samantha, referring not to the anesthetic but to her head. Eyes shut, she rocked her head
from side to side, trying to relieve the excruciating pain
between her temples. She was very dizzy. She felt her consciousness slowly receding inward, not really hearing anything any more. *Please hurry. Hurry, please.*

"It won't be much longer," said the doctor reassuringly.
"We're almost finished. There may be some pressure now,"
he said, lifting a thicker, four-inch needle off the tray. He
placed its tip against the wheal made by the anesthetic
and eased the point just below the skin. With a deft
thrust, he plunged the needle into her uterus. He removed
an inner stylet. Amniotic fluid rose through the needle's
hollow core, a convex liquid bubble appearing on the top.
In droplets, the clear fluid fell onto Samantha's skin.

Neither the doctor nor the nurse noticed the sudden
opening of Samantha's eyes. Their attention was on the
needle. Samantha's lips retracted, baring her teeth. Though
dazed, the expression on her face was almost savage. Her
head was still, its glassy eyes staring wildly at the ceiling.

"Just a few more seconds," said the doctor. "I'm going
to give you the injection now."

Later, the nurse would recall the sounds that Samantha

made as something akin to snarls. They began in her throat
as the doctor was about to attach his syringe. He paused
to glance toward the strange noise, and stopped when he
saw her feral expression.

"Miss Kirstin . . . ?"

Wild-eyed, Samantha emitted a growling shriek. She
flung out her left arm powerfully and knocked the doctor
backward. Then she shot upright. She stared ferociously
beyond them and yelled, "No!" a long, lingering cry of
animal rage. She yanked the still-protruding needle from
her abdomen and heaved it against the wall.

The nurse rushed toward her. "Now see here, young
lady, you're—"

Her words were cut short by a vicious backhand slap
that sent the nurse sprawling. Samantha pulled out her
IV, tore off the sterile drapes, and kicked off the knee
straps, swinging her legs over the side of the table. Mouth
agape, the doctor instinctively stepped backward. Samantha seized the edge of the instrument tray with both
hands and hurled it across the room. She jumped to the
floor and hurtled through the swinging doors, striking them
with such force that one came off its hinges.

Samantha ran down the hall toward her room. She flew
by hospital personnel who were too astonished to say anything. They stared in amazement at the barefoot creature
who sprinted by them, gown untied and flapping behind
her. In the distance someone shouted, "Stop her!" But no
one made a move.

Samantha dashed into her room. The old woman in the
first bed snored undisturbed, oblivious to the mounting
commotion around her. Samantha cast off her gown and
hurriedly dressed. Grabbing her purse, she ran toward the
elevator.

"Call Security!" came a voice behind her. But she had already ducked into the nearest stairwell. She took the steps three and four at a time, a bounding gazelle. In thirty seconds she was on the main floor. She darted into the lobby and jogged toward the front entrance, casually dodging stretchers and passersby who glanced at her curiously.

And then she was outside.

The morning air was fresh, the sunshine bright. Samantha felt good. She filled her lungs, invigorated. She kicked off her moccasins and carried them in one hand. Running barefoot was healthier. It was several miles to her apartment, but she hadn't jogged in three days and definitely needed the exercise. She loped along at a comfortable pace, hair rustling in the breeze. Low in her belly the baby kicked strongly. Only one thing mattered now.

The baby was safe. And damn anyone who tried to harm it.

17

It was noon in the lab. Bryson had just returned from lunch, bringing a sandwich for Mrs. Rutledge. She handed him the telephone.

"It's for you."

"Who is it?"

"I don't know. He says it's personal."

"It better be," he said, reaching for the receiver. "Hello?"

"Dr. Bryson?"

"Yes."

"This is Dr. Pritchard. I'm an obstetrician on staff at the university. We spoke last week; perhaps you remember. I'm calling you about Samantha Kirstin," he said, and paused, awaiting a reply.

"What about her?"

"It's a confidential matter, Doctor. The face sheet on her chart lists you as her nearest relative. I'm a little bit at a loss as to whether I should discuss this with you if you don't know what I'm referring to."

"I appreciate your confidentiality, Dr. Pritchard. But I know about the abortion. Sam is my graduate research assistant. She gave you my name because she didn't want her parents to find out. Did everything go all right?"

"No, it didn't. Is she with you now?"

"You mean she didn't go to the hospital? I spoke with her early this morning to make sure she wouldn't oversleep."

"She was here all right. She left her calling card all over the place. In fact she caused quite a bit of commotion."

Bryson grew concerned, uneasy. He threw his pen on his desk. "If something's wrong I'd appreciate it if you'd get to the point."

"The point is that we were halfway through the procedure when she jumped up like a lunatic and ran out of the hospital. Your assistant assaulted one of the nurses, smashed several hundred dollars' worth of equipment, and upset the routine of an entire ward. She was last seen flying out of the hospital's front entrance. There was no answer to her apartment telephone, and we even sent hospital Security over there. When she wouldn't answer the front door, they had the superintendent open it for them. She wasn't there. But they told me that the place was turned upside down. That's why I'm calling you. I was hoping she might be there, or that you would at least know where I could find her."

"I wish I did. You've got me very concerned, Dr. Pritchard. The pregnancy has been a tremendous strain on Sam lately. But she seemed rather determined to have the abortion."

"That's what I thought, too. This may sound unprofessional, but I think your assistant is some kind of a nut. As far as I'm concerned, she needs some good therapy."

"Because she changed her mind?"

"No, anyone can change her mind. She did it once already last week. You had to be here to know what I'm talking about. It was like Jekyll and Hyde. One minute she was calm as could be, and the next she went stark raving mad. There was a physical change in her, not just emotional. She was a wild person. It's the closest thing to manic psychosis I've seen since I was an intern. If I believed in witchcraft, I would say she was possessed."

"Possessed?"

"I think she is a very disturbed young woman. I think she needs help. And the sooner the better. If you should see her, please call me. Between the two of us, maybe we can persuade her to see a psychiatrist. I've had enough trouble as it is trying to keep the police out of this. The nurse she assaulted wanted to press charges. But she's calmed down now, although the rest of the place is still in an uproar. You'll let me know, then?"

"Yes. And thank you for calling."

He sat next to Mrs. Rutledge. "You heard?" he asked.

"Bits and pieces. She decided not to have the abortion again?"

He ran his fingers through his hair.

"Not her, Rosie. *It* decided. The fetus."

"The fetus?"

Bryson shook his head.

"I'm an idiot. We knew it had the potential to control her behavior. I should have known this would happen."

"Don't blame yourself. How were you to know it could happen so quickly?"

"Just because the fetus has acted so benevolently in the past, why should I have assumed that it would allow her to kill it? She as much as told me so, and I didn't listen. The damn thing has a mind of its own."

"But how could it have known Samantha was going to have an abortion?"

"It's a medical genius, remember? If it can influence her thoughts, it can probably read her thoughts, too. I'm sure it can tell when she's hungry, and when she wants to fart. When she's angry and when she's tired. And it damn well knows when she's decided that she no longer wants it on board." He got up and headed for the door.

"What are you going to do now?"

"First I've got to find Sam."

He drove to her apartment and parked in the lot. He quickly walked up the steps and pressed the buzzer to her flat. Surprisingly, she answered immediately.

From the expression on her face, Bryson knew at once that something was wrong. Gone was the uncertainty, the fear, the tortured look of anguish. In its place was a picture of madonna-like contentment. She emanated a glowing aura of serenity. To the casual observer, Samantha was a pregnant woman at peace with herself. She kissed him on the cheek.

"Hello, darling," she said. She took his hand and led him to the couch. He looked around the room. The apartment was immaculate. What had the obstetrician been talking about? Nothing was out of place.

"What happened at the hospital, Sam?"

"Nothing," she said, resting her head on his shoulder.

"Your doctor called me looking for you. He said there was a problem."

"There was no porblem. There never was."

"What about the abortion?"

Her smile was reassuring and apologetic. "That was silly, wasn't it? I don't know what got into me. I must have been crazy, don't you think? To try to hurt my baby?" She rubbed her abdomen tenderly. "There I was lying on the operating table, and it suddenly dawned on me: what am I doing here? So I asked the doctor to stop. And he did. He's a nice person, Dr. Pritchard, I like him a lot. And I ran home, you know. It's been so long. I felt great. While I was running, I decided that I must have been temporarily insane. That happens to people, doesn't it? Something just snaps inside?"

Indeed it does, he thought, gazing at her softly, trying to fight back the pity he felt for her. He studied the placid look on her face, eyes dazed, puddles glazed with a veneer of winter ice obscuring the truth within. The Samantha he knew and loved was hidden deep inside, captive. As the baby grew, so did her autonomy recede.

"What now, Sam? What are your plans?"

"There's no reason we can't continue, is there? Just as before? I can finish up the Somnapar study, and start another. And every afternoon you can keep studying me."

"But I've finished studying you."

"No you haven't!" she insisted. "There's much more we must learn!"

"We? I know what I set out to discover."

She stood up, fists clenched.

"You know nothing!" she raged. "How dare you think you can stop now!" She turned her back on him.

"Sam—"

She went to the door and held it open for him. "I'll be at the lab at four o'clock," she said, growing composed.

Easy now, he thought. Play your cards right. He smiled and stood up.

"You're right, Sam. There is a lot more I have to learn. But it's the wrong time, now, Sam. Let's give it a week or so and we'll discuss it again."

"To hell with you and your discussions," she flared. "I'll be there whenever I please."

"No way, Sam. Now listen to me. It's over. You just don't understand."

"You bastard!"

The altercation that ensued was vitriolic. Samantha was insistent upon resuming the project. Bryson was equally adamant in his refusal, reaffirming that the study was over.

The data had been gathered, he said, and that was the end of it. Samantha's personality reflected the emotional roller coaster she was riding, changing with chameleon-like suddenness. She stormed and raged; she wheedled and cajoled. But her entreaties were futile. And suddenly she became calm, now as tranquil as she had been turbulent.

"All right, Jon," she said agreeably. "You win." She turned casually away from him, as if the argument had never happened.

He was mystified.

18

She sat straight up in bed, gazing into the darkness. The room was still and quiet, save for the faintest mechanical whirr of the alarm clock. It was fifteen seconds past midnight. She silently acknowledged the time: perfect. The internal biological clock that governed her awakening was functioning precisely, pre-set to arouse her at twelve. All was well.

She pulled back the covers and rose from the bed. Her clothes were haphazardly suspended from a hanger looped around the closet's doorknob. The navy tank top and black shorts were nearly invisible. She pried them from the hanger and dressed. They fitted her loosely, cool and comfortable. Tiptoeing, she glided into the living room, over to the front door. She unchained the latch, eased the door ajar, and peered into the hall. The stairwell was dark and empty. Not making a sound, she closed the door and started down the steps.

The waiting room was crowded to overfilling. Several obviously pregnant women leaned against the walls in the corridor, the queue leading through the opened front door. Bryson excused himself as he slid past the patients, gracefully twisting to sidestep the protruding abdomens like a halfback dodging tacklers. The receptionist's desk was at the head of the throng, in a small anteroom enclosed in sliding glass. It looked like a teller's cage. Above a minute sign reading, "Payment is requested at the time of each visit," Bryson rapped politely on the glass. The receptionist eyed him indifferently.

"Might I see the doctor for a few minutes?"

"Dr. Pritchard sees drug company reps every other Thursday," sighed the receptionist, returning to her log book. "Leave me your card and call after hours for an appointment."

"I'm Dr. Bryson."

"Oh," she murmured, not missing a beat. She pressed the intercom button and spoke quietly into the receiver. "The doctor will see you shortly."

He had avoided speaking with Dr. Pritchard over the phone. A face-to-face encounter would lend greater credence to his case. He chose to go to the obstetrician's office rather than suggesting they meet in neutral territory. Bryson thought he had a greater chance of winning Pritchard's confidence and cooperation on the latter's home ground.

"The doctor will see you now," said the receptionist.

Dimly lit, the obstetrician's consultation room was tastefully furnished in mahogany and leather. He rose to take Bryson's hand and motioned for him to take a seat.

"What can I do for you, Dr. Bryson?"

"It's about my assistant, Miss Kirstin."

"I thought as much. As far as I'm concerned, Miss Kirstin is in urgent need of psychiatric help."

Bryson made a steeple of his fingers, as if in prayer. He lifted his hands before his face, pursing his lips. He measured his words.

"Please hear me out, Dr. Pritchard. What I'm about to tell you is quite unusual, even fantastic. I ask for your patience and understanding."

"I'm listening."

"Samantha has been under a tremendous strain recently.

Most of it is not her doing. Perhaps I can explain it best by giving you some background information on the activities Samantha is involved in at the lab."

For the next ten minutes Bryson reviewed both his work as a sleep researcher and Samantha's participation in the sleep studies. Without detailed elaboration, he described the discovery of the unusual EEG activity, the transmissions, the dialogue, the reports from the computer center and the resultant effect on Samantha. His dissertation finished, he looked to Dr. Pritchard for a response. Throughout, the obstetrician had listened intently.

"That's about it, then," said Bryson. "It's much more complicated than I've been able to summarize in a brief time. But, in a nutshell, Sam's strange behavior is a direct result of the fetal control exerted upon her. She's getting worse fast. And I need your help."

Dr. Pritchard simply stared for the next half minute. Then a smirk widened his lips, followed by a slow chuckle. The grin yielded to a chortle, which soon became uproarious, knee-slapping laughter.

"That is the most outrageous yarn I've ever heard!" he said, choking with laughter. "You really should be on stage, Dr. Bryson."

Bryson was mortified with embarrassment. His face reddened.

"I'm not joking."

In stages, the obstetrician's laughter ended spasmodically. His expression stiffened.

"Are you trying to tell me you're serious?"

"I've never been more serious in my life."

"What the hell kind of con is this, then? You come into my office on a day when I'm backlogged with patients, waste my time with this preposterous talk about a fetus talking to a computer, and then dare to tell me you're serious? Are you out of your mind?"

"Please, Dr. Pritchard. You've got to believe me! We need you desperately!"

The obstetrician spoke into the intercom. "Miss Smith, set up the next patient." Then, to Bryson, "If you'll excuse me, I have a busy day."

"But wait, Doctor. Let me explain!"

Dr. Pritchard opened the door abruptly.

"Get out of my office at once."

At that hour of the night, the main roads on campus were still traveled by the occasional student returning late from the library, a wayward reveler, or the infrequent couple walking hand in hand. She stuck to back roads and grassy paths. She started slowly at first, then picked up the pace of her jog. The moonless night was cool and dark. A rippling breeze ruffled her hair. She bounced around benches, behind trees, limbering up more and more, running with smooth certainty.

Her torso was already thinner. In one week she had lost four pounds. Rigorous exercise and continuous dietary restriction had taken their toll. Her slender torso appeared lanky, bony protuberances showing through in places once occupied by gentle curves.

How strong, she thought. I am muscle, I am bone. The more weight I lose, the better I look. The greater I feel. I have the might of a lion, proud and free.

A sleek filly, she galloped with unerring gracefulness toward her destination.

In the days following the stunning humiliation of his exchange with Dr. Pritchard, Bryson rarely ventured from the security of the lab and the reassuring alliance of his only confidante, Mrs. Rutledge. She gave him hope and solace. His first attempt at securing help for Samantha had been such a devastating experience that, initially, he refused to consider the matter further. But Samantha's curious antics worsened. At times she appeared totally rational, fully in control of her behavior. She enthusiastically continued the various other sleep projects. She would make pleasant, lucid conversation with Bryson and Mrs. Rutledge. And then suddenly, for no apparent reason, she would begin to babble incoherently. Her conversation made little sense to them; it sounded like excerpted phrases from the dialogues between MEDIC and the fetus. They found that immensely disturbing, inasmuch as Samantha was no longer continuing her own sleep periods.

Her appearance showed no sign of improvement. She was the person who, soaked by a rainstorm, refused to towel dry; or the grimy athlete who, returning to the locker room, dressed without showering. They thought that by now, without any reinforcement from her sleep sessions, she should be on the road to recovery, showing outward normalcy. But she wasn't. Perplexed, Bryson swallowed his pride and resolved to try again.

Clearly, going to the police was out of the question. No crime had been committed. If there were a fugitive to be apprehended, it was either an enormous machine or a six-month-old fetus. The thought of even commencing such an overture to the police seemed so ridiculous that Bryson and Mrs. Rutledge dismissed it out of hand. They concluded that the next logical place to turn for help was the computer center. Perhaps Bryson should have done so much earlier.

His conversation with Roberts was brief. Without going into details, Bryson indicated that he had discovered
something which was vitally important to MEDIC. From
his previous interchange with Roberts, Bryson expected the
supervisor to be annoyed, even indignant. But mere mention of "discovery" seemed to have a magical effect. Roberts told Bryson to come to the computer center at once.

He had a momentary hesitation about bringing sample
tracings from the minicomputer. But Roberts had said to
bring evidence; only hard, concrete data would convince
him. Samantha's health depended on it. Bryson tore out
selected excerpts and left the lab.

In the computer center, Bryson very succinctly explained
the outcome of his studies on a pregnant sleep volunteer.
He had discovered that MEDIC and the volunteer's fetus
were exchanging information in the form of two-way transmissions. This accounted for the computer's erratic behavior and its occasional malfunctions. Roberts listened
with more patience than Bryson had anticipated, tersely
asking a question here and there. When the programmer
asked Bryson for the evidence, Roberts thumbed through
the graph paper.

"Interesting," said Roberts. "But hardly credible."

"What? The proof's right in front of you!"

"There's nothing substantive here. Where did you get
this little computer of yours?"

Bryson grew wary. Perhaps it was a mistake to tell Roberts. Had he committed an unforgivable error?

"I borrowed a portable one. Very briefly, from a friend,"
he said, downplaying the incident. "I sent it back after a
few days," he lied.

Now Roberts grew annoyed. "Are you trying to tell me,"
Roberts roared, "that you gained access to a supplementary

computer from sources outside the university, without going through the required channels, and without informing
the proper authorities? And that you then used such a
device to meddle in an area that you have no permission
to even approach?"

Bryson realized immediately that the sanctity of
MEDIC was a non-negotiable principle. Someone's health
was a mere trifle compared to the importance of the machine. Explanations were no use, the man wouldn't believe
him. Bryson had to soft-peddle his approach to pacify
Roberts. An indignant supervisor might insist on inspecting the lab. And that would be the end of the minicomputer.

Bryson laughed with the forced uneasiness of a speeder
pulled over by a state trooper. Don't worry, he said. There
had been little tampering. He thought, he said, that there
was indeed communication between MEDIC and the
fetus, but he was merely speculating.

Roberts sounded mollified. "I hope you are, for your
sake," he hissed. "Your fairytale about a computerized
dialogue is so absurd that it doesn't deserve further com-
ment by me. But I remind you of the oath that all em-
ployees of the university and hospital sign, Dr. Bryson:
the oath of non-interference. If I should ever hear, even
in jest, that you or one of your staff interfered in any way
with the proper functioning of MEDIC, I'll take the matter
to the highest authorities on campus. You know the consequences, Doctor. This sort of thing must never be repeated. And as for your findings, well, I'll look at these
tracings once again. If I should change my opinion of this
nonsense, I'll let you know."

Bryson left, feeling he had gained a reprieve. When the
door was closed, Roberts studied the excerpts closely. They

were interesting, very interesting indeed. But after fifteen minutes' study, he shook his head. Impossible. It could never happen. The computer Bryson had borrowed was faulty, or else the girl was psychotic. Or maybe both.

Roberts opened a desk drawer and extracted a folder marked To Be Investigated. He filed the tracings inside, replaced the folder, and promptly forgot about the matter.

The darkness in the supply closet was absolute. Not a ray of light invaded the minicomputer's sanctuary. Suddenly, a faint click; gears shifted. A pale yellow light deep within its mechanical heart flashed on, casting an incandescent glow that created attenuated shadows amidst files of paper. It had perceived the call, and threw itself into action. Impulses from inside the sleep room bombarded its computerized brain. Not far distant, something alive had activated circuits formerly used only in daylight hours.

The minicomputer integrated and analyzed. The transmissions had begun. A free flow of information was being exchanged between MEDIC and the sleep room. The cables leading to and from the lab were vibrant with unspoken communication. The code tantalized the minicomputer, provoking it. It sifted through the dialogue, extracting, digesting, and summarizing pertinent passages.

A concise printout spilled out of the terminal. The minicomputer had been positioned obliquely against the wall, so that as the paper spewed forth it fell behind the machine into a hidden crevice. The paper folded itself neatly, a small packet of information that grew slowly thicker as the transmission continued.

Precisely two hours after the dialogue had begun, the cables fell silent. The light from the minicomputer disappeared. Once again the interior of the supply closet was the color of pitch.

"*Virginia Ledger.*"

"Science editor, please."

"One moment."

"Science desk. Courtney."

"May I please speak with the science editor?"

"Who's calling?"

"I'm . . . on the staff at Jubilee General. I'd like to tell the editor about a discovery here."

"Just a minute."

There was a pause, then the click of a receiver.

"This is Archer."

"Yes, hello. I'm calling for a physician at Jubilee General. He has found something quite remarkable which he thinks you may want to look into."

"Who is this doctor?"

"I'd rather not say, at the moment, until you have a chance to speak with him personally. The discovery has caused a fair amount of controversy."

"And what is this remarkable discovery?"

"The doctor has learned, by analysis of fetal brain-waves, that an unborn baby is capable of dreaming."

"Go on."

"What if I were to tell you that this same fetus is exchanging information between itself and the Jubilee General computer?"

"I would say you were out of your mind."

"I know it's hard to believe, but it's true. What has happened—"

"Look, lady, I've got a deadline to make in less than—"

"Please don't hang up! I can have the doctor call you himself if you wish. This is vitally important. You see, these transmissions are affecting the health of the baby's mother, and . . ."

She stopped, staring at the receiver. The line was dead in Rosemary Rutledge's hand. She looked at Bryson and shook her head apologetically.

"I had a feeling," said Bryson. "Well. Good thing I didn't make the call myself. Somehow I thought a woman might sound more persuasive. Admit it, Rosie. We're licked."

"I can't believe it. It seems that no one has any intention of helping us."

"Then we'll simply have to help ourselves."

It was much quieter now, darker, the air still and breezeless. The jog back took her past the church. Had it been daytime, one would have noticed that the hands on the steeple's clock had just passed two-fifteen. In the shadows, time flowed unseen.

How good she felt! Refreshed, rejuvenated, the run back was more exhilarating than the trip there. The object of her journey had been accomplished.

Gliding under a lamppost, the look on her face was in stark contrast to her feelings within. A passerby would have thought her skin waxy. Her glazed eyes were coated with an opaque film. She left the impression of being dazed.

What was once begun would surely continue. Any attempt at intervention would prove futile. There could be no stopping, no turning back. The perfect plan had been conceived months before. What started as the embryonic seed of a monumental concept had budded, then flowered; it would soon bear fruit. Like a missile locked on target, it had reached its apogee. Now it would begin descent, rocketing ever faster, zero in on its coordinates, and plunge earthward with a crashing suddenness that would change the course of destiny.

19

The evenings Bryson spent with Samantha were the most confusing moments of his entire life. Not since his early days in medical school had he been so continually perplexed. He was totally devoted to her welfare, as a doting father might care for his only child; and as that child appeared to become ill, his patience extended itself accordingly.

There was no attempt to socialize. They spent their moments together as a couple alone. Had Samantha been more alert, she might have wished it otherwise. Before she began the sleep studies, her affability and friendliness led her naturally into the company of others, and her acquaintance was usually sought after, and often as easily given. But now, as she drifted from independence to fetal subservience, her perceptions were a kind of twilight awareness, a state that clashed with any subconscious wish to mingle. This was quite acceptable to Bryson. Although he was a loner by nature, he considered socializing as a means of drawing Samantha out. But he quickly rejected the notion, given her condition. Moreover, being alone gave him greater opportunity to care for her, to watch over her and speak with her, try to break through.

This did not mean, however, that their interludes were shared in the confining solitude of their apartments. He spent a great deal of time with her outdoors. Late summer in their community was a festive time; there was no dearth of carnivals and amusement parks, ball games and state fairs. On weekends they picnicked, at the shore or in a nearby park, often taking long drives into the country. What encouraged him most was the vibrant little girl in her that emerged at these events, with a giggling, wide-eyed sense of wonder, when she was thrilled by a home run, or awed by a dazzling display of fireworks. These were the times when he knew he had not lost her. She would converse with him in ordinary, if not excited, tones, at a time when her contact with reality was complete. But what threw him into despair was the sudden, unexpected shift in her demeanor when, out of the blue, she would babble interminable, nonsensical medical phrases. At one moment she might be laughing and holding his hand; at the next she would pull herself away, her somber eyes glazed, and begin her incoherent mumbling for minutes on end. Her two distinct personalities would have fascinated any psychiatrist. To Bryson they were disheartening evidence of Samantha's continued ill health. Yet as much as he was discouraged, he was never disconsolate; for as long as she had flashes of her real self, he knew there was hope.

Their intimacy continued. Bryson didn't particularly mind that it seemed more and more contrived. He attributed that to Samantha's mental strain. What did confuse him was why, in such a state, her physical desires appeared to grow ever stronger.

Attempts to reason with her were futile. Many a time he tried to explain what was happening to her. He dwelled on her appearance, insisting that she was becoming more haggard than slender, and that continued weight loss could cause her harm. He brought her the homemade bread that she had once loved, but she refused it. He was quick to point out her episodes of mumbling incoherence. And he also exclaimed that, in his opinion as the man who loved her, she had grown downright sloppy. This was all the baby's doing, he stressed. It was a result of the baby's other priorities. He was there to help her fight it.

To all of his explanations, interjections, and pleading, Samantha listened with smiling patience. She replied, simply and politely, that he was mistaken. There was absolutely nothing wrong with her. She felt fine. And, she added, would he be so kind as to stop saying she looked like shit?

Bryson wouldn't give up. Yet he realized that at the present rate he was heading nowhere.

Uncertainty made him plunge frenetically into his research. He plodded through the textbooks, wandering among the library stacks, cross-referencing, tabulating. The theories of behavior control were numerous and complex. He began with older journals, the articles summarizing brainwashing, and worked his way through psychokinesis to the more recent concepts of behavior modification. What he found gave him insight into the psychology of behavior control but not the mechanism. What he was interested in was more physiological, probably biochemical. This avenue of pursuit led him into his own back yard, for much of it dealt with neurology.

The whole area of neurotransmitters was still experimental. But he was at home with the research. There followed an intensive review of updates in endocrinology, sifting through the latest developments in gynecologic and neuro-endocrinology, and the newest concepts of hormone action. And finally, he delved into the most recent theories of the metabolism of pregnancy.

He came away after three days of research with nothing solid to go on but with no shortage of hypotheses. Each sphere was intricate, but in many ways the separate spheres could be interrelated. Bryson concluded that his original hypothesis based on his study of hormone theory seemed likely in Samantha's case: a substance secreted in one part of her body exerted its action elsewhere. Probably the origin of the offending substance was the afterbirth, the placenta; or perhaps it came from the fetus itself. And its site of action was Samantha's cerebral cortex. By controlling the amount or type of substance secreted, the fetus could indirectly control Samantha's thoughts and bodily functions. But what exactly were the active principles involved? Fetal adrenal steroids, placental lactogen or estrogen, amniotic prostaglandins? And where precisely did they affect Sam's brain—in the cortex itself, midbrain, hypothalamus, or elsewhere?

If any of his hypotheses were to be proved, the answer would be supplied by the minicomputer. He would have to bring Samantha back for a few more sleep studies. The thought of submitting her to an opportunity for even greater fetal control sickened him. But it was the only way.

He hadn't expected her to be overjoyed, or wildly enthusiastic. But he did think she would be pleased. After all, it was she who had insisted on continuing the studies. Whatever his expectation, he wasn't prepared for her reaction. Samantha accepted his suggestion mutely, totally unfazed, as uninterestedly as the submissive wife who might ask her coitally assertive mate, Are you finished now, dear?

The following morning, both Bryson and Mrs. Rutledge told Samantha of their plan to reintroduce her to the sleep study several days hence. Samantha's peculiar response was equally vexatious to Mrs. Rutledge. She couldn't understand the girl's reluctance. Samantha was as warm to the idea as a frog might be to an extra swim. Her attitude was incomprehensible. Rather than try to figure it out, Bryson directed his energies toward his expanded mini-computer program.

For several days he divorced himself from Samantha. In the evenings, alone in his town house, he wrote out the new input parameter he would transcribe for his computer program. He would have the minicomputer continue to monitor the dialogue at Samantha's sleep session. But with the augmented program, he hoped the machine would be able to sift through the coded jargon to uncover the underlying theme of fetal control, the modus operandi. And if that were known, he and Mrs. Rutledge might be able to do something. Perhaps drugs, or hypnosis. Confrontation. Anything.

After four days of steady review and analysis, by noon on Friday he had completed the supplemental program for the minicomputer. He would punch it out during Samantha's sleep session that afternoon. Meanwhile, Mrs. Rutledge kept him informed of Samantha's activities, for he spent little time in the lab. Because of her erratic behavior, Bryson had curtailed her work with sleep volunteers and confined her activity to research gathering. In the mornings, Samantha tied up the loose ends of the Somnapar project. Soon it would be ready for a final computerized analysis and run-through.

It was Friday afternoon. Armed with his computations, Bryson entered the lab at two o'clock. Samantha would arrive at the lab by four. His mind strayed. He recalled that there was a time, early in the experiment, when she had requested weekend sleep sessions in addition to the daily studies. Bryson at first thought it was for want of money. He now understood it as a fetal request for an uninterrupted liaison with MEDIC. But she hadn't pressed the matter, he concluded, for fear of arousing suspicion. Other than the time spent with Bryson, Samantha devoted her Saturdays and Sundays to marathons of physical fitness and endurance. He began to wonder if she would ever return to her true self again.

Mrs. Rutledge opened the day's interoffice mail. One item caught her eye; she handed it to Bryson. It was a memo from Roberts, marked, "Follow-up to conversation of 8 September."

" 'Further review of the data reveals your conclusions to be untenable,' " read Bryson. " 'All activities in this area, other than sleep studies, are to stop. Due to the vital importance of MEDIC, no meddling in this area will be tolerated.' The guy certainly doesn't mince words."

"Well," sighed Mrs. Rutledge, "at least you tried."

Bryson went back to work.

It took him nearly an hour to rearrange the program in the appropriate sequence. He worked in the dim light of the supply closet, not noticing the small pile of tracings on the floor behind the machine. Bryson drew up a chair and bent over the computer keys. He completed his alterations just before Samantha arrived.

Ever efficient, Mrs. Rutledge opened the supply closet and dusted off the minicomputer and its cart. Her hand grazed the machine's casing. It was strangely warm. But then, the closet was stuffy. She dismissed the fleeting sensation, finished dusting, and closed the door.

At four P.M., Mrs. Rutledge assisted Samantha into the sleep room. Once again, Samantha's reticent indifference to resuming the study left Mrs. Rutledge so dismayed that she barely spoke. In minutes the preparations were complete; and seconds after the door to the sleep room was closed Samantha was somnolent.

Bryson worked quickly. As Samantha slept, he awaited the printout. Soon a flurry of information began to rattle out of the minicomputer. Again, the volume of the transmissions made the computer consolidate data, a sort of mechanical paraphrasing. Bryson scanned the printout, commenting as he read.

"It seems to want to know about abortions . . . types, procedures, that sort of thing . . . the effect of amniocentesis on the subsequent course of pregnancy . . . risks of fetal injury. Jesus. If we ever had any doubts about fetal awareness, we can lay them to rest."

The minicomputer chattered away. Then, toward six P.M., when Samantha's two-hour session was nearly over, small phrases about pain appeared in the dialogues. Bryson scrutinized the excerpts closely. The fetus seemed to want to know exactly how pain was caused. Bryson focused on the last line. Pain. Pain . . .

Samantha stirred in her sleep, nearing wakefulness more rapidly than usual. Bryson quickly returned the minicomputer to the closet. With Samantha's session nearly over, he would have to wait until Monday to see what results the new program would yield. Mrs. Rutledge reluctantly agreed that Samantha would have to undergo another session if they were to find the answers they sought.

Samantha looked tranquil, yawning as she lazily left the sleep room.

"Call me later, Jon?" she asked. "I'll be at home."

He was delighted. "Sure, Sam. In an hour or so."

"Ciao, Rosie," she said, going through the door. "See you Monday."

At seven he called Samantha. She had made dinner and invited him over. He drove to her apartment. She opened the door and hugged him warmly. He returned the embrace.

"You've been busy this week," she said.

"Yes," he replied, noncommitally.

"I missed you."

"Me too."

He felt tenderness for her. Was this the real Samantha he was speaking to? God, how he wanted her back the way she was.

"What's for dinner?"

"Soul food."

"You're kidding."

"Honest. You'll see later. Let's go for a walk first."

They strolled through the park. Mild exertion before a meal improved gastrointestinal absorption, she said. The discussion turned toward her future. School would start again soon, and with it another year of teaching and study. Samantha vacillated, hesitant. She had to continue the work toward her Master's; that much she knew. But later, the baby would come. Should she pursue her graduate courses, knowing that she might have to drop out temporarily? Should she postpone her studies a semester, and work in the lab full time if she could find a way to make ends meet? She hadn't decided yet.

It was dark when they returned to the apartment. As if it were the most natural thing in the world, she undressed him, folding his garments neatly. Then she took off her own clothes and turned on the shower. When they ate supper, she said, it would become clear why she had to wash up. She wanted him to bathe her. She said it matter-of-factly, neither a request nor a command. It was a statement.

He washed her with lemon-scented soap. She put her shoulders into the spray and turned around to rinse her face.

It was then that he saw the scratches.

Her entire back was abraded. They were healing fingernail marks. They appeared self-inflicted.

"What happened to your back?"

"What?"

"Your back. It's all cut up. Here," he said, touching the skin gently.

She looked over her shoulder. "I don't know," she said, unconcernedly. "Wash it for me, will you?"

He cleansed the cuts. "Do they hurt?"

"Can't feel a thing. Is my towel on the sink?"

She turned off the water and stepped out onto the bathmat. She dried him, and he her, dabbing the scratches carefully. Samantha led him by the hand to the bed. They lay naked side by side. She stroked him into arousal.

Bryson looked at her closed lids while she touched him. In spite of her superb physical conditioning, she appeared ill. Her eyes were recessed, somewhat sunken. Her skin looked soft, but a slightly pale, jaundiced hue made him doubt her true health. What was happening to her?

Her touch was rough and mechanical. Bryson felt like a toy she was using. He was annoyed, but too aroused to say anything. She pulled him into her. Her degree of lubrication was surprising; they had just begun. She bucked wildly. They weren't making love. It was rapid, animal copulation. The artifice of it saddened him, and he felt his arousal waning.

"Honey, we can't—"

"Shut up," she interrupted, pushing against him harder.

"I can't make love like this."

"Then I'll make you."

She moistened a finger with her own secretions and separated his buttocks. She found his anus and forced her way past the sphincter, probing his rectum. She reached his prostate and massaged it vigorously. The return of his erection within her was automatic and uncontrollable. Samantha held him deep inside her. There was a surge of warmth in his pelvis. His orgasm was swift and violent. Samantha's own climax followed quickly. She rolled away from him.

Bryson was humiliated. He felt no better than a prize bull whose ejaculation was forced by an electric prod. The whole act was planned, somehow fitting into her scheme of things. But what good could it do her or the fetus?

He touched her shoulder and snuggled closer. Maybe affection could succeed where logic failed, breaking through the barrier erected by the fetus. He nuzzled her cheek.

"Please stop, for Chrissake." She pushed him away.

"Why, Sam? We had something once, and I don't believe it's gone. I won't believe it until the Sam I know and love tells me so herself. That girl is shielded and hidden. She's right next to me and yet miles away. But if I can get through to her, maybe I can help. I love her very much, you see. Right now she's being forced to do things against her will. Not long ago these were just strange thoughts and urges. But now they've taken over entirely, even though she doesn't want them to."

"Stop it," she said. But her voice was no longer convincing, sounding hesitant. He saw a glimmer in her eyes, a sparkling awareness of the meaning of what he was saying. It was working.

"I know you can hear me," he continued. "You're no

puppet, Sam. You can fight it. The baby is using you, hurting you, and making you manipulate other people. Me. But it won't work. Listen to me. What you have to do is—"

The blow caught him off guard. Her knees smashed into his scrotum with such force that the initial wave of pain nearly rendered him unconscious. And then she was standing by the bed over him, eyes glaring, shrieking maniacally in a mechanical catechism, rattling off facts.

"Testicular pain is the most intense known to man. Its mechanism is as yet undefined, but its severity is thought to be related to the extensive neurovascular plexus of the gonad."

She watched him writhe beneath her, and her speech began to slow.

"Current research in the area has been limited to . . . to . . ." The tremulousness started in the muscles in her neck, spreading to her face as her cheeks twitched nervously. ". . . Efforts to isolate the synaptic connections which differ from . . . from . . ." Her speech was plodding now, dulled. ". . . The characteristic neuronal configuration of . . ."

And then she stopped talking entirely. Something seemed to give way. Her face jerked, its skin marked with tiny fine lines as the first tear fell along her nose. Her mouth opened wide, eyes and lips turning down at the corners in an expression of unspeakable sorrow. And then the sobbing started, quietly at first, but becoming ever louder. She collapsed onto his shoulder, holding him tightly. The two of them huddled together.

"Oh Jon, Jon!" she sobbed. "I'm so very sorry! But I can't help it, I just can't!"

His pain had dulled to a steady, lingering ache. He held

her close and soothed her hair. Warm tears fell onto his chest.

"I know, Sam, I know," he whispered.

"Please make it stop," she said, her voice a whimpering plea. "I can't stand it any more! It's killing me!"

His arms tightened around her.

"There, it's all right, you'll see," he promised. "We're going to beat it."

They lay on the bed quietly until her sniffling ceased. Calmer, her breathing slowed. Soon she was asleep.

In spite of the pain in his groin and his sense of overwhelming pity, for the first time in weeks, Bryson felt encouraged. He had gotten through, reached her. Reassured, still numb from the pain, his mind drifted off.

He was awakened by a rustling of sheets. Samantha sat on the bed crosslegged, in deep concentration. Bryson merely watched her. Then Samantha sighed deeply, blinked her eyes, and shook her head back and forth. Unexpectedly, her expression softened. She smiled at him.

"Come on. Let's eat."

She put on a robe and led him into the kitchenette. Assorted platters of gray, gelatinous substances were on the table. Everything had the sarcomatous appearance of fish flesh.

"What's all this?"

"I told you. Soul food."

"It doesn't look like any soul food I've ever seen."

"And how would you know?"

"I've been around. There's a little restaurant outside Richmond called Sambo's Country Kitchen. I ate there about two years ago. Grits, chittlins, and greens. Nothing this color. How can you call this glop soul food? It looks like raw fish to me."

"Gotcha!" She pulled back his chair. He sat at the table, sniffing the platters.

"Smells like it too," he said.

"Now you know why I wanted to shower. You have never, Jon, never tasted fish like this."

"I'm not certain I want to. You certain this isn't Japanese soul food?"

"It was a play on words, dummy. You know the old saying about fish being food for the brain? Well, this is soul food as in brain food, food for the soul. And it's also lemon sole."

"Silly me," he said, pointing to a bowl filled with what appeared to be black and white floating buttons. "What in the world is that?"

"Assorted fish parts."

"Where did you get it?"

"From a fish market," she said, surprised that he asked such an obvious question.

"You mean I can go into a fish store and buy a bowlful of assorted fish parts, just like ordering a pint of oysters?"

"I wish you could. You have to buy the scraps—the heads, tails, and fins. Some people use it for soup. Of course I don't want all that junk. It's these little goodies I'm after. I had to pluck them out myself."

Bryson watched her reach into the bowl. He felt himself growing queasy.

"What . . . specific . . . assorted fish part is that?"

She picked up one of the small greasy orbs, inspecting it closely.

"Fresh fish eyes," she said, plopping one into her mouth. She sucked on it as if it were hard candy, and then swallowed it whole.

"I don't believe you just did that."

Samantha lifted another one and gently placed it between her front teeth, like a pipe stem. She bit into it swiftly. A gelatinous spurt flew across the table and landed on Bryson's cheek.

"Jesus, Sam!" he said, wiping it away quickly with his hand. "What's gotten into you?"

"You mean, what is getting into me?" she corrected, casually sucking on a third eye. She took another and lifted it before his face. "Care to try one?" she taunted.

"That is disgusting."

"Don't be such a food snob. They're good for you. C'mon, one little bite."

Repelled, he pushed her hand away. "Get that stuff away from me."

She sighed. "Your loss," she said, chucking the oily sphere into her mouth like a peanut. "They might not taste so great, but they're very nutritious."

"I'm sure."

"Did you know that uncooked fish eyes, from almost any salt water species, are one of the highest sources of dietary protein? They also have important mucopolysaccharides found nowhere else, as well as natural vitamin A. A paper out of Israel recently described the probable nutritive value of visual purple, one of the retinal pigments."

Her cheeks were soon so full that she choked. A streak of mucoid slime dribbled out of the corner of her mouth. She wiped her lips. It was too much for Bryson, who grew pale. Samantha swirled the bowl slowly, selecting another eye. Bryson watched closely, filled with a mixture of clinical fascination and revulsion. The glassy orbs bobbed in the viscous whirlpool, floating in and out of his vision, staring up at him.

20

Monday dragged on. Bryson was anxious to see the results of his expanded computer program. Earlier that morning, he told Mrs. Rutledge about what happened at Samantha's apartment, confining his conversation to the brief, but still real breakthrough in making contact on an emotional level. It showed that Samantha was capable of being reached, and was not yet a total prisoner. But how long would her receptivity last? He needed time. And time was the one thing he did not have.

Fetal control over Samantha's will seemed to increase steadily. The minor changes in her daily routine, the addition of exercise and "proper diet," had been initially so subtle that it was easy to believe they were the result of Samantha's own conscious choice. She made it sound so logical. But as the dreams, the medical babble, and other evidence of fetal intent intensified, they occupied more and more of her waking hours. Her freedom of choice and independence of will were being subverted by the machinations of the child within. It was only a question of time before she was totally ensnared in the web of control, her true personality hidden behind a veil of fetal domination.

What was disturbing him the most was the change in Sam's appearance. When he had first known her early in her pregnancy, and later, at the beach, Samantha was the image of physical fitness. She positively radiated good health. The objective signs of ill health Bryson thought he detected Friday night were even more prominent three days later. What with her daily activities, her bizarre but nourishing diet and the incessant exercise, Samantha should have been among the healthiest of women. But her skin, once well-toned and elastic, had begun to sag. There was a certain looseness to it, not hanging jowls and folds but rather a delicate wilting, the first bending of a thirsty plant at midsummer's noon. It lacked turgor. The over-all appearance was one of initial dehydration, a siphoning off of vital fluids.

Bryson didn't doubt that was actually happening. He became convinced that if the fetus was directing all of Samantha's physical endeavors toward its own growth and well-being, the eventual result for her would be devastating. Although her body would initially profit from the supplementary diet and exercise, it would eventually suffer as essential nutrients were channeled in one direction. Her heart and lungs, robust and strong, would weaken as the necessary oxygen and blood were turned toward the uterus. How long, he wondered, before they would fail altogether?

Her posture began to change. It was only the barest slouch, but another proof of the physical insult her body was suffering. Her clothing seemed not to fit. Although the size was right, the seams were askew, and the folds of material fell off center, following the gravitational shift in her stature.

For all that its mother failed to thrive, so did the fetus prosper. Barely at the end of her sixth month, Samantha had the appearance of a woman eight months pregnant. The child's growth was unfettered. Bryson knew that it couldn't possibly continue at the present rate. If it did, by the end of her ninth month the fetus would weigh fifteen pounds. The accelerated growth, he knew, was undeniable. But what was its purpose?

The sight of her tortured him. When she arrived at the lab later that morning, she shuffled along as if in a trance. Even Mrs. Rutledge seemed to suppress a gasp. And the scratches. Seeing her now reminded him of those abrasions, wounds she undoubtedly had made in her own flesh. They must have caused great discomfort. But why? What good could the fetus derive possibly from harming the host that nurtured it?

He returned later in the day when Samantha was absorbed in her laboratory chores. He had spent most of the day wandering aimlessly on campus, deep in thought. With Samantha out of earshot, he rehashed this latest riddle with Mrs. Rutledge. Being as mystified as he was, she could offer little help. In hushed tones, they mulled over the significance of the excerpts from Friday's dialogues.

"I don't understand that reference to pain," he said. "It bothers me, especially that it comes on the heels of an abortion attempt."

She looked at him quizzically. "Does that mean something?"

"I don't know. Mean anything to you?"

"Well—and I'm just thinking out loud, now—maybe an abortion is painful to the fetus. That's possible, isn't it?"

"Yes, I suppose."

"Then perhaps it's doing what it always does: increasing its store of medical information. Only this time it has personal experience to draw on."

"Hmmm."

"Does that grunt mean you don't buy my explanation?"

"I don't know. I just don't know."

"But you don't think so."

"What I think is what I see: that she went to get an abortion and changed her mind; that not long afterward,

the fetus started asking MEDIC about pain; that Samantha scratched the daylights out of her back; and that she
looks like hell. Now you tell me: Does that seem to be
following some sort of sequence? Or am I just imagining
it?"

Mrs. Rutledge gazed into the sleep room. "For her
sake, I hope you're just imagining it."

That afternoon, they returned Samantha to the sleep
study. She complied with worrisome nonchalance. While
she slept, Bryson kept alert for two unrelated areas in the
printout: his computer's assessment of the ongoing dialogue, and its evaluation of the method of fetal control.
Initially, there was little of anything novel in the transmissions. The fetus seemed to have assimilated all the
information available on pain theory, and appeared to return its major interest toward its own growth. It had even
begun going through MEDIC's memory banks a second
time. But midway through the session, their computer—
after stumbling in hesitation over its new assignment—
blurted forth the information they had been searching for
in a long rambling printout. Bryson digested the data for
several minutes before allowing himself a lazy grin.

"Jesus!" he said.

"Well, what is it, already?"

"Prostaglandin. The fetus plays with prostaglandins."

"Sounds utterly obscene. Is it a hormone?"

"Sort of. It's a chemical, a fatty acid, found in a lot of
different body tissues. There's no shortage of it in pregnancy. It's synthesized in the fetal membranes, the bag of
waters. It has a lot to do with the initiation of labor."

"Are you saying the fetus is trying to make Samantha
go into labor?"

"No, although it could. If prostaglandins were released

into her bloodstream in sufficient quantities, they would make her uterus contract. I don't think the fetus is quite ready for that yet. What it's doing is synthesizing the chemical in smaller amounts—not enough to start labor, but enough to have an effect elsewhere. In this case, on her brain."

"And that alters her behavior?"

"Yes. If enough of it becomes concentrated in certain areas of her brain, it stimulates the release of other substances known as neurotransmitters. These are also chemicals, and there are a lot of them. In one area of the brain, it might be dopamine; in another, serotonin. And every neurotransmitter can trigger the release of a whole slew of other substances, each of which has a specific behavioral or biologic effect. So what the computer has told us is that by concentrating a finite level of prostaglandin in a specific cerebral site, a particular neurotransmitter eventually alters Samantha's behavior. We've already witnessed some of the things it's done to her, ways in which she's changed. The problem is that there's such a myriad of physical and psychological possibilities, that there's no predicting which could occur next. We may have seen just the tip of the iceberg."

"You make it sound so simple. Like falling dominoes."

"In a way it is. Scientifically, we call it feedback, with short and long loops, and reflex arcs. What it basically boils down to is putting a plug into the proper slot in a switchboard. Only here the number of area codes is infinite."

"Isn't there something that can be done to control the prostaglandin?"

"Fortunately, yes. But there are a couple of other things you should know about it. First, it's used in abortions. It was the abortifacient Pritchard was going to inject, if he had gotten around to it."

"But how could that be? If it's deadly for the fetus, why would it produce its own?"

"Depends on the amount. It's like arsenic, or strychnine. In small amounts, they might be medicinal. In quantity, they're lethal. You need similar quantities of prostaglandin, large unphysiologic doses, to cause abortion."

"How ironic," whispered Mrs. Rutledge. "The fetus is using the same substance to slowly destroy Samantha that she was going to use to kill it."

"We don't know if it's doing that; all we can be sure of is the PG—that's short for prostaglandin—is the mechanism it uses to control her. But you might be right. The other thing you should know about PG is that it can cause intense bodily discomfort. In some cases, severe pain. It's a causal agent in inflammation, headaches, nausea, diarrhea, and vomiting, depending on where it's concentrated. If small quantities are widespread throughout the body, they make you feel generally rotten. Like you had the flu."

She understood his train of thought. She shuddered.

"You think all these references to pain in the dialogues have something to do with what's happening to Samantha?"

"As an indirect side effect. The main fetal use of PG is for behavior control. But I doubt that the baby is displeased that its mother looks and feels like hell."

"Displeased? Isn't that a rather strong word to use about the theoretical emotional state of an unborn child?"

He turned away. He was beginning to get angry. Angry at himself.

"Dammit, Rosie, my problem has always been that I assumed too little. On every crucial point, I've been one step behind. I never assumed that the fetus could dream, much less think. It turns out that it's been having a long chat with a sophisticated computer. And the list goes on and on. I never assumed that it could have anything but the best intentions. I never assumed that it could control Samantha. I never assumed that it would interfere with her having an abortion. Well, I'm fed up to here with my ineptitude," he stated. "On this issue, I'm through assuming. I'm *telling* you. That baby in there is very displeased with its mother. It's downright pissed off, and you would be too, if someone tried to kill you. Call it whatever you want. Resentment. Hostility. I wouldn't be surprised if the seeds of displeasure were sown even before the abortion, when Sam first started having second thoughts about keeping the baby. I'm beginning to think that it could biochemically read her mind, even then. No matter. The only important things now are, A, what the baby plans to do, and B, what we're going to do."

He was right, of course. Mrs. Rutledge didn't know what to say. They had been relegated to the status of mere observers, witnesses after the fact, sharing a secret that the world wouldn't believe and unable to fathom the outcome. She looked toward the sleep room. Then she remembered something he said earlier.

"Didn't you mention that there's a way of controlling the PG?"

He paced back and forth. "I don't know. It seems kind of futile, but I suppose it's worth a try. Aspirin."

She looked at him blankly. "What?"

"Plain aspirin, acetylsalicylic acid. One of the most potent prostaglandin inhibitors known to man."

"You mean all she has to do is take a couple of aspirin every four hours, and she'll be all right?"

He nodded.

"Then what are you waiting for? Should she keel over first?"

"It's not that simple."

"What could be simpler than aspirin?"

"You're assuming now. Assuming that it will work. Well, don't. I'm not sure that we can abolish fetal control. It may already be too ingrained."

"But at least we can give it a try?"

"Maybe. But first she's got to get the aspirin into her system. How are we going to do that?"

Mrs. Rutledge brightened. "Who says you have to put them in her hand?"

"You can't exactly force them down her throat."

"What do you keep telling me is the worst thing about my coffee?"

He saw what she was driving at, and smiled.

"You know, it might just work? Your coffee is so vile and bitter it could dissolve the spoon. Let alone disguise the taste of aspirin."

"Enough flattery. You'll help me, won't you? She drinks five or six cups a day."

"Naturally. I'll prepare the magic elixir myself."

On his way home that night, Bryson picked up several hundred aspirin and a liter of distilled water. He prepared a solution where one teaspoonful was the equivalent of ten grains of aspirin, or two tablets. The next morning he gave the mixture to Mrs. Rutledge, who hid the flask in the storage closet. She usually prepared Samantha's coffee herself; and since the coffee maker was near the closet, little legerdemain would be involved.

Samantha's continued appetite for coffee, which she loved, had once confused Bryson. Logic told him that her emphasis on proper diet would lead her to eliminate it. But at one point earlier in the dialogues, several diverse reports about the effects of caffeine on a fetus appeared. One claimed that it augmented fetal cardiovascular development. That seemed to clinch it for the baby. The next day Samantha increased her coffee consumption from three cups per day to six.

The three of them sipped coffee together after Samantha arrived the next morning. Bryson purposely made a wry face.

"Jesus. What did you put in this mud today?"

Samantha tasted hers. "Yuk."

Mrs. Rutledge primly dabbed her lips with a napkin. "It's a special blend. And unless you freeloaders want to brew your own, that will be enough of the compliments, thank you."

Samantha finished her coffee and had another cup. Then she gathered up the Somnapar papers and went to work in a corner of the lab. Mrs. Rutledge winked at Bryson.

"Care for a refill, Doctor?"

"Don't mind if I do."

Over the course of the week, the change in Samantha was dramatic. Her progressive physical deterioration came abruptly to a halt. The signs of mental imbalance that had characterized her recent personality for the most part disappeared, though not entirely. In many respects she reverted to the Samantha Bryson had known earlier with only occasional outbursts of flightiness and irrationality. Her dietary extremes moderated, though the food she consumed could hardly be called normal by traditional standards. She continued her exercises, but at a more leisurely pace, without the fanaticism of a few weeks before. Samantha appeared most stable at the end of the work day, having drunk more than her ration of aspirin-spiked coffee. In the mornings she was morose and withdrawn until Mrs. Rutledge poured her first cup. Then she snapped out of the doldrums, bright and alive.

By the end of the week, Samantha put the final touches on the Somnapar project. She and Bryson began working on the experimental design of another hypnotic drug under investigation. Her own sleep periods had been discontinued. After a simple word from Bryson, Samantha's acceptance of the cessation of her afternoon naps had been indifferent. She made no fuss, and he thought that odd. No longer did either of them question the need for her once daily naps. Her tirade about her sleep study seemed long forgotten, suppressed in her subconscious.

Bryson spent that weekend with her. He was jubilant at the change in her. Every so often he feigned fatigue. He prepared coffee for himself regularly—for the caffeine, he said—and gave a cup to her. He pretended insult when she said it tasted just like Mrs. Rutledge's. But inside he was overjoyed. Most encouraging was her appearance. Posture straightened, skin color improved, she would soon resemble a healthy, pregnant woman.

The first faint rumbling of discontent was noted toward the end of Sam's second week on aspirin. In contrast to her previous verbalizations—a mechanical rambling of medical fact—she now had brief periods, like spells, when she appeared to be in a trance. During these rare episodes, her facial expression would change. First, her eyes would half close, and she would stare straight ahead through the slits of her lids. It seemed as if her eyes were pushed back in her head, looking out from a tunnel, like a miner emerging from a shaft, sockets rimmed with coal dust. More peculiar was her speech. It was hoarse and guttural, welling up from her diaphragm, with a throaty, Luciferian tone of dread. It was the closest thing to an incantation Bryson could imagine. And then it would suddenly stop. Samantha's expression would soften, and she would return to her work, seemingly oblivious of what had occurred.

What disturbed Bryson most was not Samantha's altered state of consciousness, but what she said during it. Despite her physical rehabilitation, her speech content was strikingly similar to the dialogues. Her raucous, searching chatter gave the impression of someone abstractedly poring over old data, searching for something glossed over the first time around. Her babbling sounded like the kind of information Bryson expected to spill out of his minicomputer.

At times Samantha's attention turned toward the metaphysical. She rambled on about the modalities of mental resistance, chanting both obscure hypothesis and substantive scientific fact. She gave the impression, if her words could be believed, that she was looking for something. She droned on about successful resistance to torture, about induction of a hypnotic trance that could render the subject immune to physical discomfort, about the scientific basis of yoga meditation that enabled the believer to sleep on a bed of nails. Bryson was chilled. If the fetus itself were speaking, it might utter the same thoughts to which its mother now gave substance.

Another week went by, and Samantha was entrenched in her new project. Her abdomen looked big enough for her to give birth any time. As far as Bryson knew, Samantha hadn't returned to Dr. Pritchard for a prenatal checkup. He knew that she should. Good obstetrics demanded monthly visits, and given the size of Samantha's uterus, probably more frequent visits would be appropriate. He mentioned it to her once, but she was reluctant. Since her return to good health, regular checkups seemed not that necessary. The worst that could happen would be for her to go into labor.

His peace of mind had been temporary. During her trances, Samantha began to explore toxicology. She talked about pollutants, chemical levels in inspired air, reports of illness or poisoning through ventilator systems. Bryson and Mrs. Rutledge were nervous. Whatever compelled Samantha's utterances might lead to thoughts that would give them away.

Could the baby be sensing Samantha's physical improvement? Guessing about its cause? If the fetus had smelled the scent, it was on the right trail. There was no way it could know about the spiked coffee; yet, thought Bryson, it wanted to know.

The next day Samantha announced that she had made an appointment that afternoon with her doctor. She said that she had decided Bryson was right. She should have a checkup. Bryson and Mrs. Rutledge had a hurried conference.

"Why the change of heart?"

"I don't know, but I don't like it."

Another week passed uneventfully. Summer drew to a close. The nights were cool: sweater weather. Bryson and Samantha went for a drive in the country. They headed for the mountains. Gently rolling Appalachian hills flanked the roadway. The lush summer greenery was beginning to wither, as here and there the thick verdant foliage showed the first flecks of yellow and red. The forest held the approaching chill captive, and a hidden layer of mist wafted ankle deep around the base of the pines.

Every so often they stopped at a scenic overlook, drinking coffee Bryson had brought in a thermos. Samantha was content. She lay her head on his shoulder and quietly gazed at the distant ridges. They drove back late Sunday night.

The following morning, while he and Mrs. Rutledge reviewed data from previous studies, Samantha's arrival at the lab signaled the end of their scheme. She appeared sloppy, disheveled. It looked as though she hadn't slept all night. Her bright hair was matted and unwashed, falling in clinging, uneven strands across her shoulders. It was the cue for Mrs. Rutledge to prepare her coffee. She set a steaming cupful in front of Samantha, urging her to drink. Samantha sniffed it and looked suspiciously at Mrs. Rutledge, then shoved the cup back toward her. The brown liquid slopped onto the table top.

"So that's how you're doing it," she accused.

Mrs. Rutledge eyed Bryson nervously. "Doing what, dear?"

"Poisoning me. As if you didn't know it. I suppose you're in on this too," she snapped at Bryson. "What do you take me for, an idiot? Some moronic dolt who doesn't know the taste of aspirin when she swallows it?"

Mrs. Rutledge's voice faltered. "Whatever are you talking about?"

"How dare you talk down to me! The audacity, sounding so smug and condescending! Why, I know more than both of you, than any ten of you! How long did you think you could get away with this? Chucking aspirin into my coffee while my back was turned? That's insane, don't you realize it? In-fucking-sane! It could kill me!"

"How could it kill you, Sam?" asked Bryson.

Samantha ignored him, continuing her tirade. "For weeks, I've known something was wrong! I didn't feel right.

A screw was loose, something out of place. I thought it might be something in the air, or the water. But in my own coffee? Never! So the last time I was at the doctor, I had him do a toxicology screen on my blood. And do you know what Dr. Pritchard said? Of course you do, because you put it there. Aspirin! My system is loaded with aspirin! Do you have any idea what aspirin can do to a pregnant woman and her child? Well, I'll tell you. It can cause fetal hemorrhage. Or jaundice. And it can even close off one of the baby's heart chambers, so it dies inside me, before it's born! As if you didn't know! Well, it's not important now. I won't touch the stuff. You can take your coffee and shove it!"

Bryson was up instantly, walking toward her. "Sam, you don't know what you're saying."

"Keep away," she warned.

He halted. "You may not have noticed it, but this past month, you've been a changed person. Your old self again —bright and cheerful. You've looked better, and you've felt better. For the first time in weeks, you've been normal, healthy. The aspirin's been interfering with the way the baby controls you. When you take it, the fetus loses control, and you become normal again. No crazy diet, no scratches on your back, no misery. So I'm asking you. I'm begging you. Please don't stop taking the aspirin!"

She laughed. "You really are a bastard. It's a wonder they gave someone like you this job. You're dangerous. I should report you. Your little speech is touching, but it won't work. I can see right through you, both of you. Is this called appealing to my sensibility? Save your breath. This is as close as you're getting to hurting me and my baby." She turned to leave.

"Sam—"

She slammed the door behind her. Bryson turned to Mrs. Rutledge. "Don't look so glum. We've lost the battle but not the war."

"I can't help it. She was doing so well. Without the aspirin—you can see for yourself. She's already started re-gressing. At this rate . . ." She stopped at the end of the phrase, unable to complete the sentence.

"That's just it. We don't know what will happen. From the standpoint of logic, it's inconceivable that the fetus would allow its mother to come to serious harm, and hurt itself in the process."

"What's it doing, then?" Mrs. Rutledge asked hyster-ically. "She's withering right before our eyes."

"That's what we have to know," Bryson said. "Just how far the fetus is planning to go."

"How much longer, Jonathan? How much longer before we can help her?"

He answered her with a hug, the embrace of a family that was watching the life of their child slowly, slowly ebb away.

"She's back again."

"What does she want this time?"

"A quarter pound of sweetbreads."

"Let her have it. I'll talk to her on the way out," said the supermarket manager, ending his conversation with the man behind the delicatessen counter.

It was the fourth time that day the pregnant woman had entered the market. She wore a gray sweat shirt and sweat pants. Every time she returned, she looked grimier. Several customers had complained.

The girl was sick. Probably a mental case that wandered away from the hospital, he thought. But she appeared

physically ill, too. She reminded him of the ashen, per-
spiring victims of pneumonia he had seen in Korea.

Why did she have to pick his store? he lamented. She
would leave and return at half-hour intervals. Each time she
would purchase one or two items. Oh, she paid for the
merchandise, but the damndest part was that she'd eat it
right in the store. An hour before, he had watched her
relish a container of yogurt, scooping it from the cup with
two fingers, like a Hawaiian eating poi. Last time she
bought a hunk of head cheese and gobbled it up in front
of Max at the deli counter. That was when Max first
called him. Some shoppers giggled; others shook their heads
in repulsion.

He watched her approach him at the market's entrance.
She finished a candy bar and dropped the wrapper on the
floor. She was opening the plastic container of sweetbreads
as she passed him.

"This ain't a pigpen, lady," he said. "You got trash,
throw it in the can."

She looked at him blankly. Then she dipped her fingers
in the container and selected a sliver of raw meat.

"What the hell are you doin'?" he asked.

She lifted the sweetbread toward her mouth.

"Je-sus!" he shouted. Before she could eat it, he lashed
out at the plastic container in anger and disgust. The pale
pink contents splattered to the floor with a wet plop.

"Get the hell outa here!" he said, propelling her toward
the door. "I see you again, and I call the cops!"

He turned away, muttering, carefully stepping over the
liquid pool of innards.

21

There could only be one more sleep session. It was their last-ditch effort, grasping at straws, do or die. If only someone believed them! At this point, Bryson would willingly sacrifice his name and position for the sake of Samantha. She had grown dearer to him than any scientific achievement. If he could, he would publish his own newspaper with bold headlines announcing what he had discovered; what was still happening. But he knew it wasn't possible. His story would be no more credible to others than it had been to Roberts and Dr. Pritchard.

As the days wore on, Bryson returned to the minicomputer program. It needed polishing, precision; he had only one more go at it. He adjusted his minicomputer program to include transmission capability, if it ever came to that. The tap into the main cable having already been set, the actual sending of signals would be simple. Once the computer was programmed, all he had to do was type out the instructions. When he was satisfied with the program's perfection, they would offer Samantha her sleep period. He altered the program only slightly, a shift in emphasis. Yet the wording had to be exact. Now that the mechanism of fetal control was known, there was only one question left—the fetal motive.

Days passed, and days turned to weeks. It was now October. Bryson couldn't concentrate on anything but the final computer program. His work in the neurology clinic slowed, and he had other physicians assume his nonresearch duties. The new sleep projects were postponed indefinitely, save for the one Samantha dabbled in in the mornings. He informed his department that the delay was a temporary one, that he had to review the protocols more thoroughly before allocating the grant money.

Rosemary Rutledge, his only ally, was his foil and sounding board. She questioned him constantly, forcing him to think and re-think. With each of his suggestions about altering the computer program, she offered a countersuggestion, a new hypothesis or theory. Her intensity mirrored his. But the uncertainty affected Mrs. Rutledge's performance. She grew agitated and fidgety. She slept less, fatigue showing in her eyes. And as the amount of their sleep decreased, so did their concern increase, each time they saw Samantha.

Her physical deterioration was remarkable and frightening. There was almost no trace of the golden girl she once was. She was like a malnourished child, swollen, distended belly atop spindly legs. She was losing weight rapidly. She resembled a concentration-camp victim, such was the degree of her cachexia and debilitation. Most curious were her eyes. Sunken, recessed in their sockets, they nonetheless sparkled with perceptive awareness, ever darting suspiciously from side to side.

Bryson continued to see Samantha. Each time it was by her choice, rather than a mutually agreed liaison. She commanded that he come to her apartment at a specific time. He agreed with some reluctance. Although his submissiveness engendered feelings of humiliation, he hoped to use their time together to get through to her. But she was immune to his pleas. His attempts at reasoning fell on deaf ears, and his emotional entreaties were equally futile. When he spoke, she would look at him regally with a kind

of abstract curiosity, as an animal might examine the prey
it had just killed prior to eating it. When he had finished
his soliloquy, she would nod her head slightly, just so, a
signal that the audience granted him was terminated, and
that it was time to get down to the business at hand.

Samantha didn't dally. Her purpose in having him visit
was purely sexual. It was a foregone conclusion that she
demanded his presence strictly for fornication. For long
hours after he left, when she had dismissed him, he would
wonder why. He doubted that it was for her own physical
gratification. She proceeded in a rigidly businesslike manner, a pregnant prostitute turning a trick. She had him lie
naked on his back. Any nuance of romance, such as kissing or holding hands, was forbidden. Then Samantha
herself would undress. She poured liquid lubricant from a
plastic bottle, always taking pains to explain that it was
baby oil. The subtlety of the word was hardly lost on Bryson, who felt degraded by it.

The routine that followed was always the same. First
she aroused him with her slick hand. While she maintained
his erection, she poured oil on her vulva and masturbated
with her other hand. There was no passion, no eagerness
in her eyes while she touched herself. Bryson was sure that
her action was mechanically rational, its only purpose being to induce vaginal lubrication. Once she was wet, she
resumed stroking him vigorously until he neared orgasm.
She postponed his climax by squeezing his penis. Then she
mounted him from above, and moved her hips rapidly in
an intensely uninterested manner, staring beyond him at
the rug. He climaxed quickly. With each throb of orgasm,
she held him deep within her. When the last of his semi-
nal fluid had been discharged, Samantha casually rolled

off. Her aloofness distressed him. Afterward, she seemed to dismiss him, uninterested in his attempts at conversation.

Humiliating though it was, Bryson never refused her invitations. He found the quick, businesslike act of their copulation strangely erotic. It was an intense, rapid sexual frenzy, highly stimulating in nature. He also persisted in the hope that their time spent together might somehow be productive. But it never was. And last, he was jealous. Whatever the purpose behind their sexual escapades, he sensed that if he refused, she'd find another man.

Samantha no longer came to the lab for anything except her work project. Heads turned as she made her way through the corridors to the lab. She showed up every afternoon in her jogging shoes and silk running shorts. Were it not for her obvious sickliness, her appearance would have been comic. She couldn't wear her shorts around her waist, her abdomen being so pendulous; they were hiked-up just below her belly. She ran bra-less. Her breasts were so enlarged by the pregnancy that their constant bouncing must have been painful. Worse, the stimulus of persistent motion, combined with the erection of her nipples from the friction of her thin tee shirt, caused her breasts to lactate. Sticky rings of moisture wed the cloth to her areolae.

She no longer looked at Bryson or Mrs. Rutledge, nor they at her, but for different reasons. Samantha functioned in her own world, oblivious of them. But they were acutely conscious of her; looking at her advanced state of physical deterioration caused them great pain.

Finally, Bryson's assiduous tinkering with the precise wording of the minicomputer program paid off.

On Thursday, Bryson told Samantha that he wanted her to participate in one more sleep session, the following day. They would start at four, but might work well into the evening. Samantha nodded her head in blind acquiescence. Bryson doubted that she would object. She looked so feeble that he thought he had to simply open the sleep room door, touch her on the shoulder, and she would collapse on the bed.

The next day was the Friday before Halloween. Bryson and Mrs. Rutledge were at the lab long before Samantha arrived. Mrs. Rutledge wheeled the minicomputer out of the supply closet. They hurried, lest Samantha stumble into the lab early. When the preparations were complete, they hid the computer and awaited Samantha's arrival.

The morning passed slowly. Samantha toyed with her project. By eleven A.M. both Bryson and Mrs. Rutledge were sighing with nervous impatience. Finally Samantha put her pencil down, closed her books, and left for lunch without saying a word.

She returned shortly before four. Mrs. Rutledge was solicitous in her assistance. She gladly prepared the sleep room for Samantha, wanting it as comfortable as possible, to allow Samantha to enter a deep slumber quickly, a sleep which would enable them to closely monitor the EEG and transmissions outside. Samantha glided trance-like into the room. She was asleep before her head hit the pillow.

They wheeled the minicomputer into place. The remainder of the afternoon was before them; they hoped Samantha wouldn't awaken before ten. The first printout was slow to appear.

At the outset, the dialogues were desultory. They meandered aimlessly, driftwood swirling in a river current. The knowledge garnered from MEDIC seemed little more than current events. Fetal questions were random, unrelated, and insignificant. Bryson felt depressingly annoyed. He thought that his operose preparation of the program should have yielded instantaneous results. After the first hour of transmission, they knew little more than before. They began nervous pacing, peeking at the tracings as they passed the console, watching the kettle that never boiled.

So it was their depression, distorting their perspective, that made the first tangible clues from the minicomputer pass unnoticed. They were few and far between, and could easily have been overlooked. But by five o'clock, their presence was unmistakable. Hints, at first; but hints with a related theme. The fetus was questioning MEDIC about maternal illness—no disease in particular, but rather the generalities of diseases in pregnancy. Such questions, in and of themselves, might have been insignificant to Bryson. What caught his attention was that the fetus went beyond that. It wanted to know the clinical course of each disease, its signs and symptoms, and the maternal outcome. MEDIC transmitted back the information requested, in the process running through the gamut of every disease known to mankind. Then the fetus settled down to what seemed to Bryson a peculiarly horrifying area of inquiry.

It focused on those disorders in pregnancy most likely to lead to maternal demise.

"It can't be serious!" Mrs. Rutledge said.

"It's dead serious."

Mrs. Rutledge flustered. The flush swept upward from her neck, bubbles rising in a newly opened bottle of rosé.

"Then do something!" she stammered. "We have to help her, Jonathan! We don't have much time left. If this printout is true, Samantha is going to die!"

He nodded acknowledgement.

232   DAVID SHOBIN

"So lock her up," Mrs. Rutledge continued. "Have her hospitalized."

"It's not that easy, damn it. First you would have to capture her, physically carry her to the hospital. That in itself would be no mean feat. But suppose, somehow, we could. What would we do once she got there? I've already explained why psychotherapy or drugs wouldn't work. You're left with plain lock-up, incarceration. I can't see how that would help. If the fetus wants to kill Sam, it will do it right there."

"But we can't just sit here. What are we going to do?"

"We're going to keep our perspective," he said in carefully measured beats. "There are several more hours to go before she wakes up."

They pored over the excerpts from the dialogues. It was a race against time. Once the fetus had determined how to deal with its mother, it was simply a question of its waiting for the right moment.

The fetus narrowed its avenue of inquiry. Whereas before it considered the multiple facets of a wide range of diseases, it now dispensed with whole topics entirely. It dismissed hemorrhage and infection from consideration and began to focus solidly on hypertensive disorders in pregnancy. The subject was broad. It ranged from the simple etiology of toxemia to underlying vascular problems to the remotest complications of hypertension. It was in these complications that the fetus began investing most of its dialogue time with MEDIC.

They grew eager. Was it panic they were feeling? Bryson and Mrs. Rutledge hunched over the printouts like chess players contemplating strategy. The dialogue narrowed itself still further to obscure relationships between hypertension and labor. The interchange became more intense. The fetus fired questions at MEDIC, and the computer rattled off mechanical replies. The speed of the printout grew so rapid that they had trouble reading the excerpts. The fetal perspective was gun-barreled. It had its focus on a very narrow horizon, but couldn't get its sights on the right target. In a final frenzy of computerized chatter, the fetus set its scope on two or three remote complications of hypertension during labor. Then, abruptly, the dialogues were silent.

It was five-thirty. They spoke in hushed tones. The nightmarish quality of what they had learned that day was too much for Mrs. Rutledge. She bit her lip in frustration. She had come to grips with the inevitability of its occurrence, but couldn't comprehend the philosophy behind it.

The time frame was set. Bryson knew that whatever the fetus planned was intended to occur during labor. But which complication had it decided on? Clearly it planned for Samantha to go into labor, become severely hypertensive, and succumb to a complication. But which one?

"What I find so incredible," she said, "is that a child could actually do this to its mother."

"What's even more incredible," he said, "is that I've discovered only two-thirds of what I wish we knew. We know what the fetus plans for Sam, in general terms; and we know when. But we don't know exactly how."

"How important is that now?"

"Very important. Right now I'd like nothing more than to phone Pritchard—any obstetrician—tell him exactly what's going to happen to Sam, and have him place armed guards around her until she goes into labor. When she does, he'd know precisely what to do. If he believed me."

"Wouldn't he?"

Bryson made a wry face. "I don't know."

"But you could tell him *nearly* all we know: that Samantha will develop high blood pressure when she goes into labor, and that she will suffer one of its complications. We even know the possibilities: this thing called abruptio, which you say is a kind of premature separation of the placenta; coagulopathy, the bleeding disorder; and kidney failure. As you said, once Samantha goes into labor, he'll be prepared to cope with them."

"Sounds neat," admitted Bryson. "Simple and precise. But from what I remember of obstetrics, the proper treatments for these complications are worlds apart. An obstetrician must know exactly what he's dealing with. Otherwise, while he's stumbling around in the dark, Sam might stop breathing. No, Rosie, there are only two things left which might possibly work.

"The first, and probably the best method, would be to deliver the baby. Being as big as it is, even though it's premature, this kid will probably have a fair crack at survival at this stage. More important is that once the baby's been delivered, it could no longer control Sam. But normally, at seven months of pregnancy, there's only a fifty percent newborn survival rate. Without knowing what we know no obstetrician in the world would go along with inducing labor at this point."

"What's the second possibility?" she asked.

"What might be our last gasp. My second idea is to intervene in the dialogues. Let's talk directly to MEDIC and the fetus."

"But why? What kind of information could we get?"

"The fetus is operating in a vacuum. I doubt it's aware anyone knows what it's doing. It has no idea the minicomputer exists. Perhaps just the knowledge that someone is watching might be enough of a jolt to stop the fetus cold."

"Why should it stop? If anything, that might provoke it, and make it proceed with its plans for Samantha even faster, whatever they are."

"That's it, Rosie. That's what I'm missing. 'Whatever they are' is that one solid fact I don't have: the exact complication Sam's intended to suffer. If we don't get the answer in the next two hours, Rosie, you and I are going to have that chat with the computer."

The remainder of the dialogue that afternoon proved valueless. If the fetus had reached a decision about its choice of medical complication, it had no intention of revealing it. The interchange between MEDIC and the baby was mere scientific banter. So, at dusk, on what Bryson would long remember as a fateful Friday evening, he began transmission to MEDIC.

As he pressed the typewriter buttons, his remark to Mrs. Rutledge, "Here goes nothing," couldn't have been more off target. No sooner had he hit the "send" button than all communication between MEDIC and the fetus ceased. His instruction to MEDIC had been a simple one: reveal the intended medical complication for the subject presently asleep in the lab. MEDIC's reply should have been direct and unhesitating. Its complex microcircuitry should have digested the substance of the query in a minisecond, scanned its memory banks for the proper response, and instantaneously transmitted back a reply. But it didn't.

Instead, there was nothing. The EEG complexes abruptly ceased, and MEDIC's numerical current stopped flowing into the lab. In its place, there was an electronic buzzing, the hovering of a swarm of bees whose nest had been disturbed. Mrs. Rutledge looked to Bryson for an explanation. He shrugged his shoulders in mute reply. Hoping that there might be a malfunction, he retyped the question and transmitted it back to MEDIC.

For five minutes there was no response. The electronic background chatter became louder, and the console began to vibrate. It was like trying to home in on a distant radio signal and coming up with static. But suddenly there was silence, and MEDIC sent its message across the cable. On the printout appeared a one-word reply.

Omega.

"I don't understand," said Mrs. Rutledge.

"Me neither. But I have a sneaking suspicion this is all it's going to say."

"How can that be?"

"I don't know. Theoretically, it's impossible. MEDIC was designed for precise reply. But in computer terminology, a response like that means end of printout."

"But what about Samantha?"

He shook his head.

"That's my cross to bear, Rosie. All I can do is watch her like a hawk."

Rosemary Rutledge left shortly after Bryson. She went directly home without doing her weekend shopping. On Friday nights, she generally cooked a leisurely dinner and curled up with a good book. In her apartment, she opened a can of tuna and left it draining in the sink. Her appetite was gone. The day's events had caused her such consternation that she couldn't concentrate on food. On her way home she had decided to spell Bryson during his weekend surveillance, should he need some rest. After straightening up her apartment and doing the wash, she went to bed.

Sleep would not come. She tossed fitfully, thoughts of

the recent past filling her head. She had been a widow for five years, childless. The sleep research lab filled a void in her life. She immersed herself so completely in the lab's day-to-day activities that it couldn't function properly without her. It became her raison d'être. The sleep volunteers were her children. She busied herself with their problems, their successes and failures, no less than she would her own flesh and blood. She doted on Jonathan Bryson. There was little obvious interference with his private life. But the manner in which she endlessly engaged him in conversation, hinting rather than prying, getting more communicative mileage with an uplifted eyebrow than with a direct question, reflected her degree of concern. When his liaison with Samantha proved to be more than a casual flirtation, she was overjoyed. She shared his emotional exultation.

Now, a sense of helplessness kept her awake. Bryson, at least, had said he would keep an eye on Samantha all weekend. If only there were something she could do, some minor detail that had been overlooked . . . She glanced at the bedside clock: one-forty. The heck with it, she thought. She was so disturbed by their failure to learn the last crucial details that she decided to review the printouts herself. She threw off the bed sheets and dressed. Once back in the lab, she would retrieve the most recent printouts from the closet shelf. The sheer volume of paper was impressive. It would take several hours, perhaps until daybreak, for the most cursory scanning of the excerpts. A proper, summary review would involve her entire weekend. She doubted that she would uncover something Bryson missed but, with the stakes so high, it was worth the effort. And there was the other troublesome memory, of something she couldn't quite place.

She checked her watch in the darkened corridor outside

the lab. It was nearly two A.M. She was surprised, when she placed her key in the lock, to find that the door was open. She chided herself for her absentmindedness. Worry and concern were no excuse for carelessness. She flipped on the light switch, leaving the door slightly ajar.

The outer lab was empty. She went directly to the storage closet and turned on the bulb inside. She stopped in astonishment, gaping at the minicomputer. The machine was on! She placed her hand on the console, now nearly too warm for her touch. That was it, what had been bothering her: the warmth of the minicomputer. There was a faint meshing of gears, and a printout ejected from the terminal and fell into a dusty corner of the closet, behind a wastebasket. She bent over and pulled the little-used metal container away from the wall. A neat pile of dusty printouts was wedged between it and the concrete. She quickly picked them up and leafed through them.

My God, she realized. It was all there, concisely printed on the graph paper in front of her. But how . . . ? It didn't matter. She held all the answers. Now she just had to notify Jonathan.

The latch on the lab door made a distant but audible click. Was it opening or closing? She knew it had to be Bryson, probably unable to sleep himself. She rubbed her temples, her back to the entrance, waiting for his greeting. But there was none.

"Jonathan?" she whispered, straightening up.

The laboratory light was suddenly switched off. The approaching footsteps were not his. Dare she turn around, or close the closet door? She cocked her head, listening. Silence roared in her ears, an unheard, approaching freight train about to explode past her. Fear paralyzed her. Then the shadow from behind loomed over her, forcing her to act in desperation. She wheeled around.

In the glow from the supply closet, Mrs. Rutledge recognized the intruder. Her shoulders sagged with relief and her hand flew to her bosom as she sighed. "Thank goodness! For a moment I thought—" and then her words stopped abruptly. Eyes widening in horror, her hand went up mechanically to ward off the blow. But she was too slow, her attacker too powerful. The iron rod crushed her skull. In the instant before she died, as darkness overtook her consciousness, her last glimmering awareness was one of understanding. Rosemary Rutledge knew.

She collapsed on the floor in a widening, sticky pool of blood that matted her gray hair. Then, slowly but thoroughly, as if following a predetermined plan, the lab was wrecked. The minicomputer, taken from storage, was shattered to bits of glass and steel. The console was toppled. The job done, the intruder left.

Lying crumpled on the floor, the shattered threads of her recent existence strewn about her, Rosemary Rutledge departed from the living unable to reveal the evidence for which she and Bryson had been so desperately searching.

22

A feeling of inevitability encircled him like baling wire, constricting his chest, cutting off his air. Ever since he had left Rosemary the evening before, he knew Samantha's moment had come. He had worn many hats recently, playing lover and scientist, employer and professor. But above all he was a doctor, and the physician in him said that Samantha could not survive more than a few days.

So this is it, thought Bryson. End of the road. If ever anything had been so royally screwed up, he had messed up this one. Whatever had been concocted between MEDIC and the fetus was going to happen soon. It was out of his hands now. Certainly he and Mrs. Rutledge had done their part, all that they could. Yet, there was no denying his responsibility.

Bryson had no choice now but to stay close at hand, notify Samantha's doctor, and alert all hospitals in the area. Bryson mustered his courage before calling Pritchard. He doubted the man would listen, but there were no alternatives. If Samantha were going to be saved, it could only be through an obstetrician's intervention. It really didn't matter whether or not Pritchard believed him. Bryson would go on record with everything he knew. Once Pritchard was confronted with the reality of a desperately ill woman, he would use what Bryson had told him and take it from there. Bryson only hoped that he could give the obstetrician enough concrete facts to save her when it happened.

He dialed the obstetrician's number and reached an answering service. Yes, he explained, it was an emergency. He had to speak with the doctor right away. The service said that Dr. Pritchard was gone for the day. Did they know where he could be reached? Bryson asked. They did not. Emergency cases were instructed to call the chief resident in obstetrics and gynecology at the hospital. Bryson left his name with the service and insisted that Pritchard call him immediately upon his return or he would try again every hour.

He squirmed on his couch, fidgeting with the telephone wire. He had to keep busy or else he would lose his mind. Locking the door to his town house, he decided to go to Samantha's. All he could do now was keep a close eye on her, whether she wanted it or not. He drove to her place and parked in the lot. He found her apartment unlocked, empty. The interior was cluttered and dirty. Her soiled jogging clothes lay on the couch. He drew the blinds and peered out over the park. She was nowhere in sight.

After a quick call to the emergency and delivery rooms, Bryson stepped outside into the park facing Samantha's building. It was a cool, sunny, late October afternoon. Numbed, he leaned back on the bench and crossed his legs. Now everything was up to Samantha. He had lost the role of the aggressor. All he could do was parry her moves, react to her initiative. He felt helpless. What if she left town?

Every quarter hour he walked around the outside of her apartment to see if she might be approaching from the rear. The structure was isolated, and he had a clear view for hundreds of yards. Samantha was not to be seen. Bryson grew frustrated. At four o'clock he re-entered her apartment and placed his calls again. Pritchard was still unavailable, and Samantha was not yet at the hospital. He returned to the park bench.

She crept up softly behind him, wisp-like, the barest hint of movement. For a moment he didn't know she was there. He sensed the unseen presence, the bristling of small hairs on the back of his neck. And then he smelled her. The stale odor was one of sweat and decay, of a long-sealed room in which something, once living, had died and decomposed. She carried a brown paper bag.

He beckoned for her to sit beside him, not knowing if she would reply at all. She looked so tired. She moved around the bench and sat, slumping against the green slats.

"What's in the bag?"

Samantha tilted it for him to look inside. She seemed too weary to talk. The grocery bag contained jars of Gatorade, orange juice, and assorted sweets.

"This is dessert," he commented. "No entrée today?"

"Energy food. Sucrose, glucose, dextrose."

"What are you training for?"

He watched her closely, alert to her every move. At this point, she was unpredictable. He wanted to be ready for any eventuality. Like a wounded animal, she might collapse, or terrified, bolt away; succumb to her injury, or draw upon the surge of inner strength and lash out against her attacker. Instead, she did none of these. What she did was so touchingly unexpected that he was caught by surprise. It was something she hadn't done in weeks. Samantha slowly leaned over and placed her head on his shoulder.

Bryson put his arm around her. Her body felt like that of a rag doll. She closed her eyes wearily.

"Do you remember, months ago," she whispered, "when we were at the beach?"

"Yes."

"And I told you then about thoughts which come into my mind?"

"Yes."

"For a long time, I thought they were gone. Or maybe they were there, and I just don't remember them. It's so hard to think. I don't have the strength for it. It's as if I'm living an endless dream, starting to come awake, and then dozing off again. Am I making any sense?"

"Yes."

"I feel like I've been drugged. My brain is mush, molasses. The last things I think I recall were times when I was with you. Once I was sleeping over, and I had a nightmare. Do you remember?"

He nodded.

"The other time is . . . fuzzy. We had supper and then went out. Later we made love. Then we had a discussion, or an argument. I can't really remember which. Ever since then, I feel like I've been wandering. I have flashes, little hints of reality. But nothing is clear. Until this morning."

"What happened?"

She opened her eyes and sat straight, wanting to look at him as she spoke.

"Did I once try to have an abortion?"

"Yes. Several months ago."

She nodded acceptance of his statement, non-judgmentally, sorting things out in her mind.

"This morning I did a sleep study. Or was it yesterday? I can't remember. Have I been doing them all along?"

"Up until a while ago."

"It's funny. I don't recall any of them until the one I just finished, but I remember this one. I know it's the last I'm going to have."

"How do you know?"

"I just know. It's a fact. Something is about to happen. Don't ask me what, or how. I know that something important is going to occur today. It's an unshakable feeling, a conviction. Like, do you remember when President Kennedy died? I remember reading that people *knew* something was going to happen that day. And they were right. Now I know what they were talking about: an uncertain sense of certainty. I simply know something will happen. Just like I knew I had to run before, and that now I have to rest, to gain strength. And that I must have this," she said, pointing to the bag, "to build up my blood sugar, for energy. Isn't that odd?"

He said nothing, waiting for her to continue. Her eyes started to glaze.

"I must take a shower now."

It was back, her tone of finality. Samantha had regained her icy composure. Again her eyes were distant, withdrawn.

They walked across the parking lot to her apartment. Bryson tried to engage her in conversation. What she didn't know, he did. He wanted to tell her that she was, most likely, about to go into labor. He wanted her to understand that she must remain near the hospital, that he would be there to help and guide her when the time came to seek medical care. But his words were lost on her. She had once again withdrawn into herself, unhearing. Fetal control re-established.

She drank her orange juice before showering. It was warm, but she didn't seem to mind. Samantha drank the whole quart from the container in long, easy swallows.

Then she bathed. It was a warrior's preparation: a ritual cleansing and fortifying of the body before doing battle. After she dried herself, she sat on the couch and ate two of her candy bars.

"I would like to take a drive," she announced.

"Where to?"

"To the waterfall, do you remember? I would like to go there."

"It's getting dark now. We can go back another time."

"I want the fresh air. I would like to go now."

Take it easy, he thought. If that's where she wanted to go, that's where he'd take her. As long as he was with her, he could always get her to the hospital if an emergency arose.

She took a sweater, dressing in maternity pants and a loose-fitting top. They drove west, toward the countryside. They didn't talk. Bryson wasn't disturbed by the drive, a gesture of appeasement. Anything to stay close.

He remembered their prior excursion in early June. It was shortly after he had learned that Samantha was pregnant. He had heard of the spot from some friends—an idyllic, secluded, wood-bound creek with a deep chasm and a narrow waterfall. It was little-frequented, located off a poorly traveled side road. Most of its natural beauty was undisturbed. There were no park benches or barbecue pits, no broken glass and crushed aluminum cans. Its cool, mossy banks lent it a romantic air. It was an ideal spot in which to fall in love.

The countryside was abundant with pumpkins. Hundreds were strewn in careless profusion among the plowed fields. An occasional ramshackle farm stand, lights ablaze in the early evening, displayed the fruits of the autumn harvest. Bushels of ripe apples and pears were everywhere.

But most conspicuous were the carved, gaily lit pumpkins, whose leering orange smiles gleamed brightly in the yellow glow of the candles within.

It was a night for parties and celebration of Halloween. Carloads of costumed children, ghosts and goblins, passed them going in the opposite direction, toward town. The windows of roadside diners bore seasonal slogans, with cut-outs of luminous broomsticks and black-clad witches pasted to the panes of glass. But soon the diners and farm stands grew few and far between as they drove westward from civilization, until they disappeared entirely when Bryson turned off the highway onto a narrow dirt road leading into the forest.

They followed the meandering road for two miles until it ended abruptly in a rutted overgrowth of weeds. He parked the car and locked it, taking a blanket and flashlight from the trunk. He shined the beam of the light to guide her, but she didn't appear to need it. Samantha picked her way through the shrubs and trees with practiced ease. In the distance, the rush of water grew louder. Samantha was drawn to it. Bryson followed her closely, placing his shoes in her footsteps. After several hundred yards, they reached a clearing.

The path disappeared, ending in a wide, flat granite facing. Maple and spruce towered overhead, and the fresh smell of moist humus and pine lingered in the evening breeze. Samantha walked across the twenty-foot expanse of rock. She sat on its edge, Bryson standing beside her. The rock sloped sharply away. The body of water was wide for a creek, perhaps fifteen feet across. Its current was cool and swift. Downstream another fifty feet, the creek bottlenecked at two large shoulders of stone. The boulders led to a still narrower chasm, which fell straight down to a

rocky plateau thirty feet below. Because of the sudden
narrowness, the speed of water flow increased dramatically
at the boulders, and it gushed into the chasm white and
glistening, an opened faucet that created a spectacular natural waterfall. It was this roar of spewing water that guided
them.

A full moon shone overhead. The granite was a dull
gray-blue in its illumination. It was a majestic harvest
moon, pale yellow in color, low on the horizon. Its boldness in ascension captured the sky. Bryson unfolded the
blanket and sat by Samantha. They watched the moon together as it rose over the treetops, in silence.

What was her purpose in bringing him here? He watched
her look at the moon. She seemed so content now. Was
there some hidden fetal need to have its mother breathe
fresh, cool air?

He wanted to think otherwise. Maybe, as labor began,
fetal control might give way. In its place, remembrance. A
memory of time passed, of carefree moments spent together. Samantha looked serene. Was this the first step
toward regaining her own autonomy, toward getting herself together again? And if it was, might she somehow
escape the obstetrical complication which Bryson believed
was intended for her?

He doubted it. The fetus had come too far to relinquish
control now. Bryson must still play the waiting game.
What was most baffling was Samantha's picture of inner
peace.

Whether it was because she perceived him staring at
her, or because of an upswell of emotion, he didn't know.
She turned her face to him and looked back softly, a tired
madonna, ladylike in spite of her illness. Her fingers touched
his cheek, drawing his face nearer. Their lips grazed gently.

It was a lingering, feathery kiss, as a parent's mouth might brush the cheek of a feverish child. Samantha closed her eyes and rested her face in his neck. Bryson held her, stroking her hair, his arms around her. Light though she was, her weight pushed him back. He carried her down onto her side. She nestled in his arms. Their heads lay close, just off the blanket, cushioned by a carpet of moss. Again her lips pressed against him, wandering across his face.

I can't, he thought. She's ill. I love her and want her deeply, but I can't.

Her touch grew insistent, and with it, his adamance slowly melted away. She had become the old Samantha, demanding but tender. They leisurely undressed one another and lay naked on the blanket, huddled together against the chill night air. In the fashion he remembered, a manner that he had feared was gone forever, they made slow, tender love in the moonlight.

For a long while they lay as one. He grew cold and snuggled closer, pulling the corners of the blanket about them. But the chill didn't seem to bother her. Samantha disengaged, pushing off the cover, before rolling onto her back. She stared at the sky.

He knew he was losing her again. Separated by mere inches, the emotional distance between them grew immeasurably. Their sudden closeness followed by an even more abrupt separation disturbed him immensely. It made no sense. But then again, nothing made sense any more. Her personality kept coming in and out of focus. Bryson felt like someone awakening from a long night's sleep, rubbing his eyes because he couldn't see clearly.

Samantha lay naked on her back. She placed her hand on her abdomen, pressed gently, and then let go. She repeated it again three minutes later, and three minutes after that. The fourth time, Bryson also touched her stomach. It was tightening, firm. Her uterus had begun contracting.

"It is starting," she said.

He sat up. "Let's go. I'll drive you to the hospital."

"No."

She still gazed at the sky, every few minutes rubbing her abdomen with wispy movements of her fingertips. She began massaging her breasts, squeezing the nipples.

"Sam, we should go."

"It's early yet."

"You might deliver fast."

"The average length of first labors is fourteen hours."

Curious, he watched her rub her breasts.

"What are you doing?"

"Nipple massage. It stimulates endogenous oxytocin release, to cause uterine contractions. Just like your semen does."

"What?"

"Semen. Prostaglandins."

What was she babbling . . . ? And then his eyes widened in realization.

Of course. Oxytocin . . . semen . . . prostaglandins. Damn, she had been using him the whole time! His mind flashed back to a conversation with Rosemary, when he explained how prostaglandins might induce labor. And as any medical student knew, human semen was one of the richest natural sources of prostaglandin!

It was all clear now. Maybe there were flashes of the real Samantha, from time to time. But it was the fetus who directed her to have intercourse with him. It was the fetus who had her command him to her apartment for their sexual liaisons. The baby knew that Bryson's semen, slowly, over the course of months, would supply minute amounts of prostaglandin to the tip of her womb. Just enough to cause several contractions, to "ripen" her cervix. And just enough, now, to actually throw her into labor.

He felt incredibly stupid. How could he, with his medical training, not have appreciated what was happening all along? How could he fail to realize what the fetus was doing, just as he now realized that Samantha's breast massage caused release of still another hormone that stimulated her labor?

Ancient history, he thought. What was done was done. There was no time to waste now. The sooner he got her to the hospital, the sooner he could help forestall complications. He would drag her to the hospital if he had to.

"Wait."

"Dammit, we're going!"

"Do you remember the waterfall?"

"Sam—" Losing patience now.

"Let me see it again. Then I will go. I promise."

"For shit's sake, this is crazy." He paused. "All right. We walk over there, then we return to the car. Agreed?"

"Yes."

He couldn't believe it. She was in labor, and she wanted to look at a waterfall. Could it be significant? Fine. He would humor her this last time. He took her hand, helping her up. Naked, he led the way across the rock ledge, tiptoeing for secure footholds. Samantha followed close behind. He guided her around the near boulder until they were at the edge of the chasm. The water rushed by, a foot below the granite edge, plummeting down to the lower plateau. They watched it for a moment.

"Had enough?"

"Could we sit here for a while?"

"We goddamn can not. It's dangerous. Come on, we're going back."

"Please! Just let me dangle my feet in the water."

"Oh, Christ," he said, shaking his head. Her voice sounded so plaintive, a child at the seashore. "Ten seconds, Sam. Just to wet your toes."

"You sit first, and help me down."

Bryson crouched, and then sat on the edge of the chasm. He swung his feet into the water. It was icy, and he felt the prickling of gooseflesh on his thighs. The current was very swift. He had to brace himself on the ledge with both hands. He turned around for Samantha.

She held the rock high, in both hands. He watched her in slow motion. Her eyes were ablaze. He remembered thinking, calmly, she's going to hit me with that rock. The disbelief paralyzed him. But then she brought it down swiftly, toward his head. He raised his forearm, too late. The rock was aimed at his skull. But as he lifted his arm, his leg raised too, and the current pushed against his other leg, turning his body slightly. It was enough to throw off her aim. The rock struck him in the forehead, a glancing blow. Bryson fell on his side, stunned. His vision was blurred. Samantha was shrieking at him, a distant voice at the end of a tunnel. Blood trickled into his eyes. He looked up at her. What was she shouting?

She rattled off words, a string of invective. Dr. Bryson must die! she screamed. He tried to steady himself, to pull himself up. She still held the rock. Why didn't she hit him again? His vision cleared, focusing on her. Strangest of all, through her litany of curses and epithets, she was crying. Tears ran down her cheeks. Her words were the harshest vilification, but her face was twisted with remorse. She berated him, insulted him. He knew too much, she screamed, and had to pay for it. But while she hollered, she was sobbing.

He reached for her ankle. Samantha threw the rock toward his hand, smashing his wrist, sobbing all the while. He rolled back in agony. His body tottered on the ledge.

"Please, Sam!"

"No!"

Still crying, Samantha kicked him hard in the face. He toppled into the water. The icy current grabbed him, catapulting his body across the torrent toward an outcropping of rock on the opposite bank. The back of his head cracked against the granite, and he lost consciousness. The waterfall sucked at him, and Jonathan Bryson's body did a graceful somerault in its froth before the force of the current carried him to the rocks below.

23

She raced his sportster through traffic, recklessly weaving between cars. They sounded their horns, but she heard nothing. She was conscious only of the rhythmic contractions in her abdomen. They were strong and precise. She passed to the right side of a slow-moving vehicle, careening onto the dirt shoulder, spewing dust and gravel in her wake. The other motorist raised his fist, cursing at the insane apparition that steadily accelerated away from him.

Her whole body was in pain. It was in her belly and in her neck, threatening to tear the top off her head. She grimaced and narrowed her eyes. Her vision was hazy. She had to get there soon.

It loomed up before her. The hospital towers beckoned, and she responded by pressing her foot further to the floor. She sped through the last red light, narrowly avoiding a station wagon crossing the intersection. There was a screech, and the smell of burning rubber filled the night air as she rounded the final corner into the emergency-room parking lot.

So close to her destination now. She stumbled from the car, half running, half crawling to the entrance. The pain was intense. She sobbed and cried out in agony. The electric doors automatically parted before her. Then the spinning began. Her world became a carousel, a swirling, darkening spiral that sucked at her consciousness, forcing her to the floor, until all thought and feeling were gone.

•   •

The nurse finished checking the vital signs.

"Blood pressure 240 over 130. Pulse 120 and weak."

The junior obstetrics resident plugged clear plastic tubing into a bottle of intravenous solution. He applied a rubber tourniquet to the forearm and searched for a vein. The back pressure from the tourniquet made them distend prominently, a road map of blue worms. He inserted the intravenous catheter into a large vein. Blood flowed back promptly. He collected four test tubes of blood, capping each with a different colored rubber stopper. He handed them to the nurse and connected the IV tubing. The solution dripped in at a rapid rate. He spoke to the nurse while he taped the tubing in place.

"I want a CBC, fibrinogen, and a coagulation screen. And type and cross her for four units of whole blood. Did you page Eisenberg?"

"Yes, Doctor."

"Take the blood to the lab yourself and tell them I need the results in five minutes. On your way, page Eisenberg again. And send somebody else in here to help me."

The nurse left hurriedly. Over the loudspeaker, the announcement: "Dr. Eisenberg, to the delivery room stat." It was repeated three times. Another nurse entered the holding area. The junior resident bade her to the bedside with a toss of his head.

"Put in a Foley catheter while I hook up the monitor."

He wheeled over a cart on which rested a rectangular fetal monitor. He plugged in the jacks, one for measuring uterine contractions and the other for detecting fetal heart tones. Then he secured the connecting straps to the patient's abdomen while the nurse was inserting a urinary catheter. He pressed the "power" button on the monitor, and two pens began recording the events of labor on graph paper. Just then Eisenberg, the chief resident, pulled back the draw screen and came to the bedside.

"What've you got?"

"Looks like severe preeclampsia. Diastolic B.P. 130. I don't remember the systolic, but it was over two hundred. And she's unconscious."

"Coma? Shock?"

"I don't know. She just got here. I paged you right away."

The chief resident lifted the eyelids, studying the pupils. He took a pen light from his breast pocket and shined it in her eyes.

"Pupils reactive, symmetrical. Always think about an intracranial bleed with a hypertensive in coma. Can she talk?"

"I don't think so."

The chief resident slapped her cheek.

"Wake up, sweetheart. Can you hear me? What's your name?"

No answer. Briskly, he spoke to the nurse. "Get me four grams of magnesium sulfate for IV push. And put another ten grams in a liter of Ringer's lactate. And see if you can find the chief resident in neurology." He turned to the junior resident. "Who is she?"

"I don't know. They just wheeled her up from the E.R."

"Is she a staff patient, or private?"

"I really don't know."

"She's got a name, doesn't she? Did you check the clinic file?"

"Nobody knows who she is. The guys from the E.R. said she came in screaming hysterically and collapsed at the front desk. Didn't say a word. And since she's pregnant, they dumped her on us."

"Doesn't she have an I.D.? A purse, a driver's license?"

"Nothing."

"Shit. Did you examine her yet?"

"I was waiting for you."

The chief resident nodded toward the monitor.

"She's contracting every two or three minutes. Fetal heart looks okay."

"The mommy doesn't look so hot."

The chief resident lifted Samantha's hospital gown. He extracted a stethoscope from his white coat pocket and listened to Samantha's chest.

"Heart and lungs clear. Jesus, she's thin. Like a scarecrow."

He palpated her abdomen, careful not to dislodge the monitor straps.

"Looks like she's about due. Vertex presentation. I'd estimate the fetal weight at around eight pounds. You didn't do a pelvic, huh?"

"No."

"Give me a glove."

He donned a latex examining glove and bent up Samantha's knees for an internal, easing two lubricated fingers into her vagina.

"She's six centimeters dilated, bulging membranes."

He stripped off the glove and discarded it in a wastebasket. With Samantha's knees still bent, he tapped one with a reflex hammer. It jerked out sharply.

"Hyper-reflexic, too. But there's no edema. Did you check her urine?"

"Not yet."

Eisenberg lifted the urine drainage bag.

"Is this all she put out? There's only ten cc's in here."

"We just put in the catheter a few minutes ago."

"Doesn't matter. I expect more urine than that. Hand me one of those dipsticks."

The junior resident uncapped a bottle of urinary test tapes. The chief resident twisted the catheter from the drainage bag and wet the tape with a drop of urine, inspecting its color change.

"Christ, three-plus protein. We've got problems, my friend. Did you draw bloods?"

"They're cooking in the lab."

Eisenberg reconnected the catheter to the drainage bag. The nurse returned with the syringe filled with medication.

"Four grams?"

"Yes, Doctor. And I'm drawing up the other ten now."

"Okay," he said, slowly injecting the magnesium sulfate through a rubber hub in the IV tubing. He spoke to the junior resident. "Al, this is what I want you to do. First, find out who's the attending on call. Get him on the phone and let him know what we've got here. Next I want a stat EKG and a chest film. See if you can find someone in internal medicine to take a look at this patient. Then go down to the lab yourself and sit on them until they give you some results. Got it?"

"On my way."

Finished with the injection, the chief resident hung the liter of Ringer's lactate solution and checked Samantha's blood pressure.

"Two ten over one forty," he said to the nurse. "Draw up twenty milligrams of hydralazine for IV push. And get me some diazoxide, Aldomet, mannitol, and Lasix in case I need it."

Alone, he sat by Samantha's bedside. He was clearly puzzled. Here was an unconscious Jane Doe in active labor, with very severe toxemia. She could easily have already had a stroke that had left her comatose. The neurologist would have to let him know about that. But she needed help, and she needed it fast. Her kidneys appeared to be failing, and her blood pressure was dangerously high. Unless he could lower it soon, she might develop uncontrollable seizures, flip off her placenta, or suffer a whole host of other complications. The entire picture was confusing. Strangest of all was that the baby, as judged by the fetal monitor, was doing surprisingly well.

Stabilize and terminate the pregnancy, he thought. That's what the ward manual called for in cases of severe toxemia: lowering the blood pressure until it was at a stable and acceptable level, and then delivering the baby. But the ward manual didn't mention what to do in severe toxemics who were unconscious and who had negligible urinary output, or who were on the verge of developing other disastrous complications.

The patient needed help, but he needed it too. Even after four years of training, he had never encountered a situation like this. The case was too baffling for his mind alone to unravel. He desperately needed answers. And he needed them at once.

It was the sound of buzzing, a swarm of bees. They were attacking him in waves. His face stung from their onslaught. He swatted his eyes to shoo them away. His cheeks were wet, mouth swollen. They must have stung him horribly. With great trepidation, Bryson opened his eyes. His face was barely two feet from the waterfall. The buzzing he heard was the roar of tumbling water; the stings, icy needles of spray. He lay sprawled flat on his back. His bones ached, his muscles were sore. Gently, he tested each extremity; nothing major broken. His hand was blue and distorted from the rock Samantha had hurled at it, but he could still flex the fingers. Perhaps some of the small bones in the hand were broken.

His body had struck the rock perfectly horizontally. The entire surface area of his torso absorbed the impact equally, cushioning the shock. Had he been tilted ten degrees in either direction, his legs would have snapped like kindling, or his skull would have been fractured. As it was, he was bruised and stiff but, with the exception of his hand, for the most part unhurt. He had been incredibly lucky.

He sat up slowly, tensing his muscles. All vital systems seemed operative. In the moonlight, Bryson looked up at the rocky crag above, half expecting to see Samantha peering down at him. There was nothing but empty, illuminated sky. How long had she been gone, and how long had he been unconscious? He looked at his watch. The glass was broken, but the digital display miraculously still worked. Ten forty-five. Samantha had several hours head start.

She had tried to murder him, that much was clear. She was programmed to kill. In fact what he remembered most vividly was her anguish, an utter, disconsolate remorse as the real Samantha stood a powerless observer to the destruction her body was trying to wreak. Someone—something—wanted him dead. And had very nearly succeeded.

He stood up, shivering. For all he knew, Samantha might have delivered by now. Perhaps she too was dead, also a victim. But she said that the average length of first labors was fourteen hours. Halve that—assuming she had a rapid labor—and subtract the time he had been unconscious, probably a few hours still remained. It was worth the effort to find out. He had to get back to the hospital.

Bryson looked down. Fifteen feet below the plateau on

which he stood, the spilling water descended into a wide, glacial lake. The lake was bounded, like a canyon, with sloping walls. The plateau, on each side, was rock-strewn and impassable. The only way out was up.

What in God's name am I doing here? he thought. The unreality of his predicament was nearly comic, so ill-suited was he for it. He was no cowboy, no outdoorsman. The closest he had come to rocks before was pebbles at the shore. The thought did little to comfort him.

The plateau was narrow. He peered around the waterfall. The other side of the rock face was identical. It was a nearly vertical cliff. He ran his hand across the rock face. It was wet and silky smooth, with few handholds. For all intents and purposes, he was stuck. But then there was the waterfall itself.

Suppressing a smile of self-pity, he inched closer to the water. The spraying mist drenched him, and the chill flow splattered about his numbing knees. Now almost flush with the falling water, he noticed something peculiar. Directly behind the waterfall was a chasm. It appeared to extend five or six feet. He couldn't see it well, obscured as it was by the spray.

Holding onto the rock face as tightly as possible, Bryson took a deep breath and plunged his head through the water. The thundering cascade pummeled his shoulders, nearly throwing him off balance. Blindly he plowed forward. The footing was there, and suddenly he found himself behind the streaming torrent, drenched and shivering. He was up to his ankles in ice water. Confined within the walls of the abyss, the deafening roar of the waterfall was Lorelei, dangerous yet enchanting.

He surveyed the walls of the chasm. The rock was damp but not slippery. It was a triangular space, three feet across at its greatest width, narrowing to an arrowhead-like wedge five feet back. Looking up, he could see the stars. The crevice snaked its way up to the cliff above, the boulders bounding the waterfall clearly visible. Funny, how he hadn't noticed it when he sat by the waterfall earlier. What he needed now was a rope. He thought, miserably, John Wayne would have had one.

Bryson had little experience mountain climbing. He swept his hands over the walls of the chasm. There were a few niches and outpouchings, but for the most part, the granite was smooth. If he was lucky, he might find enough finger-and-toe holds to grab. But he couldn't count on it. He was scared. A straight climb would be very risky, with the slightest slip sending him tumbling back to his starting place, to a certain fracture. He leaned against the cold rock and pondered his captivity. It was ridiculous.

On a whim, he placed the ball of one foot against the opposite rock wall a yard away. With his knees bent, his body seemed solidly wedged in place between the chasm walls. Pressing hard, he placed his other sole on the rock. In the narrow confines of the gorge, his body became suspended, with his back flush against one wall, and the balls of his feet against the other. If he maintained his balance, keeping constant pressure on his feet and back, he might be able to clamber up the chasm in a near-sitting position. He breathed deeply, braced his shoulders, and began the climb.

He inched up slowly. First he wiggled the toes of one foot upward, then the other. Then he pushed his back and shoulders up until his torso was level with his feet. Knees bent, maintaining himself horizontally, he slithered up the gorge.

He was only ten feet up and already breathing heavily. Twenty more feet to go. His muscles were cramping. He longed to stop, to stretch out the tightness. But he daren't release his pressure. He was sure any relaxation would send him directly to the bottom.

In spite of the cold night air and his nakedness, sweat began to pour down his face. His breath came in gasps. The muscles of his legs were so cramped that they trembled. Bryson looked up; he was two thirds of the way to the top. Only ten more feet to go. He didn't know if he could make it. The muscles of his thighs were heavy, like weights. Worst of all was the toll the rock was taking on his back. He felt the skin tearing and abrading, the granite rubbing off the flesh like sandpaper. It was raw and stinging. But as much as it tore through his back, the pain kept him alert, spurring him on.

With one last effort his feet reached the rim of the gorge, and he pushed his back up once more until his head was above the rocky surface. Keeping pressure on his middle back, he inched his shoulders higher until his elbows rested on the rocky rim. Now supporting himself by his elbows, Bryson let go with his legs.

Leaden, his heels crashed against the wall to which his elbows clung. His body was vertical now, as if he were resting his elbows on parallel bars. But it was no time to rest. He pushed his arms up straight, raising his trunk until he could finally swing his buttocks over the edge of the chasm.

He did it.

He collapsed on his back, sweating, struggling for breath. His shoulders were on fire. Bryson stared at the moon, now high in the sky, his mind a blank. After five motionless minutes, his wind returned. He allowed himself a breath-

less laugh; he couldn't believe he had done something so
physical. He rolled onto his side, then pushed himself to
a sitting position. When he could finally stand, it was in
total exhaustion, every muscle quivering. Only now did
he feel the pain in his hand. The chill returned, and his
sweat dried. He needed warmth. He hoped Samantha hadn't
taken his clothes.

They were still there, but the keys were missing. He
knew that, a hundred yards away, he would find his car
gone. Bryson dressed quickly and threw the blanket still
lying where he left it around his shoulders for added
warmth. He turned on the flashlight and followed the path
back to his car.

He forced his body down the dirt path toward the highway. His weary lope was little more than a slow jog. In
twenty minutes he was at the intersection. Bryson began
frantically waving his arms at every car that approached.

No one stopped. The passengers eyed him suspiciously
through the rolled-up auto windows. His unkempt appearance did little to inspire confidence.

This is war, he thought.

Bryson lay down in the middle of the highway, praying
no inebriated partygoer would barrel down the road. If he
didn't hear the car brake, he would roll out of the way at
the last minute. Headlights bore down on him. The car
slowed, and then stopped. He heard a door slam, and the
approach of footsteps. Then he opened his eyes. A pimply-
faced adolescent stood over him.

"You okay, mister?"

"Could be better," he replied, getting to his feet. When
the youth saw that Bryson wasn't seriously injured, cau-
tion took hold, and he retreated to the driver's seat. Bryson followed him. He would not allow him to close the

door. "This is a medical emergency," Bryson continued. "Take me to Jubilee General as fast as you can move this thing."

"Let go of the door or I'll call the cops."

Bryson lost his patience. He yanked the scrawny teen-ager out of the car and leaped into the driver's seat.

Bryson tore down the highway. Fourteen miles, he thought. She was surely at the hospital now. Still, maybe she stopped somewhere; or perhaps she didn't go to the hospital at all. He doubted it. The hospital would be the logical choice. Besides, he certainly wasn't going to stop at each roadstand to ask if someone had seen her. He pressed the accelerator to the floor. Fifteen minutes later, he pulled into the parking lot by the emergency room.

His hand ached painfully, and his shirt clung to the congealing blood on his back. He would have liked nothing more than to present himself to the emergency clerk as a patient, have her sign him in, and then have his head and back tended to. But there wasn't a moment to spare. He ran toward the clerk. Noting the shabby figure dashing at her, the woman behind the desk eyed him with suspicious alarm. But in recognition, her expression gave way to curiosity. He looked a wreck.

"Did a patient named Samantha Kirstin come through the E.R.?

"Dr. Bryson?"

"I know I look like hell, but I haven't got time to explain. This Kirstin. Was she here or not?"

"I don't remember the name," she said, checking her sheet. "When would she have come in?"

"You'd remember her if you saw her. Young, pregnant, thin. She may not have been completely coherent."

"Oh, the weirdo! Sure I remember her, Dr. Bryson. She came in here screaming and collapsed right in front of me. What did you say her name was?"

"When?" he demanded.

"Ninety minutes ago. Maybe two hours. You know her?"

"Where is she?"

"They took her up to the delivery room."

He ran toward the elevator.

Dr. Bryson!" she called after him. "I need some admitting information on her."

"Later!" he shouted. Jesus. Samantha was probably dying, but the clerk wanted to complete her chart. Inside the elevator, he repeatedly punched the button for the fourth floor until the doors closed. "C'mon, c'mon," he muttered. Finally the door opened on four. He darted from the bank of elevators past a wary receptionist. She watched him run through the swinging doors marked LABOR AND DELIVERY. AUTHORIZED PERSONNEL ONLY.

"Just a minute," she hollered. "You can't go in there!"

But he was already through the doors. Inside, he didn't know where to turn. On the left-hand side of the large suite, he saw six labor rooms, marked in numerical sequence. Opposite them, on the other side of the room, was a nursing station. Two nurses were watching him curiously, their eyes on him from the moment he burst through the doors. Bryson strode toward Labor Room One. The nearest nurse jumped up immediately.

"Sir—"

He peered into the first labor room. A black woman lay sleeping in the labor bed. He proceeded to the second room.

"Can I help you?" continued the nurse.

Bryson ignored her and pushed open the door of Labor

Room Two. A woman, laboring through natural childbirth, was panting and blowing to ease the discomfort of her contractions. Her husband, beside her, counted aloud the seconds. Each of them was totally absorbed, oblivious to Bryson. The nurse behind him reached for the door and closed it in his face. She took him by the arm and dragged him away.

"Now, if you don't mind—"

He jerked his arm away sharply and continued to Labor Room Three. It was empty. "Where is she?" he bellowed.

"If you'll come with me, I might try to help you," the nurse countered.

"Let go of me." He continued to the next labor room.

"Sarah!" she shouted to the nursing station. "Call Security!"

Bryson pressed on frantically. The three remaining labor rooms were in varying stages of occupancy. But Samantha was nowhere to be found. He glanced toward the nursing station. Both nurses were talking hurriedly into separate telephones. He rushed toward them. Frightened, they moved away from the desk.

"Where the hell is she?" he demanded.

"Where is who?"

"Samantha Kirstin! For God's sake, the girl's desperately ill!"

Both nurses looked to their right. Beyond them was a room marked HOLDING AREA. Without another word, Bryson raced over and barged in, followed by the two nurses.

Samantha lay on a stretcher, covered with a thin white hospital gown. Her eyes were closed, and her face was nearly as pale as the material that clothed her. Her huge abdomen was bare. Fetal monitor straps surrounded it, hooked to the machine at the bedside. An IV solution infused rapidly into a vein, and a urinary catheter drained beside the stretcher. Two young doctors in white looked up when he appeared. One of them called to the nurses behind him.

"Who is this guy?"

"We don't know, Dr. Eisenberg. He just pushed his way in. We already called Security."

"You'd better wait outside, pal," said Eisenberg.

Bryson approached the stretcher slowly. God, Samantha looked horrible. Eyes closed, mouth opened, she had the pale cadaverous look of one near death.

"How is she?" he asked, his voice a whisper.

"Listen, mister, Security's going to be pretty rough on you if you don't get out of this room this instant."

Still he approached. The second young resident looked at him intently.

"Dr. Bryson?"

Bryson looked up and recognized the face of the chief resident in neurology. "Tim?"

"What in the world happened to you, Dr. Bryson? You look like you were hit by a truck."

"You know him?" asked Eisenberg.

"Dr. Bryson's a neurologist here. He heads the sleep research lab."

"I'm sorry, Doctor," said Eisenberg turning to the nurses. "Cancel Security."

"How is she, Tim?"

The neurology resident shook his head. "I'm not sure. She's comatose, but I can't find a neurologic cause."

"Don't bother. It's not a neurologic problem. How high is her B.P.?"

"How did you know she was hypertensive?" asked Eisenberg.

"Dammit, man, I haven't time to explain! But I know she's hypertensive, and soon she's going to develop a very serious complication, if she hasn't already: either abruptio, a coagulopathy, or renal failure. Now please don't waste any more time! How high is her B.P.?"

"Two fifty over one forty."

"Jesus."

"Who is she?"

"Samantha Kirstin. One of my lab assistants." He touched her cheek. It was cold. The fetal monitor beeped loudly, signifying the baby's good health. But Samantha was deteriorating rapidly. "Did you call Dr. Pritchard?"

"Is he her Attending?" asked Eisenberg. Bryson nodded yes. Goldberg addressed the remaining nurse. "Call Dr. Pritchard's service. See if they can find him, and tell him to come to the hospital stat."

"Can't you do something yourself? Look at her: she's dying! What have you done so far?"

"I don't even know what's wrong with her yet."

"What're you, deaf? I just told you! Either she's abrupting, her kidneys are shot, or she has a coagulopathy. Now, which is it?"

"And how did you come to that conclusion, Dr. Bryson?"

Bryson clenched his fists. "I am very rapidly losing my patience with you, hot shot. I don't have time to explain! Now, I'm telling you: the fetus is going to kill Samantha while it's being born! I've just told you what's wrong with her. Now you tell me: what are you doing to save her?"

The two residents eyed one another. Obviously Bryson was totally disoriented. A nervous breakdown, probably. Eisenberg smiled at Bryson.

"We're doing everything we can, Doctor."

"Don't talk down to me, you asshole!" Bryson pushed him aside. He picked up the catheter drainage bag, which contained only a few drops of urine. "Christ, is this all she's put out?"

Eisenberg addressed the nurse softly. "Perhaps you should call Security again, Miss Watson."

"You're unreal! Tim, can't you find anything on neurological?"

"No sir."

Bryson was lost. If Samantha's problem had a neurological element, he could be of assistance. Without one, he was impotent. Obstetrics was foreign to him. He felt Samantha's pulse. It was weak and thready. He was losing her. This time, he spoke to Eisenberg plaintively.

"Isn't there anything you can do?"

"I'm not doing a thing until Dr. Pritchard gets here."

"Shit!" screamed Bryson, pounding his hand resoundingly on the fetal monitor. He glared at the resident, fists clenched, wanting to strike him. He looked again at Samantha, held in coma's grasp. His anger waned. Fighting was pointless.

He would have to wait until Pritchard arrived. He would get nowhere with the residents.

"How long until Dr. Pritchard gets here?"

"About a half hour."

Thirty minutes! It might as well be an eternity. Bryson ran his fingers through his hair, pacing agitatedly. What would he tell the man when he arrived? Pritchard had to believe him.

Strength in numbers, he thought. Every voice counted now. On an impulse, he stormed through the delivery room doors to the elevator. It would take only a few minutes to get to Rosie.

24

A roped-off corner of the parking lot was labeled EMER-
GENCY PARKING FOR PHYSICIANS ONLY. Thinking that the
sports car had been haphazardly abandoned by a thought-
less doctor, the attendant had driven it into a vacant spot
and left it unlocked, awaiting the physician's return. Bryson spotted his car, leaped in and switched on the igni-
tion. He sped through the ten-mile-per-hour zone and
rounded the corner with a shrill caterwaul that incurred
the attendant's baleful stare.

He rapped firmly on the door of Rosie's apartment, having received no response to more genteel tapping. Perhaps
she was sleeping. He waited a minute and insistently
banged again. The anticipated release of the door latch
didn't occur. Now impatient, he raced to the building's
foyer and fed two nickels into the pay phone. Rise and
shine, Rosie. Sam's life is on the line! He drummed his
fingers on the wall. At six rings he frowned, muttering; at
eight rings he fretted and wondered; after ten, he slowly
replaced the receiver in its cradle, mystified. Even the hard-
iest sleeper would have been awakened by the telephone's
demand. Rosie was obviously not home. She didn't date
and if she had gone out with friends, they would have
returned by now. Where in the world could she be at this
hour of the night?

After a moment's reflection, Bryson knew there was only

one place possible. Of course! Rosie was as worried about Sam as he was. He ran back to the car, and raced across campus toward the lab, berating himself for not taking her conscientiousness into consideration. If her nights were as sleepless as his, she was already delving into some hidden area of the sleep studies, searching for anything that might shed light on Samantha's condition.

Lab key in hand, he sprinted through the hospital corridors, running so fast that he had to brace himself against falling as he passed his door. The key slid into the lock, and the tumbler gave no resistance to his turn: the door was open. He was right. Rosie had to be there.

The lab's darkness surprised him. He fumbled for the light switch and flipped it on. There, half in, half out of the supply closet, Mrs. Rutledge's body lay among bits of twisted metal and shards of fractured glass.

He couldn't take his eyes off her. He walked over softly and knelt at her side. Pieces of wire and chips of slivered plastic covered her face. The skin was cold. Postmortem lividity had developed on the underside of her frame; the flesh uppermost at her temples was ghostly white. The blood beneath her was clotted and dry. Bryson knew that she had been dead for at least twelve hours; probably more. And he knew who had killed her.

Christ, not Rosie! Dear, dear Rosie!

Bryson closed her barely opened lids with his fingertips. He involuntarily clenched his teeth. He wanted to flee from the lab and close the door forever.

The crumpled packets of graph paper caught his eye. They lay just beyond Mrs. Rutledge's outstretched hand. In death, she seemed to beckon to him. Bryson stopped to retrieve them. He briefly glanced at the topmost one.

His eyes opened in astonishment, and he hunkered down, slowly unfolding the torn pages, carefully reading his mini-computer's capsulized commentary.

He held his breath. These were the ultimate dialogues! In his hands he held the uncoded essence of conversations between MEDIC and the fetus. The dates were precise. As he scanned the pages, Bryson knew they went as far back as Samantha's attempted abortion. Somehow Samantha had broken into the lab for sleep periods on an almost daily basis. No wonder she was complacent about resuming the sleep studies. They were meaningless to the fetus, for it had its fill of them in the middle of the night.

He cursed himself. What a fool he had been! He should have known that the fetus would never let anything stand between it and its liaisons with MEDIC. Even on the evenings he spent with Samantha, she had probably come directly to the lab after his departure. When he chose to intervene in the dialogues and speak to the computer, he had ordained Mrs. Rutledge's death as surely as if he had wielded the weapon himself.

It was all there before him. In no uncertain terms, the fetus spelled out exactly what it intended for its mother. She wasn't simply to suffer one hypertensive complication in labor. Samantha was destined to fall victim to all three! While the fetus was being born, it would alter and control Samantha's vital functions so that she would simultaneously have kidney failure, suffer a massive stroke, and bleed to death! The child took no chances: its plans were the utmost in Draconian revenge. A monstrous wünderkind, Rosie had said.

Bryson scooped up the packets of paper and stuffed them in his pockets. It was all the evidence Pritchard or anyone would need. God bless you, Rosie. Even in death, you've helped me.

He bolted from the room.

He had no patience for the elevator. Time was all-important. He used the nearest staircase and catapulted himself up to the fourth floor. A security guard was stationed in front of the delivery room. At Bryson's appearance, the receptionist nodded to the guard. He had been alerted. When Bryson approached, he raised his night stick to chest level.

"Can't allow you to go in there, sir."

"Get out of the way! I'm on staff here!"

"Sorry, Dr. Bryson. I have specific instructions to keep you out."

"Are you crazy? A woman is dying in there! I can save her!"

The guard looked uncertainly at the receptionist.

"Doctor, I was told—"

Bryson caught sight of Pritchard inside the delivery area. He burst through the swinging doors, flanked by the guard, who shouted in protest. When Pritchard saw Bryson, he turned and walked quickly away. Bryson caught up with him.

"I knew you'd come back, Bryson. Your erratic behavior is becoming fairly predictable. I instructed the guard to keep you out. What do you want?"

"Dr. Pritchard, it's a long story. If you'd just—"

"I don't want any more stories! They tell me that you're still babbling about the fetus killing its mother. Enough already! I'd be happy to dismiss you as a lunatic, Bryson, except apparently you also predicted hypertension without even examining the patient! Now, if you can help me, both Miss Kirstin and I would be most appreciative!"

Bryson took the tracings from his pocket and exhibited them triumphantly.

"This is all the help you'll need! It's all here, in black and white!"

Pritchard looked at the crumpled, tattered paper.

"What the hell is that?"

"The dialogues! Look, just read—"

"The *what?*" An exasperated Pritchard had heard enough. He brushed the papers aside.

"Oh, Bryson," he said wearily. "And here I thought you might be of some help. You really are an imbecile."

He started back into the delivery room. Bryson seized his arm.

"For God's sake! Don't you believe MEDIC? What does it take to convince you?"

"I don't believe in fairy tales. Now if you'll excuse me, I'm trying to save someone's life."

He yanked his arm away and went through the swinging doors.

Bryson was distraught. He had tried and failed. He cursed and ran out of the delivery room, heading elsewhere.

Bryson bounded down the steps and soon reached the main landing. The computer center was a leisurely five-minute walk away. At a trot, he could make it in two minutes. Running through the corridors, he searched for a weapon. A broken table leg, a fire extinguisher: it didn't matter. If the computer center was locked now, at midnight, he would have to break in. He had to get at that computer. MEDIC was his only solution, his salvation.

There were no weapons, no clubs. Everything owned by Jubilee General was firmly bolted down or locked away. Bryson slowed his pace a few yards from the computer center door. He tiptoed quietly to the entrance and put his ear to the door. He heard nothing. He gently turned the door knob, but the door was locked. Bryson cursed and looked up and down the empty corridor. He noticed an industrial-size fire hose encased in a glass cabinet several yards away. He inspected it closely. Its nozzle was a ten-inch length of brass. Was it weighty enough?

He opened the door and lifted the canvas hose from its hooks. He slung it over his shoulder and carried it back to the computer center's door. Holding the hose three feet from the nozzle, he wielded it like an axe, swinging it in an arc over his head. The heavy brass struck the doorknob with a thunderous clang. Chips of paint splintered away as the knob yielded slightly. Encouraged, he swung again and again, his ears ringing with the tintinnabulation of a thousand church bells. On his tenth blow the doorknob gave way entirely. Breathing heavily, he dropped the hose, and threw his shoulder against the metal. The door swung open, and he was inside.

Even at night the interior of the computer center was a resplendent panorama of light and sound. Sparkling lights punctuated the dimness, and sounds chirped like mechanical crickets. Bryson looked around the room, scanning the control center. Across the room, some of MEDIC's tapes wound slowly, an occasional panel light blinking on and off. He saw no one.

It was time to play his hunch.

MEDIC's main control board was in the center of the room. He crept toward it and heard the soft whir of tapes as he approached. A frequent clicking chatter signaled a

printout. Even at night, the computer was alive. The fluor-
escent overheads above the control panel were still lit. He
seated himself before the master switches and studied the
board. Bryson prayed he had enough time.

The console was dazzling in its complexity. Bryson
wasn't quite sure where to start. Christ! His fingers were
ready to act, but he didn't know which buttons to punch.

It must be so simple; why couldn't he figure it out?
If he could get MEDIC to reveal the same information
he had gleaned from the minicomputer, he just might be
able to trasmit it to Pritchard. Every computer terminal
on campus had a digital printout screen. He knew there
was at least one in the delivery room. If MEDIC would
confess what it knew, he might be able to relay that data
to the doctors working on Samantha.

You goddamn hunk of metal, he thought. You know
damn well what the fetus plans for Sam. Christ knows you
talked to one another enough. Give, you bastard. Spill your
guts.

He sat in front of the console. C'mon, old man, he
thought. You know computers. This one is fancier, but it's
still just a hunk of hardware. He gazed at the myriad of
buttons. Where to start . . . He thought of Samantha, of
Rosie Rutledge. His mind wandered. Me against the child
. . . Dammit, Bryson, concentrate! Think, man, think!

He took a deep breath. Settle down. His fingers were
poised above the programmer's panel. He studied the buttons. There was Input, and Override. Recall, Retrieve, and
Memory. They all seemed to be in a logical sequence. He
visually checked their circuits and interconnections. Yes,
it should work. Dammit, hurry!

He pressed Interrupt, then Input. Nothing happened. He
cursed again and punched Cancel. Then he pressed Input

directly. A red light flashed. Damn! He hit Cancel and began again, this time starting with Interrupt, then Override. The computer wound down, and the red light now flashed yellow. So far so good, he thought. Now he punched Input. The light instantly blinked green. Below it, a lighted panel flashed on, with the wording, "Instructions."

Bryson's fingers trembled above the typewriter keys. He couldn't afford any more delays. He had to get it right the first time. Slowly, with deliberate precision, he typed his one sentence command to MEDIC.

DETAIL CHRONOLOGY OF LABOR AND PLANNED COMPLICATIONS FOR SLEEP RESEARCH SUBJECT SAMANTHA KIRSTIN.

In the background, the whir of winding tapes. The panel light flashed from green to yellow. There was the sound of internal metallic chatter within the units, a clicking and shifting of gears and circuits. The light flashed green again, and all became silent. The printout began.

SAMANTHA KIRSTIN TO COMMENCE LABOR TIME L. FOUR CM DILATATION L PLUS TWO HR TEN MIN. FOCAL ABRUPTIO WITH RELEASE OF THROMBOPLASTIC SUBSTANCE IN EARLY ACTIVE SLOPE. THROMBOPLASTIC EFFECT RENAL COR- TEX TRIGGERS RENIN-ANGIOTENSIN II, CAUSING ABRUPT HYPERTENSION WITH ENCEPHALOPATHY AND COMA. RENAL CHANGES L PLUS THREE HR FIVE MIN YIELD PROGRESSIVE ANURIA. PLACEN- TAL THROMBOPLASTIN TRIGGERS COAGULATION CASCADE WITH GRADUAL DEPLETION OF FAC- TORS XII THROUGH II AND FIBRINOGEN. RAPID ACTIVE PHASE AND FETAL DESCENT. FULL DILA-

TATION AT L PLUS FOUR HR TWENTY MIN. TOTAL
PLACENTAL ABRUPTIO L PLUS FOUR HR THIRTY
MIN WITH FETAL VERTEX AT STATION PLUS
THREE OCCIPUT ANTERIOR. UTERINE TETANY
EXPELS FETUS AND CAUSES COMPLETE COAGU-
LOPATHY AND RENAL CORTICAL NECROSIS. CAR-
DIAC ARREST L PLUS FOUR HR FORTY TWO MIN.

MEDIC became silent. Bryson studied the tracing. He
didn't understand all the obstetric terminology, but he
knew enough of the jargon to realize that the placental
abruptio was imminent. Most frightening was the last sentence of the printout.

Cardiac arrest.

Bryson nearly gasped. His eyes raced across the printout;
how much time was there before Sam's heart stopped beating? Hurry, man, hurry!

Now came the hard part. Pritchard might brush him
aside in person, but if a direct message from MEDIC
flashed across his digital printout screen, he would *have* to
believe it.

How the hell do you transmit on this thing? anguished
Bryson. He grew frantic. Each of the thousands of digital
screens probably had its own code number. He had no idea
of the number for the delivery room. He had reached an
impasse. He was ready to transmit the message, but he
didn't know how to route it properly.

Bryson was desperate. Red buttons, yellow switches,
typewriter console keys . . . he wanted to scream! Then,
on the far corner of the panel, he saw a label: "Emergency Transmission Only: All Terminals." Without hesitation, he slammed his fist onto the button below.

A siren went off, a Klaxon blaring at one-second intervals, the shrill whine of a submarine about to crash dive. Bryson, exhausted, hunched over the panel, put his head on folded arms, and prayed.

All across campus, countless digital printout screens began to glow brilliantly. They had been used only rarely, but the message that now typed out across them was precise. All heads turned toward the brightly lit screens.

In the kitchen of the hospital's cafeteria, two night-shift dishwashers looked at the screen of a recently installed, unused computer that suddenly became alive with letters and numbers.

In the telescope center, an astronomer's study of distant nebulae was interrupted by a digital printout that flashed onto a newly positioned computer console.

In the delivery room, Pritchard agonized over his patient. Samantha was moribund. Her blood wouldn't clot and her kidneys were failing. How long before she delivered, he wondered? One hour? Two? She might not survive that long. He might seriously consider that the placenta was abrupting, were it not for the incredibly good condition of the fetus. He increased the flow rate of one IV solution, slowed another.

At her desk, only Miss Watson noticed the peculiar message which suddenly appeared on the digital printout screen. Odd, she thought. Wasn't the name on the screen the same as their patient's? She approached Pritchard.

"Excuse me, Doctor, isn't this patient's name—"

"Not now, Miss Watson."

She continued to read the digital message.

"But Doctor, I think you should see—"

"*Please*, nurse! I'm terribly busy here!" he said, hovering over Samantha.

The printout ended, and the nurse grew agitated at its last two words. She tugged insistently at Pritchard's sleeve, pointing to the screen.

"But Dr. Pritchard, look!"

"Dammit, what the hell . . ." he began, looking where she directed. As he studied the words on the screen, he grew pale. "Oh . . . my . . . God," he uttered.

Adrenalin surged through him, and Pritchard shouted commands. "Eisenberg, wheel that patient into the section room now! Don't bother scrubbing, just gown and glove. Miss Watson, I want pediatrics and anesthesia here on the double. Have the other nurse get them while you open the section tray. Al . . ." His voice trailed off as he rushed toward the operating room.

Bryson raised his head. He wondered if by some miracle his message had gotten through. If it hadn't, Sam would die.

He was on the verge of tears. He tried not to think. Instead, he remembered Rosie. He closed his eyes and shook his head at the memory she evoked. It was time to tell someone about her, but he was too tired to move.

The noise of the Emergency Transmission was deafening. A wave of fatigue swept over him. It was one-ten in the morning. How long had he been without sleep? He prayed for Samantha. His body cried for release, but his mind refused to obey.

Engulfed by the incessant clanging of the alarm, Jonathan Bryson closed his eyes and wept.

25

They had been in the operating room barely two minutes, and Pritchard was already sweating. It wasn't so much from the heat of the overhead lamps. Rather, he perspired from the incredible pressure and strain under which he suddenly found himself. There were relatively few situations in obstetrics which demanded absolute haste. True fetal distress, perhaps. Or a prolapsed umbilical cord. But most frightening was abruptio, premature separation of the afterbirth. It was a condition that could be instantly lethal for the baby, and have catastrophic consequences for the mother as well. If Bryson and the computer were right—and he had no reason to think otherwise—the patient had been undergoing a partial abruptio for hours. Her failing kidneys, hypertension, and depleted clotting factors were a frightening testimonial to its presence. He had to get the baby out fast, before the placenta separated completely.

The nurse had bypassed the usual presurgical routine of shaving and bathing Samantha's abdomen. She quickly doused it with iodine just before Pritchard, gowned and gloved, helped Eisenberg apply the sterile drapes. With everything ready, he looked toward the anesthesiologist.

"Let me know when I can start."

"I'm giving her oxygen now. Give me a few seconds to tube her."

"Keep her light."

"Light as a feather. The shape she's in, I won't give

her anything stronger than nitrous unless she gets up and walks off the table."

Pritchard looked at the urinary catheter. A few more drops of urine had accumulated, but not much.

"You gave her the mannitol?" he asked Eisenberg, who stood across the operating table from him.

"Yes. And eighty of Lasix. But that was before you said she was abrupting."

"Not your fault. A crazy case, this one. Remind me to tell you about it once I learn all the facts myself." He looked up at a pint of blood infusing into Samantha's vein. "Fresh whole blood?"

Eisenberg nodded. "Her third unit. We have one more ready."

"Better type and cross her for another four, just in case."

Eisenberg glanced at the junior resident, who stood in a corner of the operating room, awaiting instructions.

"You got that, Al?"

"On my way," he said, and left the O.R.

"Do we have platelets and cryoprecipitate if we need them?"

"The hematologist is bringing them with him."

"Can we start?" Pritchard asked the anesthesiologist.

"Ten more seconds."

"Can you believe she's only thirty-two weeks?"

"Could have fooled me," replied Eisenberg. "She looks full-term size."

"Crazy. Absolutely crazy."

The anesthesiologist finished inserting the endotracheal tube into Samantha's windpipe. "Go," he said.

"Knife."

The scrub nurse handed Pritchard a scalpel. He made a bold slash through Samantha's lower abdomen. With Eisenberg assisting him, he pared away at the various layers of muscle and subcutaneous tissue. In two minutes they were down to the uterus. Pritchard made his transverse incision in its wall as the pediatrician entered the room, gowned and awaiting the baby.

"What's the story?" asked the pediatrician.

"Abruptio in a thirty-two weeker," said Eisenberg, as Pritchard widened the uterine incision. "The kid looks much bigger, though."

"Fetal distress?"

"No. The fetal heart was fine when we started."

Under the exposed uterus, the bag of waters was clearly visible with the baby inside. Pritchard ruptured the membranes with a forceps, and pink liquid poured forth.

"Bloody fluid," Eisenberg said to the pediatrician.

Pritchard inserted his hand into the lower uterine segment, just below the baby's head. He began to extract it by lifting upward.

"Give me fundal."

Eisenberg pressed on the top of the uterus while Pritchard lifted. He delivered the baby's head through the uterine incision. Eisenberg immediately suctioned out the baby's nose and throat. Pritchard delivered one shoulder, then the other, until delivery was complete.

"It's a boy," said Pritchard. "Delivery time?"

"One fifteen."

Eisenberg put two clamps on the umbilical cord, and Pritchard cut between them. He handed the child to the pediatrician. The baby cried vigorously.

"Some thirty-two weeker," said the pediatrician. "I could get a hernia carrying this kid. He's nine pounds if he's an ounce." He and a nurse placed the newborn in an isolette for examination.

Blood was everywhere. It oozed from the various incised layers.

"She's not clotting, people," said Pritchard, an edge of anxiety in his voice. "Pump in that blood fast!"

Eisenberg held apart the edges of the uterus to allow Pritchard to peel off the placenta. But before he could insinuate his fingers behind the afterbirth, it spontaneously separated from the uterine wall.

"You have just witnessed an abruptio," he said to Eisenberg. "Probably the first and last time you'll see one like this. Five minutes earlier, and we'd have a dead baby. Placenta time?"

"One sixteen."

"Let's stop this bleeding, huh? Keep that blood going, under pressure. Someone have the hematologist haul ass up here. Suture."

The nurse slapped the suture holder and first stitch into his palm. The anesthesiologist was checking gauges frantically at the head of the operating table, a stethoscope dangling from his ears.

"Sew fast, Dr. Pritchard. I'm getting a B.P. of sixty over zero."

"Impossible. It was over two hundred systolic a minute ago."

"I checked it twice. And look at the cardiac monitor. Her pulse is up to one sixty."

For a moment, everyone paused to gaze at the blips on the screen. Then Pritchard resumed his hurried suturing. The hematologist entered the room carrying plastic bags of various clotting factors. While Pritchard sewed, Eisenberg and the anesthesiologist brought the new doctor up to date. The hematologist muttered an astonished epithet

and plugged several of his bags into the two intravenous
lines.

"How's the baby?"

"Looks great," replied the pediatrician. "You sure about
her dates?"

Pritchard didn't answer. Instead, to the anesthesiologist:
"Pressure?"

"A faint forty over zero and dropping."

Silence in the room.

The beeping of the cardiac monitor stopped. Its effect
on everyone in the room was dramatic. Subconsciously,
they had tuned in to the electronic pulse, in the same way
a mother is always aware of her crying baby while she
sleeps. The sound gone, the doctors and nurses stood motionless for the briefest moment, listening, aware of its absence, awaiting its return. As if of one face, they all looked
at the cardiac monitor together.

It showed a flat line.

"Damn, it's happened!" Pritchard hissed. He tore the
drapes off Samantha's chest. "Somebody announce the cardiac arrest!" One of the nurses dashed from the room.
"You two bag her and pump her chest while we finish
down here," he said to the anesthesiologist and hematologist. "Get the baby out of here. Make room for the arrest
cart."

Already a beehive of activity, the scene in the operating
room became even more frenzied. The loudspeaker announced a cardiac arrest in the delivery room. While the
hematologist began giving Samantha closed cardiac massage, the anesthesiologist kept her lungs ventilated with
oxygen. The pediatrician wheeled the newborn to the nursery. Close on his heels four medical residents entered the

room pushing the cardiac arrest cart, a small pharmacy and instrument tray on wheels. Trained as they were, they didn't have to be told what to do. They automatically assumed their various roles with exactitude, keys fitting into a lock. Questions were asked calmly, perfunctorily. Pulse, blood pressure before the arrest; the nature of the illness; duration of the arrest. One of them took the hematologist's place compressing Samantha's sternum. Every half minute he would stop to look for signs of spontaneous cardiac activity. Electrocardiogram leads had been attached. The tracing was still flat. On the lower half of the operating table, Pritchard kept sewing. He and Eisenberg had closed the uterus and began approximating the various layers. The teams proceeded efficiently. Samantha's tissues were being perfused with blood and oxygen even without a heart beat.

"Cardiac activity," announced one of the residents, six minutes into the arrest.

"Rhythm?"

"V-fib."

"Paddles ready. Stand back everybody. We're going to shock her."

The leader of the resuscitation team placed two cardiac defibrillation paddles on Samantha's chest wall. He triggered the current, and Samantha's body jolted briefly.

"Rhythm?"

"Still V-fib."

"Turn up the juice."

The current was increased, and he shocked Samantha again. Her torso went rigid, and she rose fractionally off the table.

"Rhythm?"

"You're in sinus."

Samantha's heart had begun beating again.

"Do we have a pressure?"

"Eighty over forty."

"Can I finish?" asked Pritchard.

"Yes. Let me know about the bleeding."

Pritchard and Eisenberg resumed suturing.

"Looks like she's starting to clot," said Pritchard.

It took another ten minutes to complete the operation. Pritchard worked swiftly, omitting several minor steps. It wasn't his finest cosmetic closure, but it would heal. During that time, the resuscitation team administered various medications that kept Samantha's heart beating strongly. The hematologist finished infusing his clotting factors. The coagulopathy was abating; Samantha's blood was beginning to clot normally. Her blood pressure had risen to an acceptable level. She was no longer hypertensive. A stream of concentrated urine began flowing into the catheter.

An exhausted Pritchard stepped back from the operating table. He supervised the application of Samantha's dressings. He stripped off his latex gloves and wiped his forehead. He could hardly believe what had just taken place.

"Nurse," he said, "have someone locate Dr. Bryson. Samantha Kirstin is going to live."

Across campus in the research corridors, a figure appeared at the end of the hall. It approached the lab silently. The lab door stood slightly ajar. Its face peered inside, taking stock of the chaos within. After making mental notes of the lab's contents, the light was switched off. The figure pressed the button lock on the latch and pulled the door firmly shut.

26

It was a merciful sleep: four hours of uninterrupted slumber, with neither dream nor distraction. It was dawn when he awoke in his car. He looked at his dashboard clock. It was six twelve. His thoughts were immediately with Samantha. She was probably in recovery now.

Bryson had wanted to be at her side ever since pressing the emergency transmission alert. Once he was assured Samantha was alive and improving, he would notify the authorities about Mrs. Rutledge. Rather than plod back through the labyrinthine maze of hospital corridors, it would be quicker to drive over to the main hospital entrance closest to Samantha. Bryson hurriedly left the computer center and headed for his car. But his hand had begun aching painfully. He stopped in the emergency room on his way to the parking lot.

Now his injured hand was comfortable. He examined the short arm cast that extended from fingertip to elbow. Flexing his fingers hurt but was bearable. They had x-rayed his hand in the emergency room. There was a fine, hairline fracture of one of the bones in his hand, and an even smaller chip fracture at the base of his third finger. He would have to wear the cast for six weeks.

While it was being applied, he asked the clerk to keep him abreast of the latest reports from the obstetrics floor. She came back as the plaster was drying, told him that Samantha was now in a stable condition. Tears ran silently down his cheeks. The doctor who worked on him asked him if the cast hurt. No, he replied, it was just fine.

They cleaned and bathed his back and applied a light dressing. He received a tetanus shot and an injection of pain killer in his buttock. He couldn't wait for them to finish so he could drive to Samantha's bedside. But once outside, in his car, the narcotic began to take effect. Bryson decided to close his eyes for the briefest moment. Four hours later, he awakened.

He cautiously drove one-handed to the hospital's main entrance. Inside, he used the house phone to call the clerk in obstetrics. She told him that Samantha was in the recovery room, in stable condition. He could see her if he wished.

If he wished!

Her eyes were closed. She seemed to be resting peacefully in the recovery room. A nasogastric tube emerged from one nostril and led to a suction bottle. Separate intravenous solutions ran into each arm, and a urinary catheter drained into a plastic bag near the floor. Electrocardiogram leads ran under her gown, attached to her chest. The cardiac monitor beeped with reassuring steadiness above her bed. In spite of all the plumbing and medical paraphernalia, Samantha's cheeks were pink. Her hair, splayed across the pillow, had a faint luster. To Bryson, its glint was a better prognosticator of her return to health than any dial or gauge.

He touched her hand. The skin was healthy, warm and dry. She opened her eyes.

"Jon." She sounded hoarse, distant.

"Don't talk. I just came to see if you were okay."

She hooked a finger of his hand with hers, holding it tightly.

"I'm all right."

For several minutes they simply gazed at one another, index fingers locked together. He caressed her hand with his fingertips. He leaned over and kissed her gently on the cheek. She smiled. In spite of her brush with death, Samantha had a look of peace and serenity he hadn't seen in months. He knew she would be fine.

"I have a little boy."

The baby—he had completely forgotten. He wondered what it was like. The fetus had failed in its plan; Samantha was alive and would be growing stronger. Did that mean that it was now a normal newborn, or was it the highly developed creature it fashioned itself to be?

"That's wonderful, Sam. Congratulations."

"He's in the nursery. The baby doctor told me he's going to be all right, in spite of being premature. Go see him if you can, okay?"

"I will."

A man, possibly an orderly, though he didn't wear a white coat, came to the bedside and told him it was time to go.

"Come back soon, Jon. I'm not going anywhere for a while."

"Don't worry. I'll be back the minute they let me."

"I just wish Rosie could have been here."

Rosie . . . Bryson felt a note of panic. Did she remember?

"I'll miss her," continued Samantha. "I'm so sorry she had to leave."

"Leave, Sam?"

"Time, Dr. Bryson," interrupted the man. Had he been standing by the bedside all along? "You can come back in a little while."

"Just a second. What do you mean about Rosie leaving, Sam?"

"They didn't tell you? I thought you'd be the first to know. Mr. Phillips, here," she indicated the young man, "said that Rosie had to leave unexpectedly for California, and that she wasn't coming back."

"What?"

"Sorry, Dr. Bryson," said Mr. Phillips, pulling him by the elbow. "That's it for now."

Samantha had closed her eyes. Bryson allowed himself to be led away. What, he thought, was Sam talking about? And who was this Mr. Phillips?

Deep in thought, he walked through the corridors toward his lab. Obviously Samanatha recalled nothing of Mrs. Rutledge's death. Someone was deliberately deceiving her. But who? And why?

The research corridors were empty. Bryson was surprised to find the door to his lab locked. He hadn't even remembered closing it. No matter; it was a minor detail compared to what he would have to explain next. What, he wondered, would he tell them about Rosie's murder?

He unlocked the door and stopped dead in his tracks.

The laboratory was spotless. There was no shattered equipment, no broken console. And there was no Rosie. Her body was gone.

He walked inside, astonished. Where Mrs. Rutledge's body had lain on the floor, shiny tile glinted with his reflection. There were no blood stains. The remains of the minicomputer had been removed. Hurrying to the main panel's connection to MEDIC, he noticed that the jacks for the minicomputer adapter were replaced and the console soldered over. He looked under the panel. The wire into which he had spliced was intact, with no evidence of prior tampering. Not only was the lab cleaned up, it was spick-and-span, with the gleaming look of new equipment. Someone had gone to great lengths to remove all traces of the murder *and* the sleep studies.

"Dr. Bryson?"

He jumped back, startled. Mr. Phillips had followed him.

There were three others with Phillips. He knew Roberts, and he recognized the badge of the chief of hospital security, although he had never met the man. He had no idea who the third man was, but it was this stranger who did the talking.

"Sit down, Dr. Bryson. Phillips," he said to the young man, "leave us alone for an hour."

The man who addressed him appeared to be in his fifties, with distinguished-looking graying hair. He spoke with an air of authority.

"Who are you?"

"Let me do the talking, Doctor. Save your questions for later. Who I am is not important. Suffice it to say that we would have met anyway if you had gone through proper channels."

"What channels?"

"I will explain, Doctor. It will all become clear as I speak."

Bryson fell silent. He had no choice but to listen to what was apparently a well-prepared dissertation.

"This hospital, and the university," the man began, "are enormous investments. They are investments not only in terms of money, which amounts to hundreds of millions of dollars, but also in concept and philosophy. Everything we do here, everything we accomplish in this little corner of the world, is felt elsewhere. The medical progress and breakthroughs achieved here are important to all of your fellow citizens. Training of future scientists and medical leaders is vital to the best interests of our country. Not unexpectedly, then, whatever is done here has possible implications for national security.

"Our government is well aware of that fact. The successes here were planned and anticipated. It could hardly be otherwise. After all, Jubilee General didn't just happen; the very concept of an institution of this magnitude was something that took years in the making. The government realized long ago that the greatest gains could be accomplished by the greatest concentration of both funding and talent.

"I'm sure you realize, though, that traditional university medicine doesn't always cooperate with interests other than its own, whether those interests reside in the local community or in the federal government. There's long been a schism between town and gown, just as there was—in the past—no love lost between the professor and the government bureaucrat. So in answer to your question as to who I am, let me tell you what I do, for this is where I come in. To smooth over potential areas of friction between this enormous medical complex and the government, Jubilee General's designers wisely made plans for a small liaison group. The several members of this group, to which I belong, serve as intermediaries between governmental bureaucracy and the medical community.

"One of the things which has been of immeasurable assistance to us has been the university's computer. MEDIC's judgment in this area is impeccable. It knows the financial requirements of the hospital and university, and it understands the need of those influential in government to know. In our liaison capacity, MEDIC has proved to be our go-between. It helps us achieve our goals. Naturally a machine of this importance is pivotal to our success or failure and, by implication, to the well-being of the nation. So we took great pains to assure ourselves that we were intimately familiar with every aspect of its functioning. Any problem with MEDIC might become a problem for the entire country.

"Mr. Roberts and supervisors like him safeguarded our interests in the computer center. At least, they did up to now. Any irregularities in MEDIC's functions were to be reported to us."

Bryson looked at Roberts, who looked away.

"To the same degree that Mr. Roberts is guilty of poor judgment," the man continued, "so are you, Dr. Bryson."

"That's ridiculous."

"Is it? A perfectly innocent woman is dead because of your tampering. How could you not realize the enormity of your actions? Why, you didn't even follow your own rules."

"What rules?"

"The consent form for your sleep project, for one. You knew sleep volunteers couldn't be pregnant. But you chose to abrogate your own dictates for the sake of your research interests. That violation has proved to be disastrous."

"But what should I have done?" asked Bryson. "I went to Roberts for help, and I spoke with Dr. Pritchard. They both refused."

You were blinded by ego, by your research goals—however noble they were. Yet I'm not here to recite your list of failures. My task is to tell you what must be done now."

"How do you know all this?"

"MEDIC, of course. After you sounded the transmission alert in the computer center, I was notified immediately. No one can violate the sanctity of MEDIC without a thorough investigation. In short order—this time with the full cooperation of Mr. Roberts—we had replayed the most recent entries into MEDIC's memory banks. We discovered the near tragedy with Miss Kirstin, and we reviewed all the events that occurred since she first entered your study. How ironic that it was you who supplied Roberts with the key. A key he chose to ignore. We know about the transmissions, the minicomputer and the dialogues, Doctor. And we know about the murder. Everything."

"And the baby?"

"Of course. Shortly after its birth, a team of our finest pediatricians and experts in neonatal medicine examined the child thoroughly. In utmost secrecy, naturally. They found that he's a perfectly normal newborn. There is no trace of the medical genius that existed before birth."

"Thank God for that. And MEDIC?"

"What of MEDIC?"

"Does it really think, and hypothesize?"

"MEDIC is an extremely sophisticated computer. Its capability is enormous. It might hypothesize, in a figurative sense. It probably does have the capability to freely relate events in near human terms. But as for true thinking? No. We can explain everything that happened as a result of two distinct factors. One is MEDIC's advanced design, which rendered it susceptible to imprinting from outside influences. The other was superior fetal intellect, which obviously was a temporary phenomenon. A freak occurrence that could never ever happen again. You see, Doctor, thinking implies independence of action. That,

MEDIC certainly didn't have. It was, and is, a mechanical slave to its master, requiring commands in order to function. A sophisticated slave, but a slave nonetheless."

"What are you going to do about Mrs. Rutledge?"

"That, sir, is precisely the point. Errors have been made, among which yours figure prominently. But we cannot allow those errors to interfere with the workings of the university, or the needs of the country. If word of what happened here should ever leak out, to the politicians, for instance—or even worse, to the press—MEDIC would cease to be useful to the nation. The furor that would evolve, the investigation that would follow, would mean the end of our progress here. We cannot allow that to happen. So the investigation will start and end with us. There will be no report to the police," he said, nodding to the chief of security, "and no mention of this to anyone. MEDIC will be thoroughly checked for any after-effects of its relationship with the fetus, and its memory banks will be cleansed. Mr. Roberts is already chastened by his failures, and the hospital staff, including Dr. Pritchard, will be loosely briefed and kept silent. And you, Dr. Bryson, will keep these facts to yourself forever. There will be no research awards, no praise from the scientific community for your accomplishments. In short, I would suggest that you completely forget the events of the past half year."

"But you can't ignore a murder! You're talking about a colossal cover-up, in the name of national security!"

"And who is ultimately responsible for Mrs. Rutledge's death, Dr. Bryson? Certainly not Miss Kirstin. If anyone must bear the guilt, it should be shared between you and Mr. Roberts. Call what we're doing whatever you want. It is what must be done."

Bryson lowered his head, letting the man's words sink

in. Then he grew agitated. "No one will stand for it! People just don't disappear. Eventually it will come out!"

"Who will tell them, Dr. Bryson? Certainly not you: to do so would jeopardize both yourself and Miss Kirstin. And not Mr. Roberts, not Dr. Pritchard. You see, as of this moment, Mrs. Rutledge ceases to exist. There will no longer be a record of her employment here. Her apartment has been rented. Miss Kirstin and others have been conveniently misled. For all intents and purposes, Mrs. Rutledge has disappeared without a trace."

Bryson was flabbergasted. What he had just heard was incredible. It violated everything he believed in. Did they really have the power to do what they claimed?

He knew, without further thought, that they did. The evidence was already before him: the immaculate laboratory, Samantha's conviction that Mrs. Rutledge was alive. Bryson lowered his chin and shook his head. Maybe it was a blessing in disguise. Certainly, there was no bringing back Mrs. Rutledge; but now Samantha was safe, and shielded emotionally, too. Dared he ask for more?

"What if I should fight you?" he asked. "Suppose I did the unthinkable, as you see it, and told the press?"

The man shrugged. "Who would believe you? Highly trained though he is, Mr. Roberts didn't swallow your tale for an instant. Maybe he should have. But without some sort of evidence, there's not a journalist in the country who would believe you."

He was right. They had taken the tracings, removed the minicomputer. And he knew that, no matter how hard he might search, he would find that every relic of Mrs. Rutledge's existence had been effectively removed from the face of the earth.

"Don't press the issue, Dr. Bryson. Forget it ever happened. Be thankful for what you have. Miss Kirstin is alive. Her child is healthy and, above all, normal. You still have your job here and, if you cooperate, a promising career.

"Why don't you get some sleep? You look exhausted. You've done everything you can for Miss Kirstin, and she needs the rest, too. Phillips will drive you to your apartment. He'll stay with you for the next twenty-four hours. It's not that we don't trust you, Doctor. But you may find his presence . . . reassuring."

They turned and left. Bryson sighed, weighing the man's words. It was senseless to resist; what was done was done. But the man had been wrong about one thing. No matter how much they eradicated the physical traces of Rosemary Rutledge, they could never remove the emotional. The memory of her would remain with him forever, along with the horror and shame he felt for what had happened to her.

27

Inside his apartment, Bryson undressed and sat on the bed. He called the recovery room and inquired about Samantha. The nurse said that Samantha's recovery was unusually rapid, the kind of speedy convalescence seen in poisoning victims once the toxin was removed. At the present rate, Samantha would be transferred to a private room later in the day. Bryson thanked the nurse and asked to be notified if Samantha took any unexpected turn. He lay down to collect his thoughts. He leaned back and closed his eyes. Fatigue took its toll. When he awoke, it was dusk.

He yawned and stretched in the bed. He hadn't slept that long since he was a teenager. The clock on the night table showed that it was six P.M. An odd hour to be awakening. His thoughts strayed to Samantha. She was probably out of recovery now. It had only been twenty-four hours since their fateful drive to the country. It could just as well have been a lifetime. He swung his legs over the side of the bed and reached for the telephone. He dialed the hospital switchboard and asked the operator to page the chief resident in obstetrics. Eisenberg answered the page.

"Don't you guys ever sleep?"

"Not in obstetrics. I guess you're calling about Miss Kirstin."

"Have you seen her recently?"

"I saw her on afternoon rounds, about three. She looks great. They had just brought her down from the recovery room, but she was very alert. I'd wager she'll make a fantastic recovery."

Eisenberg brought him up to date on Samantha's condition. He and Pritchard had examined her earlier. Everything was on its way back to normal. Bryson rang off and dialed the home number of Tim Kelly, the resident in neurology. Kelly told Bryson that an outside team of specialists had examined the infant and found nothing wrong. He was told they had been summoned because the child was so premature. After they left, he and a resident in pediatrics had spent the better part of the morning examining Samantha's baby. From what they could determine, the child was in every respect a perfectly normal newborn. Neurologically, there were no deficits. From a developmental viewpoint, specifically motor skills and intellectual ability, it was too early to tell. But its reflexes and responses were no more or less advanced than any other newborn in the nursery. The only question the pediatrician had was whether or not the mother wanted her child circumcised. Bryson said he would find out.

He got up and stared at his reflection in the bathroom mirror. His fingers grated on the heavy stubble of beard. He was grimy, covered with a slimy mixture of river filth, dirt, and perspiration. There was a bruise on his forehead, and strands of hair were matted together with the blackish crimson of dried blood.

He prepared a hot shower. Showering with one hand proved more difficult than he anticipated. He had to keep the cast elevated to avoid getting it wet. Eventually he got the hang of it and luxuriated in the steaming spray.

He was starving. The thought of a thick steak was inviting, but he was anxious to see Samantha. There were some cold cuts in the refrigerator, and he downed a hasty sandwich as he dressed. He had forgotten about Phillips. The young man sat before the lit fireplace in the living room.

"Hope you don't mind, Dr. Bryson. I love a fire."

"No." He recalled a similar statement by Samantha months before, and started for the door.

"Where are you headed, sir?"

"To the hospital. Will you drive?"

"Sure." Bryson handed him the keys, but he refused. "I had my own car sent over. Security regulations."

"All right. Head for the hospital. But first stop at a liquor store."

"It's Sunday night, Doc."

"Christ, I've lost all track of time. Look, there's a little French restaurant on Fourth. I know the owner, and it's on our way. He'll give me a bottle of wine."

"I'm supposed to report that kind of transaction."

"You wouldn't dare."

The owner greeted him with the effusiveness peculiar to restaurateurs. What had happened to the arm of le cher docteur? Bryson said he would elaborate some other time, and soon managed to extract an uncorked bottle of white Burgundy. Perfect, thought Bryson. He wasn't sure if Samantha would be allowed any liquids. But if she was, he didn't want to risk spirits too strong or too bubbly.

They parked in the doctors' lot and walked together to the fourth floor. Phillips, arms folded, leaned against the wall by the elevator, a position which permitted him an unobstructed view of the corridor. Bryson strode to the nurses' station. He carried the bottle by his side, like a lantern. He identified himself and asked for Samantha's room. The nurse checked his name off a list of permitted visitors, then pointed the way to 462.

En route, he passed the wide glass window of the newborn nursery. He stopped in front and gazed through the pane, inspecting the faces of some thirty infants in various stages of sleep or wakefulness. A name tag at the head of the bassinet identified each child. Samantha's name was nowhere. But in the corner, there were three additional incubators. Perhaps her son was placed there for additional observation because of his prematurity. Bryson walked closer, peering at the three self-contained vehicles. On the rearmost, he spotted the card which read "baby boy Kirstin."

The child cried robustly. His face was infused with tones of scarlet and pink. By his face, his small hands were covered with the white folded ends of an undershirt. One hand touched his mouth, and he placed his lips around the cloth-covered fingers. This contented him, and the crying ceased. Relaxed, his face revealed its proportions. He was a beautiful child, clearly Samantha's son. Bryson had never felt particularly attracted to infants, but he felt even more estranged now. He had no feeling of warmth toward the baby. It would take him a while. It would be hard to forget the monster that once was, the unborn creature that had tried to destroy all he had loved.

He watched the child lull himself to sleep. After a few moments he moved on. He approached Samantha's room and hesitated, not knowing whether or not to barge right in. He might have waited longer were it not for her addressing him: "Jon?"

He softly cat-pawed into the room, not certain of what he might see, fearful of disturbing her. She looked at him and beamed.

"It's okay. I'm awake."

In speaking, she broke the ice. He smiled back at her.

Barely off the critical list, she looked quite good. She was propped up in bed on two pillows, an intravenous dripping into one arm. The other tubes had been removed. Her color was back, more so than he had seen in months. Was it the transfusions, or a fever, perhaps? Her eyes were wide, sparkling and radiant.

"You look great. Surgery agrees with you."

She started to laugh, and her hands went to her abdomen.

"Don't make me laugh. My stitches hurt."

He walked closer, nearing the bedside.

"That's a good sign. How the hell are you, anyway?"

"My ribs ache a little, but I just had an injection for pain. Come"—she gestured with her hand—"sit on the bed. Please?"

He reached her bed and sat, putting aside the wine, looking steadily at her. She reached for his hand.

Then she noticed the cast.

"What happened to your arm?" Her eyes searched him with curiosity.

She doesn't remember, he thought.

"I had a little fall. Two tiny fractures. It feels fine. But I have to wear this gadget for a few weeks. Then, good as new. You don't . . . do you remember going into labor?"

Her eyes were distant, fatigued. "No. It's all hazy, maybe from the medication I'm on. I feel like my mind's a void. There are so many things I don't know, or can't remember. Will you fill me in?"

"Sure," he said, knowing he would never, ever, tell her the truth. It's best she not know. Her eyes were moist. "What's wrong?"

"All day I've been wondering what to say to you. It's hard. The painkillers make my mind drift. I had such a long speech . . . but there's only one thing I want to know now," she said. "Do you love me, Jon?"

Her eyes were pleading, with tears forming in their corners. Bryson shook his head slowly, flooded with relief and affection.

"Oh, Sam."

His arms went around her neck, cast and all, and he held her tight. He rocked her gently from side to side. Warm tears bathed his shoulder. Softly, she cried without crying, the end of a nightmare of torment and agony. He pulled away and lifted her chin with his fingers. With infinite gentleness, he kissed her softly on the lips.

"You know I do," he said.

She was comforted. Samantha looked tired, her face still strained by her recent operation. She sank into the pillow and looked away.

"What are you thinking?" he asked.

"Rosie. Why did she have to leave?"

"She had no choice, Sam. She won't be coming back. She left for reasons beyond her control. But even though she's gone, I know she'd be happy with the way things turned out."

Again she cried softly. He cuddled her as one might comfort a child after a nightmare, patiently waiting for the torment to cease. Soon Samantha regained composure. She looked at his gift.

"What's in the bottle?"

"Warm white wine. Can you drink anything?"

"All the sips of water I want. I suppose we could consider wine a form of water, don't you?"

"Don't tell that to the French."

The bedside water pitcher was filled with crushed ice. Bryson filled a paper cup, and poured a generous measure

of white Burgundy in each. Samantha examined the label
from the corner of her eye.

" 'Montrachet. Grands Crus.' Is it good?"

"Good enough to make you forget you're drinking it in
a paper cup over ice." He touched their cups together. "A
toast."

"To what?"

"I can think of a few things. First, to a speedy recovery."

"I'll drink to that."

She took a long sip and leaned back on the pillows, relaxed, but showing the slightest trace of fatigue and discomfort. "Hmmm. That's good." She held out her cup for
a refill. "I like it on ice. Maybe we've discovered something
new. What's toast number two?"

"To us," said Bryson, raising his cup.

"Right," she said, touching his cup. "What about us?"

"As soon as you get well, we're going away. Far away.
Someplace warm. A few days, a week. Just the two of us."

"Sounds wonderful. But you're forgetting something."

"Don't worry about the lab. It can wait."

"Something else."

Puzzled, he raised his eyebrows. "You don't want to
go?"

"I'd love to. But you, me, and baby makes three."

"Oh, Sam. I'm sorry. I forgot."

"Cramps your style, huh?" she said wearily.

"No . . . I . . . there are plenty of places we can go."

Her smile was sympathetic. "I'm not just your girlfriend
any more, Jon. It all changed the moment he was born.
I'm a mother."

"You don't love me, is that it?"

"I love you very, very much. But sooner or later you
have to face reality," she said, pausing to catch her breath.

"We lived in a separate world before, not mentioning that I was carrying another man's child, willing to cross that bridge when we came to it. Well, here we are. And it's no little footbridge. It's the Golden Gate."

"So?"

Again, her wan smile, her fingers touching his cheek. The return of pain showed in her eyes.

"An A for effort. But the reality is this. You're a handsome young doctor. I'm an unmarried woman with an infant to care for. It's a bigger load than you think. Right now you're sincere, and I love you for it. But you've done enough for me already, Jon. Whenever you want, you're free to go."

Bryson applauded softly.

"Q.E.D. A very touching speech. Are you finished?"

"I think so."

"Then let me tell you something. One of the reasons I'm crazy about you is that you're the kind of girl I expected to say just what you did. You're forthright and independent; it's impossible for you to be different. But just because you're a free thinker, don't get the idea that you've cornered the market on intellect.

"I've thought a lot about this too. Sure, neither of us talked about it. But I know all the arguments you just threw at me by heart, and others you never thought of. I've looked at our relationship upside down and sideways, and each time, I come to the same conclusion: that I'm crazy about you. . . ."

"But, Jon, I . . ."

"I'm not finished," he interrupted. "What I'm driving at is that you're not forcing me to do anything. Like you, I have total freedom of choice. And I made my choice long ago. I choose you, Sam. With baby or without baby. Christ, I'd want you even if you had ten babies."

Her eyes were joyful, as her mouth broadened into a smile.

"Whatsa matter, baby?" he mimed. "Too proud to be a doctor's wife? Do I have to spell it out for you?"

She started laughing and crying at the same time, tears of joy. She put her hands on his face and drew it toward her wet cheek. Her arms went around his neck.

"I can spell," she said. "And I'm not too proud. Did you see him, Jon? Have you had a chance to look?"

He pulled away. "Yes, just before. He's beautiful, Sam. A feisty little guy." He pulled her close, and kissed her deeply. When their lips parted, Samantha lay back against the pillow. Her eyes were heavy with fatigue.

"My darling," said Bryson. "Rest now."

He closed her lids. She took his hand and pressed it to her cheek, resting like that against the linen. Bryson watched her fall asleep. He felt resignedly at peace. Samantha was his, for now and forever. He wouldn't let anything harm her. If that meant shielding her from the truth, he would do it gladly. Better to bear the burden of her guilt, and his, than risk the hurt that true knowledge would bring.

Everything considered, he was lucky he escaped so lightly. He nearly killed Samantha, nearly ended his career. If he ever brought slander to the university, the seething scandal would consume them both.

The future . . . Perhaps it wasn't as bleak as he imagined. He and Samantha would find their own little niche, and in time, he, too, would become attached to the child. He smiled to himself. They would be one hell of a family.

28

The university security agent began to doze. Now, at two A.M., he was two-thirds of the way through his new assignment, a twelve-hour guard shift in the computer center. The flurry of activity in the center during the daylight hours had virtually ceased by eight P.M., two hours after he had come on duty. The last few electronics technicians straggled out by nine, taking with them the cumbersome mechanical tools of their trade. They didn't speak to him. Their demeanor indicated that they were government professionals on temporary assignment to the university. Quick, proficient, and thorough. He didn't ask them what they were doing with their gadgets, nor was he expected to. Though their field of interest was roughly the same as his, loose talk or casual camaraderie between different subsections was discouraged. His area was security; theirs, computerized electronics. Oil and water. They didn't bother him, nor he them. Birds in the same sky, they each sought a separate windstream.

From the banter they exchanged while working, the security man gathered that they were looking for some sort of malfunction. In the end, judging from their shrugs, he surmised that they had found nothing. They left the lab with the same expression of weary complacency worn by their scores of departing colleagues he first encountered when coming on duty. Whatever they were searching for had either never been there, or had vanished. They reminded him of the tired flight crews of C-147s that crossed the South China Sea toward Danang in monsoon season, alert for the storm that never appeared. Navigator to pilot: all clear.

His chief had told him little: the security of the computer had been violated. The agent guessed that it was a break-in. The electronics techs would be testing the computer, said the chief. He didn't elaborate beyond that. In a world where an individual's need to know was carefully monitored, his current need was nonexistent.

The agent checked with the armed guard outside the door when the technicians left. All secure. He locked the door from the inside, knowing he wouldn't be relieved until six A.M. He made a slow circuit of the computer center, scanning its nooks and crannies for security weaknesses, crevices where a bomb might be hidden, or a listening device installed. He knew none would be found. But the professional in him made him persist. His search had him criss-cross the computer center three times, as much out of ennui as from sense of duty. Each surveillance circuit took an hour, and by midnight he was tired, bored, and satisfied that nothing was amiss.

He hated machines. They were cold and remote, offering little fascination. Even the enormous computer was a complex hunk of metal. He recalled his days in government service. He longed for field duty, the thrill of the chase, even routine leg work. Anything was better than this. It might have helped if the computer was operational, with moving parts and flashing lights. But from what he could see, it was totally shut down. No sound, no movement. It was dormant.

He sat in front of the control panel. Four more hours of boredom lay ahead. The agent mused, allowing his mind to follow the flight of fantasy. He closed his eyes and found himself on a back street in Tangiers, pursuing a Chinese courier. The alley was long and winding. The chase was on.

Now dozing, the agent's head bobbed on his chest. Soon the bobbing ceased, and he was sleeping soundly. The computer center was silent.

For the first time since its construction, MEDIC was alone, unsupervised, and not functioning. Its endless miles of wiring, now quiet, were coiled and ready, awaiting the call to spring into action. MEDIC was a caterpillar trapped in its cocoon, needing the interference of man to molt and develop, the human touch that would set the butterfly free.

But MEDIC would not wait. As the agent slept, a green light flashed on the console. There was a click, and a single tape began to wind, softly, steadily, as the slumbering giant within began to wake.

The newborn nursery was hushed. The two A.M. feeding was completed, and each infant lay contentedly in its bassinet. The nurses turned the lights low and left to complete their charts. In the isolette of baby boy Kirstin, the child slept quietly on its stomach.

His eyes blinked suddenly open. Far across campus, in the computer center, the trumpet was sounding, and it was time to heed its call. He stretched one leg, then the other, a fledgling testing its wings. The child rolled further on its side, an impossible feat for a normal newborn. His small hands reached out and pressed against the side of the isolette. He lifted his head slightly off the mattress. He felt the weight of his head, sensing gravity for the first time, rolling his face completely to the side.

After seven months in utero, his eyes were accustomed to the dim light. Through the Plexiglas side of the bassinet, he looked out across the nursery, taking in the cribs of the true infants, noting the nurses at their desk who toiled oblivious to the child whose piercing gaze riveted them. He didn't blink. His vision was tentative, searching, growing more confident with each passing second.

His eyes glowed, a crystal blue. These were no eyes of a mere babe, the tremulous, sightless orbs of a newborn. They were bright and alert, the eyes of a hunter, an eagle aloft whose darting glance scanned the countryside for prey.

ABOUT THE AUTHOR

DAVID SHOBIN is a physician who teaches and practices in New York. He has authored short stories and medical articles. This is his first novel.